The Elf Child

Lyndi Alexander

Clan Elves of the Bitterroot
Series - Book II

Urban Fantasy Novel from
Dragonfly Publishing, Inc.

The Elf Child

Clan Elves of the Bitterroot Series - Book II
Urban Fantasy Novel

Trade Paperback Edition
EAN 978-1-936381-11-1
ISBN 1-936381-11-7

Published in the United States of America by
Dragonfly Publishing, Inc.
Website: www.dragonflypubs.com

*Clan Elves of the
Bitterroot Series*
(in order):

The Elf Queen
[Book I]

The Elf Child
[Book II]

The Elf Mage
[Book III]

Special Terms

ELVISH DICTIONARY:
Denami: *Beloved*
Lelan: *The Clan, the People*
Nian: *Male elf*
Neris: *Female elf*
Solurd: *Crabapple-like mountain fruit*

ONLINE GAMER TERMS:
OMG: *Oh My God*
Toon: *Game Avatar*
MMORPG: *Massive Multiplayer Online Role Playing Game*

With gratitude to Eric, who has the patience and devotion of Astan, but most importantly the heart and soul of Lane Donatelli

PROLOGUE

HE wanted her dead.

All the years he had been alive, Grigor Biren had wanted—something. An ever changing vast something that seemed just out of reach. He had never been able to define exactly what would leave him satisfied.

Until now.

He wanted her dead. Jelani. The elf queen. The child of elven Linnea and human Vincent Marsh. Raised human and then returned to the Bitterroot Mountains of Montana to ruin everything.

Here he cowered, cold and shivering, just before winter set in. Alone in the forests. His powers gone. She had taken them when she had taken control.

The old king had exiled his own son Bartolomey, scattering his followers to the winds. Grigor had believed Bartolomey's promises of power and influence, but when his mentor had been deposed, Grigor was also robbed of everything for which he had worked.

She had stolen his dreams.

She lived with the Lelan now, the clan, in the forests north by the lake. Partnered with that fool Astan Hawk, she believed the two of them would usher in an age of prosperity for the elf clan as they reunited families divided by the schism of a quarter century, as humans reckoned time.

Bartolomey had been unable to preserve his followers, their numbers insufficient to accumulate the life force needed to connect with the soil. Barely fifty strong, the elves in the fractured remains of Bartolomey's group began to age as humans did, and they began to lose their powers.

Those who fled Bartolomey's rule included many of the old wise women of the Circle and the youngers, as well as the sleepers who had gone into nothingness for twenty-five years until the queen could be restored. Being more numerous than those in Bartolomey's group, they had remained resilient, even living among the humans.

Now Jelani and Astan had summoned all the members of the clan into the forests, even welcoming many who had followed Bartolomey, spineless worms willing to crawl back to beg forgiveness.

He would never debase himself in that way.

No, Bartolomey had been right. The clan of the Bitterroot had coexisted with the soil in these mountains for many centuries before the white settlers had come west, before the natives had built their tepees among the trees, back when animal life was plentiful and the headwaters were young. The leader of the elf clan should be one who had lived among these animals, these rocks, these trees, all his life.

Not some half-breed naïve and inexperienced outsider who suddenly appeared on the horizon.

Not a city dweller masquerading as a queen for as long as it pleased her before she abandoned them for her next adventure.

Not someone who cruelly stole powers from others, leaving them cold and alone in the forest.

The breeze picked up, waving the fragrant pine tree branch where Grigor had curled up to brood about his wounded fate. No proper ethereal elf house for him, not any more. He sniffed the cold air. A late autumn rain was coming. It was time to find some cover.

He climbed down the pine and turned away from the open spaces, seeking shelter further into the thicket. He could hunker down and debate his course at his leisure. His plans would come together with a little more thought and planning.

Grigor knew this: If it was the last thing he did before he froze to death on the barren mountainside, he would make sure she never hurt anyone again. He would take her life, as she had taken his.

He had set the clan back on the right path. They would see he was not a villain, but a hero. They would all see.

It was just a matter of time.

CHAPTER 1

ASTAN Hawk stood on the mountain ridge overlooking the city of Missoula and took a deep breath of the chill October air, crisp and clear at this altitude, free from human pollution and smog. The maples below had faded from their brassy gold and orange to a duller brown as the days passed. Soon the vision of Missoula would almost blend into the earth.

His feet firmly on the soil, Astan stood connected with his past and his clan.

Strength came to the clan through these lands, not through the cold concrete and stone of the city. The fact that the clan returned here after the exile of Bartolomey showed the value of the sacrifice made by his father Daven Talvi and the other sleepers, their devotion to duty well rewarded. The elves had come home.

Not only had the elf clan left the city for the Bitterroot, but it once again had a queen. Jelani Marsh had followed her mother Linnea to rule the clan, as tradition dictated.

Even Astan had to admit this queen challenged tradition.

Raised in the human world, ignorant of her past and her heritage, Jelani had not been prepared to deal with the schism of the elf factions and their reunification. Likewise, hidden from the evil Bartolomey in the human city of Missoula, Astan and the other youngers had not been privy to the intrigue that had left the former queen trapped inside a Douglas fir.

So it was just as well that he and Jelani had gravitated together out of need, understanding, and a mutual attraction that had grown into a deep love.

The former barista had changed in her months with the clan, finding her peace within. And why shouldn't she? She had come to the land her mother had called home. How could one of elven blood have survived in the city among so much that was unnatural and not be torn?

In Astan's years with his grandmother Djana and the Circle on the outskirts of Missoula, if he hadn't been able to escape into the mountains whenever he wanted he might have been a little crazy, too. Despite what logic and plans might determine, one's heart always knew the truth of things.

He took another deep breath as he studied the hillside below him. Everything seemed secure. The faint sun warmed his face. He closed his eyes and enjoyed the moment. In the days to come, the temperature would drop steadily and the real snow would fall. Not the light flakes that swirled around him now, but a cold cover, deep and protective. Then every trace of warmth would be cherished.

He sighed and moved off along the ridge, his eyes scanning for danger. Jelani returned to his mind. Not that she was ever far from it.

As the summer came to an end many of the youngers had envied his position as the chosen partner of the young queen. Even Astan's father Daven Talvi had once hoped to win her hand. Why had they all been so anxious to inherit a headache? He couldn't guess.

She did not mean to cause trouble. Of this he was certain. Thrust into the unfamiliar position of queen, she struggled to meet the competing needs of the clan. His first impressions had been correct ones. Her intelligence made her a good student. But like the rest of them, Jelani had much to learn.

Astan had walked Jelani to the Circle's gathering, leaving the bed they shared earlier than he would have liked. But they knew Djana expected compliance. He had left Jelani standing in ankle-deep fallen leaves at the entrance to the Circle's chamber. Djana had come to the door and drawn Jelani inside, dismissing Astan with the same tart look she had used since Jelani chose him over his father Daven.

Although Djana, his father's mother, his own grandmother, had raised him from infancy after his father had gone into sleep and his mother Veraena had disappeared without explanation, she had grown cold since they returned to the forest. Her disdain hurt, but Astan struggled not to show it. Jelani was his family now.

Despite his status as guardian and mate of the queen, Astan found both his grandmother and his father had relegated him to a subordinate status when it came to Jelani. He could comprehend the need for the Circle to instruct the new queen on her royal duties. They understood the needs of the clan. But he was tired of Daven usurping his role.

Certainly, Astan could show his beloved the clan's history, teach her the language, and bring her to the heart of her people. He had been patient for several months, knowing some transition period was necessary.

It was time for him to rectify the situation.

A rustling behind him stiffened his back. Adrenaline rushed through his veins. Ready to leap aside, he turned with a speed practiced over many years of intense training.

Hand upraised to strike, he scowled as he saw it was only Beckley, another of his elven family.

The burly elf with the rumpled blond hair chuckled as he saw Astan's reaction. He pulled his jacket closer around him, brushed the wet remnants of snowflakes from his hair, and walked over to stand near Astan.

"Jumpy?" Beckley asked, surveying the land. "I have sensed nothing on the mountain. That means it's something else." Beckley cocked a brow. "What's *she* up to now?"

"*She's* with the Circle."

"Mmm." Beckley's eyes narrowed as he looked down into the valley.

Astan knew Beckley had the gift of far-sight. Like the hawks that inhabited the Bitterroot Valley, he could see a greater distance than most elves or humans. But even Beckley couldn't see into the shaded Circle's chambers in the center of the woods.

"What does that mean?" Astan's tone was sharper than he had intended.

"They're up to something." He eyed Astan. "You're her mate.

Can't you make her see what they want makes sense for us all? Mother says the Circle has twisted itself into a knot trying to teach Jelani to bend to their will."

"Why should she bend to their will? Is she not Queen? She has the best interest of the clan at heart!" Annoyed, Astan rubbed his forehead as if he could erase his frustration. "She hardly sleeps nights worrying about what might happen to all of us if we do not proceed thoughtfully."

"Perhaps she has not yet learned how to speak to the Circle members." A glint of amusement shone in Beckley's eye.

"You know her."

Beckley chuckled again. "Yes, I do, brother. Despite the strangeness of her ways, she is something special. And you the lucky one to win her heart. Grigor was—" He stopped, choking off the rest of the sentence.

Astan's stomach twisted at the reviled name, reminded of one of the worst days of his life. Grigor's treachery had killed two humans. He had nearly executed Astan, his father Daven, and Jelani. Astan saved Jelani in the end and had even healed Daven's wounds. But he had not forgiven himself for not being able to protect those to whom he owed that duty.

Beckley, one of Grigor's favorite playmates as they had grown up together, had never crossed over to follow Bartolomey. His loyalty had remained with the Circle thanks to the influence of his mother Rashia, the clan's midwife. Now Beckley stood as one of Astan's most trusted subordinates in the clan.

"Grigor is a traitor," Astan said, his voice tight with remembered pain. Surely the chill that played an arpeggio along Astan's spine was not caused only by the passing winds. "He chose to embrace hatred and bloodshed. It was right that he was expelled from the clan."

The two of them stood several minutes in contemplative silence, watching a small group of white tailed deer cut across the slope below them. The herd, mostly females, had more than the usual number of fawns running among them.

As he observed the deer, he felt a series of flicks across his mind, an odd sensation he had known since childhood and one he had experienced much more often since Jelani had come to live in the mountains of the Bitterroot. The flicks came to him first as sequenced visuals that seemed like random images. Then, like the construction of a jigsaw puzzle, a gradual collective of images merged until a meaningful context allowed him to understand the message.

Flick. He saw the deer in his mind, but the leaves were still green around them. An earlier time. Many fewer deer. Only a couple of fawns.

Flick. Jelani in the woods, kneeling by a sapling.

Flick. That sapling by summer's end, twice as tall, bushy and full.

Flick. The elves, gathered at midsummer by the headwaters of the river, their numbers increased by those returned from their travels.

Flick. Back to the deer before him.

Analysis presented an answer before he considered the repercussions of his thought process. Jelani's acceptance of her role with the clan and the subsequent growth of the forest, even the clan itself, had also translated to the fauna of the woods. She had made this happen.

"Astan?" Beckley asked, jiggling Astan's elbow. "Where are you?"

Drawn back to the October afternoon on the mountainside, Astan blinked in surprise. "Sorry. Just thinking, I guess."

"Lost in a flight of milkweed floats, I'd say." Beckley grinned.

"I'm not sure what it is." Astan shared a quick explanation of the phenomenon. "I remember being able to do that as a child. I'd just know things. See how they worked. How situations came together. The last few years, it hasn't happened nearly as often. Now it's started again."

Beckley's chubby face shifted into a contemplative mode. "Hmm. Being back in the forests, you think?"

"Perhaps."

"The Circle may be able to help you, if this is your true ability. Djana, Daven, and the others. They taught me how to sharpen my own skills."

Astan nodded, but inside he rejected that path. The Circle interfered enough with his life. He had noticed that his time with Jelani sharpened his thinking process. He would continue to study that possibility instead.

The two elves moved along the ridge, in harmony with the wind as it blew past them, with the soil under their feet, with the birds gliding and hanging motionless in the currents above them.

"Do you think it's true?" Beckley asked, after they had crossed about half of the ridge. There was an apprehensive undertone to his words. "Do you think Grigor's actions have set him against nature to such a degree that he has become human?"

Astan frowned. "Who said that?"

"My mother and others of the Circle. The old tales teach that elves who lose their connection with the soil through violence will forfeit their elven power."

Astan had asked himself the same question. When the elf clan had fractured before, each part had become weaker than the whole. The strength of the clan elves of the Bitterroot was in numbers, a collective sharing of power. None of them had seen Grigor since the day Bartolomey was exiled. Who knew if he even lived? Surely an elf alone, without the restorative group bond of the clan, would wither and fail.

"Perhaps it is so," Astan said. "Better that he stays away. Surely he wouldn't have the courage to hold his face to the sun again in sight of the clan." He clapped Beckley on the shoulder and forced a smile. Why waste breath on the traitor? Time for a change of subject. "We'll deal with that question when it arises, my friend. What brings you to this summit?"

"My task it is to bring food for the clan tonight," Beckley said. "I've already scouted the western woods. Terzon's coming up the back side of the ridge. Several possibilities for a wild pig or two. Surely one would offer itself so that the clan might grow."

Astan eyed the small group of deer which had moved farther down the mountain. "I have some time before Jelani comes. Let me help you. With our combined efforts, we should be able to feed everyone."

With a last look at the valley below he headed down, Beckley at his heels. Today, at least, he would be satisfied that he had done everything he could to promote the welfare of the clan. Tomorrow would be soon enough to instigate his battle with the Circle for the right to control Jelani's future.

CHAPTER 2

JELANI Marsh, now the elf queen, perched on the barest edge of a broken tree stump.

She looked out through the semi-opaque walls of a room created by elf magic, wondering how long the dozen old women wrapped in their worn layers of brown and green clothing really wanted to debate the proper administration of collected herb lore. Again.

Lucky Astan. He had left her to scout that morning, so he was free to run and breathe and be. She, meanwhile, drowned in bureaucracy.

Somehow Jelani had imagined the day-to-day life of a queen, elven or otherwise, might be a bit more glamorous. Running with a herd of wild elk. Flying with eagles. Exploring dark crystal caves. That would have been fascinating. Instead, she spent most of her time sparring with the women of the Circle about boring duties and responsibilities.

Barely six months since she had discovered her true elven roots, she learned the fate of her mother and father. Both had been killed by her mother's evil brother Bartolomey in his bid to rule the clan. She had seen them both one last time in midsummer, when she had fulfilled the clan's prophesy and rescued her mother's life force from the tree where it had been cached for twenty-five years. Just before dear old Mom and Dad decided to ditch the earthly plane to spend eternity together in the ether and dumped the whole mess in her lap.

Before she had become the new queen of the Bitterroot clan, Jelani had been a somewhat self-centered working woman with a few carefully chosen friends. An orphan with no family, she had tried living with her stepmother and failed. She had tried the

University of Montana and dropped out. She had tried taking wedding vows and got dumped.

Queen experience? Not much.

Elf experience? Now that she found a little more rewarding. Daven Talvi, whose skills included the talent to unlock the minds and abilities of others, had taken Jelani into the woods and released her elven gift on a grand scale. Her 'green thumb' affinity with plants of all kinds burgeoned into the capacity to heal the damage to the Montana forest caused by human loggers and natural catastrophes. Watching an acre of logged land sprout up with young trees over a matter of days warmed her heart.

Unlike Circle time.

Jelani sighed and shifted her weight on the wide stump, trying to stop the tingle in her thigh that warned her leg was about to fall asleep. The 'room' centered around a familiar pattern of fallen trees that provided the Circle a meeting place. Most of the elf women, the *neris*, were many years older than Jelani. She couldn't understand how they could possibly find sitting on the rough tree bark to be comfortable. The greenery soothed the eye, but occasionally she thought she would be willing to give her firstborn for a plain folding chair.

She had steered the conversation to practical matters, like the assurance that food stores were gathered in sufficient quantities for all elves who sought to rejoin the clan now that Bartolomey was gone. She had encouraged them to use their familiarity with the lands specifically to target projects that she could use to enlist human help from the city or state governments. She had proposed that they create some written record of family lineage so those who were returning could trace their heritage, herself not the least.

Things that she imagined should concern a queen.

The Circle elders, however, increasingly veered off into the complex elven tongue they used among themselves, a tongue in which she had only acquired the basics, and ignored her sincere suggestions.

Even the Earth Liberation Front, the human eco-terrorist group Daven and Astan had used to help protect the old forests while seeking Linnea's hidden location, would have to be pleased at the new growth. They all wanted the same thing. Perhaps they could have worked with the clan, too. But the Circle wouldn't consider it. So many possibilities, so many closed minds.

Choking back her frustration, Jelani made one more attempt. "I would really rather talk about the plan to make sure we're all set for winter with enough food and space for everyone. Surely, we can talk about herbs later in the year. The season's just about over, right? I mean, we'll have snow a foot deep in a matter of weeks."

The stares of the elders, carefully devoid of emotion, pierced her. Djana's teeth gnawed her lip in a gesture Jelani recognized, one that meant she had much to say but believed it prudent to withhold words of another disappointment from a girl deemed not up to the task of ruling.

Jelani studied their silent faces, wondering what they expected. She was the queen, right? They should listen to her, perhaps even follow her. They should not just dismiss her, as they so often did. "Well?"

Djana released her lip, her voice tight with weary impatience. "Jelani, we need to assure that all will be as it needs to be. As it has been through the ages. We will come to your concerns in time."

A wave of frustration rushed over Jelani. "Look, you asked me to be your leader, right? I didn't volunteer. I didn't put my name on the ballot. You drafted me and put me in charge. I'm doing the best I can. When you let me!"

A susurration of mild protest rippled through the group along with the soft rustle of movement and boots tapping on the earth. Djana's lips pressed together in annoyance. Sitting board straight on a fallen log, she carried much more of the regal air of a queen than Jelani could ever hope to muster.

"All things in time, Jelani. The young are so impatient." Djana relaxed her face into a denigrating smile and the others followed suit.

"Don't patronize me," Jelani snapped. "You know the first time something goes wrong, you are all going to blame me. I would rather be blamed for something that I have done, instead of something that's been 'through the ages.'" A thick paste of sarcasm coated her words, and she hoped they really heard it. "You know it seems to me that business as usual hasn't worked very well for you recently. Remember? You lost your king, your queen, my father, and your homes to your old friend Bart. Is that how you want things to go?"

"Not proper, not proper at all," muttered gray haired Rashia.

The others fidgeted and clucked assent.

"You want proper? Fine. I'll just sit here and shut up. Fewer headaches for me." Jelani crossed her arms. "Bunch of dried up old sticks," she mumbled in a sour tone.

But she should have known that would not pass unnoticed. Even though elven ears were not as pointed as she had expected them to be, their hearing capacity was sharp in the extreme. Djana shot her a look.

Jelani did her best to ignore it. Overhead, pine branches whispered in the wind, providing some distraction although the cool breeze wouldn't penetrate the protected area Djana had conjured. She needed to get back out among the trees. At least there she could be useful.

Djana shifted her weight, leaning forward gracefully to pick up her carved wooden cup, exuding calm to extend to the group in the way she had of insinuating her wishes into the others. Jelani hated that manipulative ability, having been its victim several times before she had learned to protect herself. When Jelani had asked Daven if persuasion was one of Djana's elven gifts, he never answered. That said it all.

"We attempt, as always, to instruct you on all the matters you need to know. There is much for you to learn. As the queen, your duty will be not only to follow the laws of the clan, but to teach them to your daughter as well, so that she, too, will know the ways of the Lelan."

Daughter? What daughter? A flush of annoyance drove Jelani to her feet and it took everything she had not to stamp her worn black boot on the ground. She had determined long before that she wasn't parent material. She had grown up without her own mother and she had no desire to follow in the footsteps of her stepmother. And her father? Well, Vincent Marsh had been anything but usual.

"Yeah, but see, we've got years to deal with that, right? Maybe even after we decide where to stuff the dry herbs." She made sure her tone of voice indicated she didn't mean in the usual storage places. "Meanwhile…."

Djana rose to her feet as well. Jelani noticed that the gray streaks of hair at Djana's temples had faded since they had returned to the forests. All the elves seemed stronger and even younger since they had come back. Something must be going right. Something she was doing perhaps?

"Maybe you should take a walk and collect yourself, Jelani," Djana raised a hand to the heavy long black hair, of which she was so vain, and lifted it back over her shoulders. "Since these matters which we believe are of importance do not interest you we can finish without you. Daven will tell you anything you might need to know later."

"I can't wait. Really. You all enjoy, hmm?"

Jelani marched toward the sheer portal, drowning in aggravation. As she escaped, she let her footsteps connect with the ground, draining her frustration into the soil and leaving only gratitude for her freedom. If they didn't want her help, she would take off the rest of the day.

Outside the space where the Circle met, the wind chilled her cheeks. She had not yet mastered the elven skill of body temperature control. When in harmony with the soil and each other, elves could maintain themselves at the right levels in the extreme heat of summer or the snows of winter. The ability to warm and cool their blood to remain comfortable just came with the elf body, a creation that very much resembled humans in size, shape, eyes, nose, mouth, and other outer appearance.

But inside their perfect skin these mountain elves exhibited subtle differences from their human neighbors. Their bone structure was less dense, which allowed them to tread more lightly. This, along with their elven nature, gave them a gait that made them appear to glide over the forest floor as they moved.

Like Astan, those trained in the combat arts could increase or decrease their connection to the soil, giving them more personal gravity if needed or less if they needed to climb a hill quickly. Since they had returned to the clan lands, many of the elves had developed a narrow ring to the outside of their eye's pupils, metallic shades of gold, silver, and copper. Daven had explained that this enhanced elven night vision similar to that of pumas and cougars.

None of these physical changes had carried over to the half-breed yet. Jelani had practiced and practiced, tried to follow the steps Djana and Astan explained, but she had not been able to accomplish the body warming. She never left home without a heavy sweater.

Her mixed heritage had not prevented her from cultivating other elf traits though. As she made her way to the top of the ridge where she sensed Astan waited, she recalled the time in early August when Daven had taken her into the mountains north of Seeley Lake to show her how the elves lived in the open. This could be summed up in one word.

Magic.

Daven had told her that elves could conceal themselves from human eyes and, in fact, coexist with humans who hardly ever noticed them. But she'd had no idea then of the extent of this ability.

"Have you ever been walking in the forest and heard something you couldn't identify?" the tall, hazel-eyed Daven had asked. "Or felt movement ahead you couldn't trace to a living creature? Even felt like you were being observed?"

"Of course. Branches fall, you know, stuff like that. The wind. It doesn't mean something was really there."

"You'd be surprised, Jelani, at what humans don't notice in the wonder of the world around them."

They had walked off the common trail to the elven compound. When they arrived, he had asked her to take off her shoes and socks. When she balked, he laid a hand on her shoulder as he had when they first met, to communicate through telepathy. *Jelani, trust me, as you always have. You can see my heart. You know I wouldn't let you come to harm.*

If she believed one thing about him, this would be it. She removed her footwear, her toes warm against the earth. "Now what?"

He crouched, setting three runes on the ground between them. "Shhh," he whispered. He dug in the earth until he had loosened a handful of dirt, speaking softly in the elven tongue. Jelani caught a few of the words but most of it passed her by. When she thought she could hold still no longer, Daven took the dirt in his hand and pressed it onto the top of her feet, continuing to speak elven words, his tone one of reverence.

Startled, she would have pulled away from him, but his hands gripped her feet keeping them still.

"Close your eyes," he said. "When you open them again, you will see as the elves do."

Not at all sure what would happen, she took a deep breath and closed her eyes. The touch of his hand grew warm, almost hot. Is this how he had healed Crispy? She waited so long to reopen her eyes that Daven prompted her.

"Jelani?"

"I'm scared, Daven. What if everything is all, I don't know, purple or something? What if I don't have this sight because my dad was human? Maybe I'll go blind because I'm not supposed to see anything."

His hands were warm on her feet. *Sense your body, tense and stressed as the city dwellers live. You belong here among natural things. This is your birthright. You have become one with the forests, with the soil. You are of the Lelan now.*

Right. Her, not worried? Not anxious? Not alone? Couldn't happen.

But she wasn't a coward. She opened her eyes and discovered a different world.

She and Daven had come up a single trail that led to the area. Now, as she looked behind them, she could see a dozen imprints snaking across the grass around them. The deer, the elk, even rabbits left distinctive marks and patterns on the green blades that made it clear to her what had stepped there. She looked behind to see her own footprints, heavy and destructive, the plants crushed under the weight of her boot. Daven's passing, however, was marked only by a shadow on the grass that faded as she watched.

But that wasn't all. Her new sight revealed patterns in the trees, many of them set close together to create small enclosures. Looking up, she saw gossamer platforms extending between the branches, the elves on them hardly noticing her below through the nearly opaque walls of their chambers. For the first time she saw elf children. Their tinkling laughter lifted her spirit.

"Kids? There were kids out here the whole time?" she asked in amazement.

Daven smiled, raising a hand to the curious toddler above, whose attention had now been captured. She laughed and scattered a handful of flower petals over them. "We didn't all come out of a glass slipper, you know. We procreate much as humans do."

Looking around, she considered the view. As her eyes adjusted to their new sight, she saw more and more dwellings in the trees. Surely their walls were like those of the Circle chambers, diaphanous but sturdy with magic, keeping out the elements. She winced as the small ones ran in what seemed to be open space above them, awaiting their death-defying tumble to the ground. But their magic kept them safe.

"You just live in the open? Just hang out?" She shuddered. "I don't think I could do that."

"We did not believe you would. That's why we have created a special place for our new queen."

They continued into the woods to the foot of a Douglas fir that was so tall it hurt her neck to crane back to see the top. Astan waited there to meet them, a warm smile on his face.

Her eyes narrowed at the negative thought that came to mind, even though she couldn't believe Astan would be involved with something that could hurt her. "You'll shove me in a tree, like my mother?"

"Of course not, *denami*," Astan said. "This is specially created for you. For us." He gestured at the trunk. "Look closely."

She eyed the rugged bark, suspicious, but at last saw the outlines of a door and three dots spaced closely together. When she reached for the dots, she found them separated by an interval that comfortably matched her fingertips. Contact with them gave her fingers a little tingle. Then the trunk split open without the crack or noise she would have expected, the two sides raising and separating.

"Come into our home," Astan said softly, taking her hand. They entered the opening to discover a small cottage of several rooms, complete with windows.

"Now wait a minute," she said, stepping out to examine the trunk of the tree, no more than four feet across. She looked back inside at the roomy space, which held several chairs, a small table, and some cabinets. A fireplace was laid out but not burning. An open space in the back hinted at a bedroom. "How did you do this?"

"We want to make our queen happy," Daven said. "Welcome, Jelani."

She could hardly believe what she saw. The space reminded her of something Snow White might have stumbled upon in the woods. Except this was elves, not dwarves. "Is this the only house like this? Just for us?"

"No," Astan said. "Others exist, but none are quite so suited to humans. The Circle has gone to some length to keep your comfort in mind."

Grateful at the concern for her wellbeing, she marveled at the creation, her one frown prompted by the fireplace. "You want me to burn a fire inside a tree? That seems counter productive somehow. Even if we didn't die from smoke inhalation."

A laugh burst from Daven, amusement flickering in his eyes. Shaking his head, he patted her on the shoulder. "You are quite right, Jelani. Burning an actual fire in this enclosure could be dangerous to you and the tree as well. One of the elders has left you some flash dust."

He demonstrated the use of the gift by opening a small glass box on the mantel. Inside was some nondescript powder that looked like well-dried ash. He said a few words in elvish and tossed a pinch of the powder onto the hearth and a fire appeared.

"Whoa." Jelani stared at the flames, and then came near. No smoke came from the fire, and heat came only as high as the fireplace enclosure. While the room warmed perceptibly, the heat faded as it approached the walls formed by the trunk of the tree that housed her.

More magic.

"You're going to teach me that abracadabra part, right?"

Daven crossed his arms and studied her. "I'll teach you all the magic you can learn, my queen."

Astan bristled, as she had seen him do more often as the days passed. The Circle might have appointed Daven as Jelani's unofficial tutor, but Astan was her mate, her partner, her love. She tolerated Daven's constant presence in her life for one reason. His son Astan was all hers.

And thanks to Djana dismissing her from the interminable droning of the morning meeting, she could choose to share the rest of the day with him.

Her mind came back to the present, as the trees cleared near the top of the ridge. She spied Astan in dark silhouette against the morning sun. An eagle cried out, gliding overhead, and she looked up in time to see it joined by a second, swooping lower and then turning to fly above the first in a move that identified them as a mated pair.

Astan watched them too, one hand blocking the sun from his eyes, his dark brown jacket unbuttoned and open to the wind.

While he was distracted by the eagle, she ran silently the last few yards and tackled him. They fell into the light snow and started to roll down the hill. Astan scrambled for some purchase, finally catching a loose root that stopped their free tumble.

Breathing hard in panic, his brown hair rumpled and face flushed, he grabbed her arm and pulled her close. "What in the name of—"

Coughing and wiping her frozen cheeks, she laughed at the alarm in his dark eyes. "Tag, you're it."

"What?" He blinked at her in total puzzlement. "I'm what? Why?"

She pulled herself up onto her elbows and snuggled close, enjoying the feeling of the cold fresh air on her face. "Didn't you ever play tag when you were a kid?"

"Tag?"

"Yes, tag. On the playground. Someone is 'it.' They chase everyone. If you get tagged, then you're 'it.'"

Astan's eyes changed. He lost that worried look. "So because you touched me, I'm it."

"Exactly." She leaned over and kissed him lightly on the mouth. He tasted of the wind. "Tag."

"You know my grandmother took me from the human school when I was still very young. But let me see if I understand this." He pulled her close, arms warm around her, and kissed her. "Now you're it."

She kissed him again, more deeply this time. "You've got it! Tag! Mmm. How long can we play this game? As long as the Circle can talk and talk and talk?"

He held her for a long moment, then grinned and let go, hoisting first himself, then her, upright. She brushed a dusting of snow off them both.

"Actually, I'm surprised you're here so soon." He took her hand and walked a little farther up the ridge so they could see the whole valley, brilliant in golden aspen leaves and dark green pines against the snow.

"They kicked me out." She bit her lip.

"What?" His frown held the beginnings of a thundercloud. "You're the queen."

She sighed, frustrated. "Astan, I was more than ready to go." She studied the trees in the valley below, inhaling a deep breath of pine scented air. "With so much to do to bring the clan into harmony before winter sets in, I don't understand why they spend so much time dealing with petty crap. This is the kind of stuff that got my mother killed, right? Insignificant jealousies, politics, who's who, instead of what's important. We've brought the area back to health. We've gathered in another hundred of the scattered ones. And more are reported to be ready to return. This seems more important to me. Honestly, I just don't get it."

"Nor do I." Astan was silent for a long moment and then he squeezed her fingers. "Did you see the new growth along the river? The place where you walked yesterday?"

Satisfaction bubbled up into her heart. "Really? So soon? That's wonderful!" She wrapped him in an impulsive hug. "Can we get out of here?"

"Where do you need to go?"

"Into town. A couple of hours' escape would let this settle. I could go by my—"

"You'll do no such thing. I'll take you. Let me tell Hidal I'm leaving." He waved a warning finger at her and turned toward the other side of the ridge, trilling like a bird in several short bursts. An answering call came from below.

"All right. Let's go." He started down the hill, his hand under her arm all that kept her from falling at the pace he set. She didn't care. They were together and alone, and during those moments everything would be right in her world.

Now that Jelani had joined the clan in the hills, she visited the city less often, but today she definitely needed to see some of her human friends. Someone who made sense after her days with the Circle. She knew he understood, although he had no need for the city any more.

"You don't have to come, Astan. I'm perfectly capable of finding the coffee shop." She said it with her head cocked to the side, her hands on her hips. Then she added that little smirk he really hated, the one that meant 'don't be stupid'. Their easy relationship endured such teasing, as long as she didn't put herself in danger. His dedication to her safety did not bend. She knew this about Astan, and allowed for his opinions and actions, so true to his nature. She hoped he would do the same for her.

He brushed back her dark hair, long and curling now, as suited a *neris,* to study her brown eyes. "What are you up to in town?"

She caressed his face, feeling warm and cherished. "If I told you everything, then you'd never be surprised, now would you?"

"Surprises come in many forms, *denami.* Some nicer than others."

The endearment made her smile. "We're talking about Iris. How dangerous can it be?"

"Another makeover?" He laughed softly.

Jelani's best human friend, Iris Pallaton, a tall blonde social worker, prided herself on her fashion sense. She had been very complimentary as Jelani's choice in clothing had evolved since becoming the clan's leader, donning a new palette of colors that echoed the earth tones of the wild in lieu of her former predilection for black. Of course, Iris took personal credit.

"I hope not," Jelani said. "I don't know how much more change I can stand."

"You know I love and cherish you as you are. Or as you were. Or as you will be."

His smile shone through his eyes, brightening his whole being. She slipped into his arms for a tender kiss that promised much more when she returned.

How to wheedle her man into giving her what she wanted? Humor was usually the best weapon. "Now I am your Queen, and I am giving you an order. You will walk me to town to visit my other loyal subjects."

He eyed her, his face stoic.

Not working this time. "Oh, come on, Astan, please? Just for a little while? I need a break. You do, too! Coffee, you know you love it."

He made a face. "Fine. I'll leave you just outside town at the bottom of Pattee Canyon Drive."

* * *

They traveled cross-country, arriving outside town in mid-afternoon.

As soon as they were in cell-phone range, Jelani used some of her last remaining contracted minutes to invite Iris for coffee. Iris, enthusiastic, agreed to meet her at the old coffee shop where Jelani used to work.

"I'll be back by sunset," Jelani promised.

"See that you are." Astan buttoned the top of her green, down-filled jacket as if she were a child. "You don't want to force me to come looking for you."

She pulled away hurrying down the road toward the city before he changed his mind, trying not to think how each step brought her closer to freedom. She felt his intent gaze watch her every step.

"Don't worry!" Jelani scolded.

But she knew he would. It was what he did.

CHAPTER 3

AS Jelani walked along South Higgins toward the coffee shop, the rumble of the passing traffic rattled her right through the ground into her feet, despite the thick soles of her hiking boots.

The number of cars on Missoula roads surely had not increased that much since she had moved to the forest with Astan. Maybe she was just no longer accustomed to the noise after three months with the clan. The pure mountain air away from Highway 93 was full of natural sounds, nothing like this.

"Worse today," she murmured resisting the urge to cover her ears and protect herself from the roar of the engines.

Worse today, worse today, worse today echoed in her head as she walked, falling in with the rhythm of her steps. She desperately scoured her brain for a different song, something to relieve her mind and distract her.

There. The tune Astan had written and played for her on his little reed flute. A poignant little refrain in a minor key that he had told her was inspired by the sometime sadness in her eyes. The notes wrapped themselves around her heart and buoyed her up so she could continue.

Maybe she just needed some of Butterfly Herbs' special chocolate hazelnut coffee. It had always been her favorite for the two years she had worked there and she felt deprived lately not to be able to brew a pot whenever she felt like it. Tea she could make over the fire. The Circle kept her supplied with an assortment of herbal flavors. But the electrical apparatus for espresso derivatives just was not part of the magic.

The familiar sights of Missoula, a city of aging hippies and surprising pockets of diverse culture, insinuated themselves into her awareness as she walked. On the west Higgins Avenue bounded the historical district that held the University of Montana and many huge old Queen Anne and Revival homes Jelani had always admired. As part of the old city, Higgins was also home to several historic landmarks like the Lucy and Bluebird Buildings, as well as the standout eight-story Wilma Theatre building farther up the block.

She had lived in the city seven years, since she was eighteen when she had traveled west to attend the University. The science department had been thrilled at first to have Vincent Marsh's daughter apply to their program. Sadly, she was not the gifted naturalist he had been. She dropped out after her second year.

Not that a fancy college degree would have done her much good, considering how things had ended up. She imagined Djana and the others would find her even more useless if she started quoting them reams of data on statistical probabilities.

Her best friend Iris waited outside the front door to Butterfly Herbs, talking on her cell-phone, her voice thick with concern. A heavy winter coat in an impossible shade of cerulean blue concealed her willowy figure. Her jaunty knitted hat sat askew atop her head. She hugged Jelani awkwardly around the phone and continued talking.

"No, Mandy," Iris said, "I don't think it's a good idea that you leave home just now. Why? Because you're sixteen and you don't have a job, that's why!"

Jelani smirked at her friend's beleaguered expression. Iris was at her best when handing out advice. She loved her job as a counselor and life coach. Naturally empathetic, she gave of herself until Jelani was surprised there was anything left.

"I'll get your latte," Jelani said with a wink and went inside.

The store hadn't changed much. Heavy glass jars along the walls held treasures of herbs and spices both common and rare, as well as a wide variety of teas and coffees. The cashier must be new. She didn't look familiar. How long had it been since Jelani had visited? She could not honestly remember. Weeks, at least. When she didn't have to be anywhere at any given time for days at a stretch, she found it easy to fall into the elves' lack of formal schedule.

Time among the clan seemed to pass at a different rate. While they still marked sunrise as the beginning of a day and sunset as the end, weeks and months were much fuzzier. Seasons seemed to be significant divisions of note. Those she could follow.

As summer had changed into autumn, the elves had seemed to shift into unhurried mode, a slower pace, as if the cooler winds had thickened them somehow, like syrup. Astan explained that most of the elves, like humans, tended to be homebodies during the harsh winter months, waiting for the spring sun to thaw their sylvan world once again.

The store employees weren't completely unfamiliar. Jelani spotted one former coworker operating the espresso machine.

"Hey, stranger!" Bailey called, as Jelani approached the counter.

Jelani slipped off her coat, hanging it on the hook at the end of the benches. "Hey, yourself."

"You're looking good. That man must be treating you right." The curvy dishwater blonde's smile warmed beyond what she normally used for her customers. "Why didn't you bring him with you?"

Jelani shrugged, knowing she could have demanded that Astan come. But Astan never had liked this place. "He had other things to do."

"Funny not seeing him and his friend here any more." Bailey finished off the preparation of a cappuccino with a swirl of whipped cream and a dusting of cocoa. Then she handed it to her waiting customer.

"I bet it's a lot quieter these days without me and my merry band." Jelani bit her tongue, trying not to remember the crazy times, and waited her turn.

"What can I get you?"

"I need a large chocolate hazelnut coffee with cream and a cinnamon latte. Skim. No whipped cream."

"You got it."

Jelani looked around, fighting the sting of tears in her eyes as she allowed herself to miss her old life, just a bit. She had left her job here after a week or two as the leader of the clan. It was impractical to try to be two places at the same time.

But every time she came to the coffee shop, she thought about where she had been standing, right where Bailey was, when she first met Astan. She met Astan's father Daven, just outside the back door in the alley. She confronted the clan's enemy, Bartolomey, and his creepy mate Malina at the table next to this one. And she had even bought Richard a cup of coffee at that cash register the day he had agreed to take her to the jazz concert at the university for her twenty-fifth birthday. The day that had changed everything.

"How much longer do you have at school?" she asked Bailey, wanting to shake those memories.

"This semester and then one more. Then I am done, baby!" Bailey laughed. "I can officially join the ranks of the unemployed with a college degree and student loan repayment book in hand."

Jelani grinned, but the smell of brewing coffee sank slowly into her stomach with an unusual sense of nausea. She swallowed hard, willing it to pass. As desperate as her cravings for coffee had been during her time in the woods, she would drink this cup if it killed her. "I'm sure it won't be that bad. What's your major? Accounting?"

"That was last semester." Bailey sheepishly smiled as she swirled cinnamon into the espresso. "Definitely hotel management this year."

"Oh." Maybe Bailey displayed some real insight into her future career after all. Jelani just smiled and nodded. None of it was relevant to a day walking from sunrise to sunset among the plants of the Bitterroot forests.

She dug into a pocket for her dwindling stash of human currency and found six one-dollar bills. She put them on the counter with a handful of change, enough to pay for the coffee and a generous tip. "I wish you luck, anyway. There's a small investment to get you started."

"Thanks!"

As Bailey handed Jelani the two coffees, Iris entered the shop shivering. She slid into the booth without taking off her coat and laid her phone and purse on the table. Jelani joined her, setting both cups on the table. Iris fairly pounced on hers, wrapping bare fingers around the warm cup with a groan of satisfaction.

"That child will be the death of me," said Iris.

"Nonsense. You're a miracle worker. Look what you did for Crispy."

"You know as well as I do that wasn't my handiwork. I'd put five years into conquering Ron's agoraphobia before your elf friends came along." Iris sipped her coffee despite its temperature. "Daven managed to heal the gateway from all those years of abuse and drugs in one hands-on session. Once we got past that obstacle the rest was easy." Iris smiled.

"Crisp told me you don't even see him professionally any more. That's wonderful."

"That is wonderful," Iris agreed. "How is Daven, anyway? Do you think he'll ever have a spare evening away from rebuilding your magic queendom to go on an old fashioned human date or two with me?"

Jelani laughed and rolled her eyes, sitting sideways on the bench, knees bent and hugged close to her. "You and men. I swear."

"What? Nothing wrong with men." The blonde's smile never faded. "You seem to be happy with yours."

"Astan?" Jelani felt a rush of heat into her cheeks. "I'm not so sure he's happy with me. He's always nagging me about this protocol or that. About how I don't walk through the woods the right way. Still working on the elvish language, but I'm not much more fluent than your average eight year old yet. Even though Djana and the Circle shove it down my throat daily along with their awful predilection for homemade herbal teas."

She sighed and took a long whiff of the coffee in her hand. Heaven. Coffee and chocolate together had to be one of the most incredible combinations ever. She sniffed again, finding her stomach had settled, and the aromas were even more distinct than she remembered. Every little nuance of the mocha mix seemed to announce itself in a separate layer. Even the sweetness of the raw sugar she added overcame a bitter note she had never noticed before.

Iris wagged a finger. "That tells me how they feel about you. How do you feel about him?"

How did Jelani feel about Astan? Her lips curved into a smile. "He's wonderful. He's patient. He's funny. He's steadfast. I could trust him with anything. He'd never let anything happen to me."

She remembered how Astan had come to her rescue when Bartolomey would have killed her. She had learned all she needed to know about his character that day.

"And?" Iris persisted, her eyes sparkling sapphires of curiosity.

"And what?"

"I saw your bedroom. What's he like as a lover? What kind of magical qualities do elves bring to lovemaking? Are they gifted in many ways?"

Jelani stalled, reluctant to share any personal detail of the wondrous but sparse private time she and Astan shared. "Are you asking about Astan or planning to seduce Daven?"

"Jellie. I'm wanting to make sure you're okay."

Iris reached across the table and took her friend's hand. "Lane and Crispy, they're worried about how infrequently they've seen you in the past months. And I am, too. You look different. Thinner. Your hair has grown like wild vines, double the normal rate. You've changed." Her fingers closed tighter on Jelani's and she squeezed a little. "If they're not treating you right up there, I want to know. You've still got your place here, right?"

Jelani nodded. "Till the end of the month. Djana had some money saved and covered it for me, just so I didn't freak about making a complete break right away. Then? Well, then I guess I'll stay full time at our place in the forest."

"Who wouldn't want to? It's gorgeous. What magic can do for you." Iris sat back with a little envious sigh.

Jelani allowed herself a moment of satisfaction. Magic. A crazy notion. Before she found that glass slipper she had never believed in magic, elven or any other kind. Back when she first met the elves, she and Iris and the Boys had all wondered what elves did all day and night in the forests and how they survived the elements. Now she knew.

"How are the Boys?" Jelani asked.

"Like I said, they're worried. Lane's talking about trying to get a camera of some sort out in the woods to keep an eye on you."

"Oh, really?"

Jelani wouldn't put it past him. Pudgy computer geek Delano Donatelli, Lane to his friends, had more than his share of paranoia. Not as bad as his roommate Crispy, so called because of his fried years as a teenager. The two had lived together in foster care, and when they had aged out of the system they decided to share a place. Until very recently, Crispy had been categorically afraid of even so much as a venture onto the front step of their apartment.

But as Iris had said, Daven had convinced him to open up to the world again.

"Where's Lane going to get a power cord to run out that far, hmm?" Jelani laughed and drank more of the coffee, feeling the warmth settle in. Her body seemed to relax, not the usual response people had to caffeine, but when she had soaked in the amounts of coffee that she had over the years this was what she defined as usual. Perhaps her chemistry had changed. Natural might be healthier, but it certainly wasn't her normal.

Iris lifted her cup to Jelani. "Once he conquers that obstacle, I think you're done for. Then he's your problem."

Jelani remembered Astan's careful interference with Lane's various electronic devices, including his webcam, and decided not to worry too much. "If it makes him feel better, more power to him."

"But seriously, Jellie. Are you sure you're okay?" Iris' face showed genuine concern.

"Why do you keep asking? I'm fine!"

"Still snappish, I see." Iris' phone buzzed on the tabletop and she glanced quickly at its face and sighed.

"Don't answer it," Jelani said, suddenly desperate to keep Iris with her, holding the remains of her human life close.

The phone vibrated as it played some folk-rock guitar tune as a ring-tone, and then it stopped. Guilt clouded Iris' face. "All right. But only for a few minutes. I know what the office wants."

She slipped off her coat.

"Good. We just got here." Jelani relaxed into her seat, clutching her cup. "So much to catch up on."

Iris studied her, nodding. "Tell me what you've been doing."

"Me? Well, you know, trying to learn the clan's native language. I guess we were lucky that they'd had to live in town for so long. Most of them speak human English fairly well. But as soon as they got back to the forest, that changed." She sighed. "Right now, I have all these Circle gatherings where they all get together and talk and talk and act like I should have some idea what answer to give. I hardly ever do."

That didn't sound very interesting. Jelani frowned. What else occupied her time? She need something to convince Iris that all was well.

"I've been, um, healing the forest," Jelani said.

"What? The forest? You mean like putting bandages on trees?" Iris leaned forward, elbows on the table. "How are you doing that?"

"You know how I always was good with plants, right? Somehow, up there on the mountain, I can make the forests grow. Even in areas where the loggers have clear cut. Daven shows me what needs to be tended and I do it."

"Are you kidding? How?"

Iris appeared genuinely interested so Jelani explained her hours walking through the forest, stopping when she found a tree damaged by human intrusion. A touch from her hand, a few minutes communing with the plant, and she could actually persuade it to produce fresh sap and feel it begin to flow inside the trunks again, spreading to the impaired areas, bringing nutrients to rebuild and more to carry away the wounded cells. The sensation amazed her.

This was the gift Daven had promised her all those months ago and she was grateful for it. She hoped to prove herself worthy of it when the old biddies would let her.

"What a blessing," Iris said softly. She frowned a moment, as if trying to remember something. "An article in the *Missoulian* last week quoted some local environmentalist saying something about a change for the better in the general ecology. I don't remember the details, but maybe this is what they were talking about!"

"I know. It's like what I did for the animals at the Wildlife Rehabilitation Center. Something that I believed was just an affinity for injured creatures, but now that I'm among the clan, it's blossomed into something much more powerful."

"Does Daven say why?"

"Djana said when the clan reunited they became attuned to the soil once again. When the clan comes into harmony, their life force is shared among them and strengthened. Then each individual's powers become stronger as well."

"A whole societal shift. That's amazing."

"I know. But then they say that the more I increase the health of our surroundings, the more the clan will heal too."

"A chicken and egg thing."

"I guess." Jelani fidgeted, uncomfortable bragging about her accomplishments. She debated telling Iris about the frustrations of the Circle, like the confrontation that morning, but didn't want to be a whiner. Any handle she gave her human friends to judge her unhappiness would upset them. All the same, she should be able to be honest with her best friend. "You know, being a queen doesn't come with a manual. I'm not sure I like it."

"Oh, honey." Iris's voice filled with sympathy and she came around to Jelani's side of the table to hug her. "I'm sure it's overwhelming. But after all you've gone through, I don't suppose you can just walk away."

Jelani shook her head, clinging to her friend. "I've thought about it, Iris. I've thought about it a dozen times. More. But there are so many things in my life that I've just quit because they were hard." She took a deep breath and let go. "I don't want to do that any more, Iris. I have been so fortunate to learn the truth about my past and to receive these gifts. I want to see this commitment through to the end."

"Good girl! I know you can do it!" Iris wore her social worker smile. Jelani tried not to mind. "You've been my friend all this time. And Lane's. If you can survive that you should be able to manage those elves."

"I mean to. I just have to stick with it."

"Astan will help you through it. He cares about you so deeply."

The thought of her companion lifted Jelani's heart. "I know he does."

"I know what we'll do! After Lane finishes the book he's writing about your search for your mother and all that happened, we'll get him to write you a manual on 'How to Be a Queen'. At least it'll keep him off the streets." Iris gave a light-hearted musical laugh.

Jelani laughed too, though she knew the chance of Lane being on the streets was pretty slim. He was pretty much tethered to his computer bank.

"He'll like that. I'll tell him he has to interview all the old wise women of the Circle. He can go all D&D on them."

"Exactly." Iris moved back to her side of the table. "I know you didn't ask, but from a professional point of view, you've made most of the steps of community integration, honey. You've found housing and employment, well, of a sort. Healing nature is a good objective, I think! As queen, I'd say you've got civic involvement."

"I'd say." Jelani rolled her eyes. "More than I ever expected."

Iris grinned. "You've achieved certain expected social roles since you've partnered with Astan, and you've got his family connections now. Even the annoying ones." She counted off on her fingers. "Peer support?"

"Which peer would that be? I'm too human to be an elf. Too elf to be human." Why did she sound so lame? She was happy.

"Yeah, that's a problem." Iris's brow scrunched up into a quizzical knot. "But you still have your health."

"Oh, huzzah," Jelani groused.

"Hey, health is important. All that fresh air and fresh food will make you outlive us all." Iris finished her coffee as her phone rang again. She studied the vibrating object with a malevolent eye. "I've got to get this."

Jelani shrugged, understanding the needs of a job.

A job. Like hers?

Strolling through the forest showing plants how to heal themselves did not seem like work, though it certainly served a purpose both for the clan and for life on the planet in general, one for which she would likely never get credit. And certainly never be paid.

But she had to admit she didn't really miss her phone ringing all day and night with the demands of others imposing on her time. Much less stress in the woods, taking life as it naturally unfolded.

Iris stepped away from the booth speaking quickly and quietly, and then snapped the phone closed. "I've got to go, honey. Promise not to take so long before you come back!"

"You all should come out to the woods," Jelani replied, trying to cover a hint of pathos that crept into her voice. "Crispy can fix up my father's cabin. We can have, I don't know, a sleepover."

"That will be great. You take care." With a quick kiss to Jelani's cheek, Iris grabbed up her coat and purse and she was gone.

Jelani felt her absence like a sudden sucking vacuum of space leaving her vicinity, a gaping hole where warmth had been. Tears stung her eyes and she turned away from the room, not wanting anyone to see.

When she had regained control, she glanced up to find two uniformed Missoula policemen watching her from the counter. The sense of déjà vu was too much to bear. One of them approached her table.

"Hey, aren't you Richard Snyder's girlfriend?" he asked.

She stared up at him, taken aback at the question. This guy almost looked like Richard with the same close haircut, the same build, the same pseudo-rakish tilt of the uniform hat. Though she had gone out with Richard several times, she never considered themselves boyfriend and girlfriend. But Richard had, right up until Grigor shot him for coming to her rescue.

"Me?" Jelani sputtered. "No, not really."

"Huh. I could of sworn it was you. Didn't you think so, Jay?" He turned to the other officer, who nodded. "It's a shame what happened to Richard up there in the woods."

Jelani swallowed hard feeling her coffee rebel in her stomach at the thought of Richard the last time she had seen him, blood spreading across the shirt under that awful plaid lumberjack coat. She didn't want to think about him or that awful day. She had to get out of here. Right now.

"See you!" she called to Bailey on her way out.

Almost at a run, she burst through the door to the street. As she slipped on her coat, she half-expected the officers to follow and arrest her for what had happened to their colleague.

But they didn't come. She had escaped.

CHAPTER 4

HAUNTED by Richard's senseless death, Jelani walked the streets of downtown Missoula, wishing that her watering eyes were caused by the sharp fall wind.

"I'm not unhappy," she muttered to herself. "I'm not."

She crossed at the traffic light onto Orange Street, hardly seeing the people walking past her. The storefront windows were decorated for fall, some already for Christmas, and her heart resonated once again with the markings of human culture. Her thoughts spun into a whirlpool of confusion. Although she loved her new life, she missed her old, too.

As she continued to study the displays, she found the lights too bright. They hurt her eyes and she had to look away. She walked ahead, hugging her arms close to her body. The noise of the city's passing traffic continued to press on her awareness. It was too much.

She realized what she truly craved at the moment was the soft gurgle of a mountain stream. Just the focused thought of the peaceful green of the forests, the rugged brown rock of the mountains, calmed her. She often spent hours each day absorbed in the beautiful country of the Bitterroot Valley, from the lakes in the north, south through the mountains, east to the forests, listening to the conversation of the trees, the animals and the breeze. That was her life now.

Because she missed Iris and the Boys, she had tried to get them out to see how wonderful life in the forests could be.

After an 'adjustment' of their eyes so they could truly see the magic, the three of them had come to inspect the tree house Daven had charmed for her. Iris had *oohed* and *aahed* over everything, including Daven.

Crispy, now a regular visitor to the forest, accepted the new vision with equanimity, more interested in the cleaning and preservation of a tree house than the science or magic of it. Lane was the problem, as always. Whenever they could pry him out of town to the mountains, his fingers twitched with phantom pains, as if his computer keyboards had been amputated from them. But the tree house had been too much.

His dark eyes had taken one look inside, and he had retreated out into the open. "No way, Jelly Bean. That's just not possible. Not possible. I don't care what the Doctor does on television. Now I've accepted some crazy stuff from these elf pals of yours, but this goes right over the line. You're going to walk in there, and when whoever's controlling this thing falls asleep at the switch, bam!" He clapped his hands together startling them all, including the elves in the canopy overhead. "It's gonna slam in on you, and you'll be a pancake."

But it hadn't, despite Lane's dire predictions. Jelani had spent many a restful night in her little place, most of them with Astan close by. Even her black cat Azrael had made the permanent move out from town and he approved one hundred percent.

If it was good enough for Az, it should be good enough for her.

It was good enough for her. Most of the time.

A nudge of enlightenment shook her outlook. What did she expect when she put herself smack in the path of nostalgia for a life she had left behind? Why leave herself wide open to regret the choices her parents made for her when they fell in love so many years before?

"I should know better," she muttered.

Feeling a little dizzy, she leaned against the brick wall of the bank building. Caffeine. The coffee had tasted so good that she had swallowed it right down. Now, what a rush! Iris was right. After the natural organic food she ate in the forest, the heavy-duty coffee hit her like cocaine. She must have detoxified herself, thanks to Djana's flavorless herbs. And she had now sullied her 'pure' body with the evil brew of beans.

"Huzzah for health," she said with a weak smile, trying not to close her eyes. That would just make the spinning worse.

A man in a dark suit spied her as he came out of the bank, stepping close to catch her elbow in his hand. "Are you all right?" he asked, his eyed narrowed with concern.

Startled, she resisted the paranoid response to crack him in the chin. He was a well-meaning stranger in a city where people actually cared about someone they didn't know. Missoulians were pretty lucky in that respect.

"I'm fine, thanks," she said, making the effort to inject warmth into her reply.

He let go as soon as she spoke. "Someone I can call for you?"

"No. Really. I'm fine." She forced herself away from the wall, standing as tall as she could for someone five feet, three inches. Running a hand through her hair, she pushed it back from her face to demonstrate that her death was not imminent. "Too much coffee," she added, feeling a smile develop on her lips brought on by the annoying heat of a blush.

"Not hard to do around this town." The man broke into a grin. "You take care, honey." With one final look to assure himself that she meant what she said, he turned away and headed north up Orange Street.

"Don't call me 'honey,'" she mumbled, but not until he was out of earshot. His concern had seemed genuine. She should be grateful, not grumpy.

Jelani walked in the opposite direction, idly angling toward her apartment. She could stop and see the Boys, but in her current frame of mind, Lane might manipulate her into further upset and regret about leaving the city. Better to pick up some more of her belongings and then head back.

She passed the carousel, a huge merry-go-round built by hundreds of volunteers in the 1990s, and stopped a moment to watch the people making the circuit on the lustrous painted horses. This was no kiddie ride. The hand-decorated ponies flew around that ring, pleasing adults as well as children. Jelani and Iris had themselves boarded many times, sitting in the outermost row to score rings from the green Chinese dragon that extended itself so temptingly toward the riders. Jelani caught the gold ring on occasion. She usually donated the free ride to a nearby child.

Better not try that with her head already spinning.

A small self-mocking laugh saw her to the bridge and she walked briskly across, admiring the Clark Fork below. The leaves of the aspen on both sides of the river shone a warm golden yellow in the sunlight. She had canoed and rafted on this branch of the Columbia River many times during her years in Missoula. The river swelled in the spring to the point that surfers actually came out to enjoy the water. But the water at that time of year was much too cold for her, even with a wetsuit. She wasn't crazy.

Her gait developed into a rhythm allowing her thoughts to wander. They settled on Astan Hawk. She had held back the depth of her true feelings, not confessing them to Iris. She still couldn't believe that she had found this love that filled her so completely. Through her teens and even into her twenties she had tried relationship after relationship, only to watch them fail. Astan touched something vulnerable in her. Maybe his own insecurities brought them close. They both felt they had so much to prove to the world.

Astan was every bit a hero, devoted to duty and the clan. But especially to her. He was acutely good at 'handling' her, a knack he must have learned from his father. Or perhaps the message from the magic vessel left by Jelani's father, the one naming Astan as the Guardian of the clan's young queen, had somehow given him the ability to know her deeply. Daven might teach her what the Circle wanted her to know, but Astan led her heart to the Lelan.

With a hollow echo the door swung open into her nearly empty apartment. Her eye caught what was missing instead of what remained, adding another layer of sentimental gloom. Lane and Crispy had confiscated much of her furniture, with her blessing. Even her used possessions constituted an upgrade for them, so she was pleased they had a good home. She would be able to visit.

She had taken her papasan and her bed out to the woods via Lane's red beater truck. She donated her plants to the wildlife center, since she never knew exactly when she would be back to water them. But her closet remained half-full and the nights in the mountains had been very cold of late.

She selected half a dozen sweaters and shoved them into a grocery bag along with most of the remainder of her collection of hand knitted socks. For seven years she had gathered them. Those socks were often the only splash of color she would wear. Iris had contented herself with that small triumph back then but constantly hinted Jelani needed more color in her life. Jelani had found that the hues of the mountains suited for blending in, and those were enough colors for her at the moment.

Surveying what she had left, she considered her needs. She and Astan never shivered a moment in the tree house. Heat seemed to rise through the ground beneath them in some kind of geothermal effect. Through the chilly nights she had Astan and a stack of blankets to keep her warm. In her outdoor travels through the autumn landscape, though, warm socks would come in handy.

She picked up a few more personal items, things to make her new place feel like home, and some cat toys Azrael had left under the now missing sofa. He might enjoy something familiar to bat about, though he had certainly found new animal friends to play with in the woods.

Despite its beauty, she left the dreamcatcher Astan's grandmother Djana had given her, the one with the blue jay feathers. The delicate woven object swung from the ceiling on its long string right over where her bed used to be. While the Native American dreamcatchers purported to block bad dreams while one slept, somehow Djana's creation facilitated the reach into a sleeper's mind to bring on dreams. She had tried to influence Jelani to choose her son Daven as consort, before crisis made it clear Astan should be the proper companion of the new queen.

"No, thank you," Jelani whispered. Yanking it down, she tossed the dreamcatcher into a wastebasket. "Plenty of bad dreams all on my own."

With her hands on her hips, she surveyed the detritus of her life.

Nine more days and she would have to clear out the rest.

Time to say goodbye to Jelani Marsh, failed college student and directionless float about, ignorant of her true heritage. Time to say goodbye to all the unhappy years when she felt unfettered and undefined, waiting for something or someone to show her a reason to have hope, to believe that her life could mean something.

That person, or the Lelan at least, had come. Her purpose had arrived. Now it was up to her to live that dream. She remained determined to succeed.

Jelani glanced out the window at the golden orb of the sun as it crept downward toward the horizon. If she was going to succeed without worrying Astan, she had better move.

She shoved the bags with her chosen items into her old black college backpack, strapped it on, and hurried out the door.

CHAPTER 5

GRIGOR Biren marched through the woods on the lee side of the Swan Mountains, nearly oblivious to his surroundings.

Thick layers of brown leaves crunched under his feet, scattering chipmunks into their hiding places as he passed. Some small part of his mind not engaged in plotting or feeling sorry for himself watched for fallen branches with his remaining instinct for self-preservation. Passing over decaying limbs, he walked with too heavy a step now to travel at an elven pace. Several times during the last seven days, he had caught his ankle, leaving bruises and aches behind.

It had been two days since he had found more to eat than just the seeds of the lower level pine trees and a handful of multi-legged insects. Plenty of cold water bubbled up through the ground into streams that fed the soil, but the trout avoided him. An elf alone. An elf without his gifts.

At one time he had been able to control the water and its effects on the land, but no more. He was as helpless as any human lost in the forest. He had not even been able to fashion an elf shelter. Instead he had dragged a large fallen tree branch over to a boulder and braced it with other pine branches before lining it with moss, above and below, to keep out the cold rain. It was the type of emergency cover a human might make. Not worthy of a child of the soil.

Movement overhead caught his eye. Two magpies circled for several moments and then dove for the tree line. Their loud bickering, a nasal *nack-nack* traded back and forth between them, revealed where they had gone. While they often fed on ticks and maggots, they also ate carrion.

Hungry enough now, Grigor would, too.

He crashed through the underbrush in search of the birds' landing place and nearly tripped over the dead elk before he saw it. The birds scattered, scolding him for the intrusion. Avoiding the staring eye of the great beast, he fell to his knees and plunged his hands into the animals' soft guts. Trying not to smell the days old meat in his hands, he shoved it between his lips ordering his jaws to chew the stuff, all the while feeling nausea inching up his throat.

The taste of the spoiled meat finally sank into his tongue and he spit it out, his stomach emptying on top of it. He went to wipe his face and found the smell still on his fingers. He vomited again. Sick, he rolled away from the carcass.

"Grigor?"

He stopped retching and froze behind a tree. Who out here would call his name? And a female, at that. The voice was familiar, but in his rattled state he could not picture a face.

"Grigor, what are you—"

Light footsteps came around the tree and a shadow fell across his face. He looked up to see the *neris* Fontine, his former lover, her face twisted in disgust as she watched him.

"Oh, Grigor." She covered her mouth with one hand and turned away.

Barely able to get to his hands and knees, he heard the rush of water close by to the west and crawled in that direction. Thankfully, she didn't follow.

Where had she been? What was she doing here?

He fell into the rivulet before he saw it, its waters shockingly cold. His breath stopped for a moment. Forcing himself to focus, to recover quickly before she was gone, he ducked his head in the water and scrubbed his face and hands and even his long tangled and neglected hair. How could he have known she would follow him out here? He had not seen another elf of the Lelan in how long? Two seven-days? Four? Longer?

When he had finished, he dragged himself out of the water, breathing hard as he lay on the wet earth, praying to the old trees themselves for the strength to endure.

"Are you all alone?" Fontine asked but did not approach.

Grigor considered the brief glimpse he had gotten of her standing over him, her hair long and golden, her eyes the color of wet shale just as she had been when they both followed Bartolomey. When he had loved her.

"What would you expect? We were cast out." He choked on the words, or maybe it was the reek of his clothing.

Living in the open did not provide him much incentive to remain neat and clean. A quick search around the glade found some herbs with a mint smell. He rubbed them into his clothes with his hands, hoping that Fontine wouldn't find him altogether repellent.

"We were invited to rejoin the clan," she said.

A rustling from her direction warned she was coming his way. Grigor straightened his hair the best he could and got to his feet.

"We belonged to the true clan," he said, words thick in his torn throat. "We followed the one who led the clan all those years despite the hatred of the Circle. Now those of us who still stand behind our beliefs are scattered to the wilds."

He had looked for the others, Bartolomey's partner Malina, Erdest, Terzon, but they had vanished without a trace. As far as he had been able to run, he had not found them.

Fontine stepped out from behind a tree, her delicate features just as he remembered them. Her beauty tore at his heart. Clean, combed, perfect, everything any *nian,* any elf man, could desire. As sunlight shafted through the trees, she studied him with a shocked expression.

"Oh, Grigor, look at you. So thin. So broken." Tears pooled and became luminous in her eyes.

"I've survived, despite exile," he said, trying to convince himself as well as Fontine. He took in her full face, her new clothing. "You seem to have done well, abandoning the principles in which we believed to join the traitors."

She jerked as if he had slapped her.

"I made a decision to live," she protested. "Look at you. Alone, without the shared life force to keep you strong. Without the company of others to warm your mind. You're eating dead meat, by the Lady!"

"'By the Lady'? Do you mean the Queen?"

She looked away, her gaze dropping to the ground. "She's not evil, Grigor. What has happened isn't her fault. It's simply the providence of the circumstances of her birth. She's just a girl trying to serve the Lelan."

Afraid to come closer lest he repel her too much, Grigor shoved his hands in what was left of his pockets. "We thought we served the Lelan, too. You and I, back in the forests with Bartolomey. We believed in his cause. That his rule was just, since his sister Linnea was gone."

"But have you seen what Jelani's done for the forest? Even places we thought were dead, she's brought them back to life, Grigor. She's changed everything." Fontine looked at him again, chewing her lip, as if she didn't trust her own words.

"We thought we would change our world, too, as I remember. Change everything. You and I, Fontine. You and I." Grigor closed his eyes a moment recalling the feel of her skin under his fingertips, the berry taste of her red lips, the way her gold hair caught in his hands when they coupled.

"No!" Her tears fell, as she backed away. "I can't! Don't make me think about that time! We cannot change things now. I must serve the clan as it exists, so that we may all live."

The space between them seemed to expand into a chasm much wider than truth. "Fontine, please don't go! Please." He felt the sting of tears in his own eyes. "Please don't leave me again."

She hesitated, halting her retreat.

"What can there be between us Grigor, if you will not come to the clan? Would you wish that I live here with you? Two alone? Two on the road to a starving death? Would you share your dinner banquet of maggots with me?" Her voice broke and she covered her face with her hands.

Her horror, evident in her trembling fingers and the stricken eyes she revealed, pulled at his gut. For just a moment he saw himself through those gray eyes. Pale skin, hollow cheeks, ragged clothes. A far cry from the cocky young First of the youngers.

Silence stretched like a gauzy strand of spider's web, delicate at first glance, yet too sturdy to permit them to speak. So easy to give in to those eyes, remembering how the warmth of love could shoot them through with a deep fire.

Just say yes. Be with Fontine again. Be part of the clan again. Live.

But he couldn't do it. The clan was wrong. The 'queen' was wrong.

Now that he had seen Fontine, he did not want to lose her. He had to keep her coming back, whatever it took, deceit or worse. He looked up, feeling more vulnerable than he could ever remember in his life.

"I'll try, Fontine. Will you stand by me? Help me see how it is?"

She watched him, suspicion a slash in her furrowed brows. "You want to reunite with the Lelan? Rejoin the clan, become one of us again?"

"Isn't that where an elf belongs?"

"Of course, but—"

She had not moved from her retreated position and one foot was poised to run. He knew how fast she could be gone. With her elven power she could vanish in several beats of his heart.

"Maybe if you ask them, Jelani and Astan. Just to make sure their welcome is sincere." Grigor held out a hand. "You know if I just walked in they'd never trust me."

She shrugged. "Maybe you're right."

"So will you come see me again? You know, to tell me what they said?" He was careful not to look her in the eye, trying to appear contrite. His muddled brain forced thoughts along the channels of his mind, showing him possibilities. Reconnecting with Fontine could benefit him in more ways than just his personal comfort. She could be a window into the new group. If he played her right, she could lead him straight to their weakest points.

"I don't know, Grigor." Her toe tapped a staccato rhythm and then she let her hand slowly swing toward him. "Maybe. I'll try. I'll bring you some clothes. Some food."

"You always were the best. I miss you, *denami*." He caught her hand in his, the supple skin like warm silk. He let his rough fingers slide up and down hers sending her faint remembrances of their time together, attenuated by the fading of his power. Their previous connection allowed him access, at least. Hopefully, it was enough.

She stood with her eyes closed for several minutes, experiencing with him, though she did not move any closer. "I'd better go," she said at last as she pulled away her hand. "I'll come soon."

"Until we meet again, then." He took a step back.

"This is for the best, Grigor, you'll see."

She was there another moment and then moved away almost faster than he could observe.

After her departure, her absence seemed so complete he wondered if he had hallucinated her appearance altogether. He returned to the clearing, finding the magpies back at their meal. His stomach turned and he made an about face, running away toward the mountain and his shelter in the forest. His heart beat with a stronger rhythm now that he had shared physical contact with another of his kind. He ran with a lighter step, skimming over the smaller fallen branches.

Fontine had promised to return with real food and clothing.

This was only the first step in his plan for revenge. Something else would come to him. He felt an upswing in the tempo of his life force. His luck was beginning to change. He knew it.

He wasn't alone any more.

Half-giddy with hunger, he ignored the cold to stop at the river and stripped off his filthy clothing, scrubbing it against some large flat rocks to remove the worst of the stains and odors. Fontine had returned to him. He could hold on to the beautiful young elf. He knew he could. He had always known just how to win her heart. The effort required on his part would be minimal.

A reminder of better times. A kind word. Attention to his hair and clothing. Or even better, letting her tend to him, letting her see his false contrition, letting her 'save' him. Yes, that was the best.

His body shivered like a branch of aspen leaves in the wind, as he finished washing his clothes in the icy water and hung them atop his makeshift shelter. They would smell good enough to let

Fontine get close to him next time.

He ducked inside his shelter, wrapping up as best as he could in the pile of rags he had for blankets. Oh yes, he wanted to get close to Fontine again. As he closed his eyes, exhausted and weak, he thought about her, how her skin felt against his, the taste of her mouth, the small sounds she made when they coupled. Memories took over. While they couldn't feed his empty stomach, they distracted him from it long enough to fall into a sleep full of lusty dreams.

CHAPTER 6

"ASTAN just leave me alone. Please. Stop asking me to endure one more minute of this. I can't do it."

Curled up in the papasan chair with the blue patterned cushion, Jelani pulled a wispy green elven blanket over her head.

Astan's stomach tightened into a hard unyielding lump. For days now, this inexplicable cloud hung over the *neris* who comprised his morning and night. If it lasted much longer he would cross over into madness.

"Jelani, the Lelan believe in you. I believe in you. Why can't you believe in yourself?"

She didn't respond.

The end of the month had arrived and Djana had decreed she would no longer maintain Jelani's city dwelling. Jelani had no money because she had given up the city job she no longer needed. In the forest human money meant nothing. Up until now, she had been happy with that. Joyous even some days. He imagined the loss of connection with her former surroundings might have something to do with the alteration in her good spirits. But she would not say. She only cried.

He could not understand Jelani's change in behavior, her easy tears, her aversion to food, her surrender to a tired sorrow. He had tried to access his recurrent ability to form a picture of a situation but her unstable aura seemed to disrupt his focus.

The Circle looked to him to deal with the queen and he believed he tried his best, but Astan could not defeat her mood swings and lack of interest. Bands of stress tightened around his chest until he thought he could not take another breath. His hands balled into fists. He tried with every part of his essence not to explode at her.

He was the Guardian. The Vincent had said so. The old queen, Linnea, had put Jelani's hand in his.

He should be able to talk to her.

She should listen.

No matter what he tried in the last few days, she always seemed to face her future with something between anger and agony. Over the last months he had always been able to get through to her, even on those days she and the Circle met in battle like two mountain rams in head shattering collision. He would hold her hand or sit with her shoulder to shoulder, simply being present, showing his support and love in silence. Before long her pixie smile would surface and she would again become the one he recognized as his light and love.

"*Denami*, I thought you liked this house. Daven said—"

She didn't come out from under the blanket. "It's not that! I can give up the apartment. I've given up the city."

"What is it then?

"You wouldn't understand. It's just how I feel."

His hand, in the act of rubbing his forehead to deflect the growing pain inside, fastened on his hair. If he pulled hard enough to yank it off his head, would that lessen his frustration? Baldness wasn't an issue. He had plenty of hair. Since they had returned to the forest his brunette hair had grown longer and thicker, nearly shoulder length. He even knew that Jelani would have no loss of feeling for him if his head was as bare as a vulture's. What they shared transcended physical appearance and even the need for words.

But he could not translate the language of this new, weepy, exhausted, hopeless Jelani. He did not know what to do. He couldn't take it any more.

"If we cannot satisfy you, then move back to your people and leave us alone!"

Furious more at himself for losing control than at her stubbornness, he turned and stalked out of the tree home. When he reached the fresh air, his pace accelerated into a run. That's what he needed, to retune his body to the soil, to feel the breath in his lungs, to synchronize the beat of his heart with the natural world, to work through the exasperation until he was drained. Then maybe he could try again.

The sweet clean scent of pine needles under his feet began to recalibrate his mental equilibrium. The farther he got from the area where the clan lived, the better he felt. He hated their expectations of Jelani because he resented the way they treated her, despite how hard she tried. Whenever she didn't meet their standards, Djana would give that look of disappointment, as though he had failed alongside his mate.

The two of them shared a past, both believing they were orphans until their true histories were revealed, when Jelani had acquired twenty-five years of age. His father had been suspended in a magic hold for those years, his mother missing. Her father had been murdered, and her mother nearly lost to treachery. The conflict to resurrect the clan had changed the dynamic of the Circle, as they rallied to challenge Bartolomey for his usurpation of the clan leadership.

But that battle had passed. Jelani had returned to live as a child of the soil, as had they all, in the Bitterroot. She had accepted the duties and responsibilities of her position as Linnea's daughter, queen of the clan. If Djana and the others would only let her perform that function. If they could get past whatever had changed her attitude and threatened to pull her under.

He stopped his headlong run, out of breath from the upward haul. Panting and bent over at the waist as he looked over the valley below him, he could pretend for the moment that he was alone in the world.

"But of course, you're not."

The voice came from behind Astan. It was a deep, full-bodied sound tinted with humor.

"Father," Astan said, allowing his breath to catch up with him as he turned. "I should have expected I could not escape the Circle even in the open air."

"Of course not. The clan is one." Daven Talvi grinned, full of good humor. He wore a heavy leather jacket that strained to cover his broad shoulders, and dark pants along with light elven made boots of deerskin. The worn bag of stone runes Daven always carried, hung from his belt along with a short dagger in a sheath.

Before Astan could step aside, Daven laid a hand on his shoulder. With Daven's usual perception and ability to read others' thoughts, Astan could not keep his father from knowing the subject that troubled him.

She is quite a challenge, my son. His mental voice held comfort and encouragement. *Yet your feelings for her run deep.*

"They do," Astan admitted, pulling away from his father's touch. Any *nian* had the right to keep some of his most intimate thoughts and feelings to himself. "I don't understand her any more. She's emotional. She's irrational. Just weeks ago she seemed happy to live among us, to prepare for her role, accepting all you and Djana have taught her. I have done what has been asked. I would let nothing happen to her. You know this."

He moved away from Daven and climbed a rocky outcrop, seating himself pointedly higher than his father. A simplistic and perhaps childish move, but one that put him in a superior position, a little more comfortable than feeling as he usually did, that he could never measure up to the standard Daven set. His father was held in such high regard by the Circle. To reach that benchmark was nigh impossible for any average son.

Daven said nothing, but the slight upward twitch at the corner of his lips might have meant he understood Astan's purpose for moving there. He sat on a rock, closer and lower than where Astan sat, and took the runes from his belt.

Opening the bag, he poured several into his hand without looking at them, rolling them on his palm with his fingers, almost idly. Astan knew that his father's magic connection with those stones left nothing to chance.

"You have no reason to hide your thoughts from me, Astan." Daven looked out over the valley below. "We are no longer rivals for the heart of the queen. She chose you."

Astan's stiff jaw refused to allow him to reply. He believed Daven intruded too much into his son's private affairs just by the nature of his instructive involvement with the queen.

Astan knew that the self-condemning words waiting to break out of his mouth would advance his cause no further. He did not blame Jelani for her current state. He blamed himself.

He closed his eyes and concentrated on the feeling of wind against his face, unobstructed here on the rock. It was just cold enough to chill the outer layer of skin, but not to penetrate his warm clothing.

Daven did not seem to take the hint. "Moreover, Jelani's father Vincent and Linnea's father Lorenz chose you as the Guardian. The task is yours."

"Even though you could do it better?" Astan shot back, stung. "I know that is what Djana believes."

Not that she would come out and say it. As one of the elders, Djana knew her place. But that constant displeasure in her dark brown gaze, the pressing together of her lips when he spoke of Jelani, all told Astan that he had not performed as the Circle expected. What was it she wanted from him?

"Djana and the Circle have their beliefs," Daven said, as if reading his son's mind without physical contact.

"She said you would be better suited to teach Jelani what she needed to know about the clan," Astan snapped, the reply driven by anger and frustration. "About the magical powers she might have, about our society. Surely I could have taught her those things, but the Circle wanted you. She should be pleased."

Not reacting to Astan's sharp tone, Daven continued to twist the stones in his hand. "That pleases her. You must agree Jelani's gifts have been freed in a remarkable manner. She has saved much that was lost."

"I know. We celebrate the rebirth of the forests whenever we walk together."

Astan knew that Daven had unlocked Jelani's abilities, just as he had freed her friend Crispy from the trauma of his past abuse. Daven's elven gift seemed to be to determine, diagnose, and augment abilities in others. Although Astan wanted to resent Daven's 'interference,' he knew his father was likely best suited to help his beloved Jelani with her coming of age in the clan.

But that doesn't mean I couldn't have done it with a little guidance.

Having the Circle shove Astan aside just enlarged the chip on his shoulder. Maybe a direct approach would work better. What was he lacking? "Do you know what it is the Circle expects of me?"

Daven cast a speculative look. "My son, would I serve you well by telling you what that may be? Or is it a lesson you need to learn as you would peel a *solurd*?"

Astan growled at the implied brush off, sharing Jelani's frustration with the pedantic mysteries of elven teaching. If Daven wanted him to act as if he was full-grown and not a child, why did he continue to play these games? Why couldn't he just speak frankly? It was one trait that Astan found more evident in Jelani's human friends, especially Lane and Crispy, than in his fellow elves. Even if the truth was unpleasant, they seemed to have no trouble sharing it.

"So you do know," Astan surmised.

"If I did, I would still let you find the truth in your own way. This is the way a lesson is firmly learned."

"Thanks a lot." Miffed and resentful of the all too human pique he felt, Astan blew out the air in his lungs and leaned back onto the granite behind him. With his hands behind his head he stared up into the sky. It had been a brilliant blue earlier that day, but now was heavily shadowed with gray clouds moved in from the west. At the higher altitudes several inches of snow would fall by night.

Elven skin didn't freeze the way human skin would when left to the elements. Being one with the soil, they shared the warmth of the earth, even in the worst blizzard. That did not make it perfectly comfortable, however. Most of the elves designed some sort of shelter for the winter months. None as snug and secure as what he shared with Jelani. For that, he needed to thank his father, which again rankled him.

His mind focused on returning before dark to make sure Jelani was well and warm. Perhaps whatever had brought her tears had passed.

Daven chuckled and Astan's temper flashed. "What?"

"You bring us honor with your devotion to her, you know,"

his father said. "She is so special, and always in your thoughts. Even above your own care and safety."

"So?" Torn between defensiveness and embarrassment that his father might find him weak, Astan sat up, his eyes burning.

"So, I am proud, my son. You have grown up strong and true, even when I could not be by your side to help you."

Daven chewed on a greenstick as he spoke. Astan knew the spicy interior of the stick would bring a mild flow of calm to the one who tasted it. He chose not to partake, preferring his mind to remain sharp.

Although if Jelani continued to madden him with her mood changes and unpredictable motions, he might well ask for some of the elven ale Beckley was well known for brewing. It did not dull the senses, while it relieved the heart. Perhaps Jelani would benefit from a tall mug of brew as well.

Despite his own hidden resentment, Astan sensed his father's praise was sincere. He climbed down from his perch. Guilt rumbled around in his chest, tugging at his heart. "I always regretted growing up without a father, without a mother."

Daven nodded. "Sad I was to wake from my years of sleeping to find that your mother had vanished into the human world, leaving you with your grandmother. Veraena was a child of light. Not a day goes by that I don't feel the pull of her loss."

As a child Astan was told simply that both his parents were gone. For years he'd had no idea that either of them still lived.

Once Daven had been reborn with the help of Jelani's blood, he learned the truth about his father. His mother's disappearance, however, had remained a mystery.

Djana and the other *neris* believed that Veraena may have hidden elsewhere in the wild when she did not remain in the city with the rest of the Circle. But it was not until they had returned to the forests that one of Bartolomey's former followers had revealed her escape to the outside world.

"Do you think we could look for her, Father? Jelani's friends have many routes of access to the human world."

Daven took a deep breath. "Perhaps. But first we have much to rebuild and repair inside the clan. This should be our priority.

Veraena's blood will call her back once the clan is strong. All those who have left our clan will feel the growing power base drawing them back. We must be ready for their return."

Putting an arm around Astan's shoulders, Daven squeezed just a little as they looked down into the lands of the Lelan.

"Let me say this, my son. Of all the youngers, you are unique. The runes have told me that you have before you a path that will take you far, bringing great dangers and great rewards. Your heart must be strong and you must hold true to what you know is right, no matter what the risk. Many obstacles stand in your way, some the likes of which you have never encountered before. Strange magic moves beneath the branches of our trees and the Circle seeks to protect us all. None of us see the future in clarity."

He continued with his mind voice. *The most I have to offer you as encouragement is that we all believe in you, Astan. You are the chosen one, by whatever means, by the crossing of stars or the intersection of bloodlines or the sheer luck of fate. I do not believe we could be in better hands.*

His father released him and stepped back, studying him. "Indeed. Now, get you home to your lady and make sure she is prepared for what is to come." Daven's smile radiated warmth and faith, echoed in the depths of his hazel eyes. Then he turned and he was gone.

Alone on the mountain top Astan felt cold wind sting his eyes. Was his mother out there somewhere? He had heard stories of her at the knees of the wise females of the Circle, a *neris* said to be of strong magic and dark promise. If they found her, would it change their lives? Would Daven find a new reason to live?

Might he leave Jelani for Astan to teach, as any *nian* would his partner?

His eyes scouted the horizon in all directions, slowly, as he wondered what eyes he would need to see far enough to find Veraena. Then he started back down the mountain hoping Jelani's sadness had passed.

Daven was right. There was much to do before such tangential tasks could be pursued, no matter how close to the heart they might be. Surely the time would come.

CHAPTER 7

MOVING day.

The sky was clear and blue overhead. They had been spared the snow Crispy had obsessed about all morning. Jelani had helped carry out the first several loads of clothing and remaining small items of furniture from her Camelot Court apartment, but as the afternoon had progressed she felt worse and worse. Something was not right.

Her stomach aching, she hunched over on the steps, miserable.

Probably just nerves. Stress. I am leaving the human world officially, as soon as this day ends.

"That's the last of it."

Lane Donatelli came out of Jelani's empty apartment and looked down at her. "Jelly Bean, you don't have to do this, you know. The coffee shop would give you your job back in a heartbeat. You can enjoy the hustle and bustle and car fumes and pollution inversion like the rest of us."

When she didn't reply, the big man lumbered down the stairs. He wedged his ample backside next to hers on the step and put an arm around her. "Honey? Tell old Brother Lane what's on your mind."

Jelani groaned, her stomach coiling on itself as if snakes twisted through it. "I feel awful."

Skinny Crispy Mendell watched them from ground level, his eyebrows twitching. "Poisoned. She's been poisoned."

Lane rolled his eyes. "Really, Crisp? And when was that? We've been right here with her for the last three hours. She drank some water. Ate some peanut butter crackers. And whatever that tea was she brought from home."

Crispy scowled. "This is her home."

"I know that. Believe me, I've tried to convince her."

Listening to them bicker made her head hurt, too. "Shut up!" Dizzy, she tried putting her head between her knees, but bending that far just set off her nausea. "Move, Crisp. Now!"

He skittered out of the way and Jelani threw up all over the steps. She wiped her mouth with her sleeve, embarrassed and still sick. Spots floated before her eyes and she weaved where she sat on the concrete. She supposed she needed help but she didn't know how to ask for it or even what kind of help she needed.

Lane got to his feet slowly and stared at the dark mess she had made, a steaming pile of liquid almost black and gelatin like. "Whoa. I don't think that's normal, Jelly Bean."

He lumbered to ground level, taking his cell-phone out of his jacket pocket to speed dial someone. "Crisp, run up and grab one of those towels out of the box on the landing. Give her something to wash her face, all right?"

Jelani, her world in a whirl, felt rather than heard Crispy inch up the stairs past her. She could not open her eyes. Blackness hovered around the edges of her awareness.

What is wrong with me?

The next thing she knew, a damp towel was shoved into her hand. After wiping her face, she let her hot cheeks lay on the cool wetness, eyes closed. Somehow that felt better.

A car pulled up into the blank whiteness that was the field of her active consciousness. The screech of brakes followed, and flashing red lights shone through the surface of her closed eyelids.

She heard voices around her. Crispy. Lane. Then Iris. Other voices she didn't know asked her questions. She could not generate answers. Then she felt herself lifted and put onto a flat cloth covered surface. That movement focused her enough to speak up.

"Lane?" Jelani tried to move and found her arms and legs confined. She struggled, desperate. "Lane?"

His worried voice was close to her ear as others urged her to be still.

She felt the sting of a needle in the back of her hand.

"Honey, we didn't know what else to do. We called the ambulance. They're taking you to the hospital. Just to get you checked out."

"No, I can't," she murmured but another wave of nausea hit and distracted her.

"I'll try to find Astan, honey. Don't worry." Iris voiced rang through the chaos.

Don't worry, don't worry, don't worry.

The words echoed in her head as the ambulance pulled away, accented by the blare of the siren. Then Jelani's world faded away.

* * *

BEFORE her eyes opened again, the sounds of a hospital emergency room sank in.

Beeping. Impossibly loud beeping, just above her left ear.

Bustling feet down past the end of her bed.

Crying of a child in pain or fear off to the right.

Something pinched the index finger on her left hand. Her right hand was warm, very warm. She realized as she came fully awake that someone was holding her hand, someone familiar.

Astan.

She opened her eyes and turned to verify her impression. He stared down at the floor, his lips silently moving. Relief flooded over her as she saw him. Her fingers twitched on his and he looked up, startled.

"*Denami.*" He was on his feet in a second. "Finally, you are awake. I have been imagining all bad things."

Her voice came out in a whisper. "What happened? What's wrong with me?"

Iris slipped into the curtained area and came to her side, exchanging mysterious glances with Astan. "Oh, sweet Gaia! You're awake. How are you feeling, honey?"

Jelani assessed herself, feeling the nausea still lying in wait, but the dizziness gone. "I don't know. I'm all right. I think."

A white-coated man, with a brunette nurse in an oversized

colored print smock at his heels, pushed through the hospital curtain. Iris ducked aside, but Astan remained positioned at Jelani's side like a guard dog.

The muscular doctor with the silver movie star hair surveyed the small curtained space through horn-rimmed glasses, and then crossed to Jelani's left side. "Feeling better?"

"I think," Jelani repeated, not willing to be certain just yet. She studied his impassive face for some clue to what he was thinking. For the first time she noticed several adhesive bandages on her arms and an I-V pole hung near the head of her bed, the plastic tubing snaking from it to her left forearm.

"Hmmm." The doctor murmured something to the nurse who then tapped something into the electronic pad in her hands. He reached out and pinched the skin on Jelani's arm between his fingers, and then looked at her hands. "How long have your lips been dry like that?"

The question seemed odd. Weren't emergency rooms for matters of life and death?

"You're dehydrated," the doctor said. "How long have you been vomiting?"

Her shoulders twitched. Maybe those two things could be related. Dry lips and dehydration. She really wished her thoughts would come together a little more.

"I don't know. Several days. I've been nauseous for a couple of weeks now, but it seems to be getting worse. Maybe. I don't know. An ulcer or something?"

The doctor eyed her a moment. "Some reason to think you have an ulcer? Does your stomach burn when it's empty or full? Do you drink a lot of coffee?"

"Ha. No, not any more," she said with a hint of wistful longing. "I get stressed pretty easy. Too many meetings with the Circle. All that—"

"A new job," Iris interrupted with a fingernail jab at Jelani's right shin. "Lots to learn and all."

Had she really been about to tell the doctor that she was training to be the elf queen? A silly giggle escaped her.

The doctor's eyebrows wiggled and came together in a hairy

V shape. "New job, then?"

"Exactly." She squeezed Astan's hand wondering if she could do anything to erase the worry that had settled on his face like a solemn mask. "So, can we go?"

"I'm waiting on the results of some blood work. Then we'll see." The doctor eyed her, turned his gaze on Astan and Iris for a moment, and then swept out of the room.

The nurse hesitated at the curtain. "When was your last period?"

"What? I don't know for sure." Jelani tried to think back. "Should be last month, right?"

As she set her mind to remember she realized it had been several months, back in late July, about the time she had been initiated as part of the Circle. Djana had even insisted that they wait for the ritual until it was her time of the month. Something about the phase of moon, she had said.

When she told the nurse the date, a knowing look came over the nurse's face and she vanished beside the white curtain.

"No way," Iris gasped.

"What?" Jelani frowned, wishing she had more energy. She would just check herself out of the hospital. Dehydration? Give her a bottle of water. Or just give her some tap water in a glass. It should not warrant a trip to the emergency room.

She tried really hard to forget the splat of black vomit on the sidewalk. It was not something she ever wanted to experience again. She guessed one of them must have told the doctor about it, since he had asked her about throwing up before they had gotten to menstrual cycles.

"That's not the first time I've skipped. I used to in high school all the time."

She realized belatedly what conclusion Iris had jumped to, and her eyes focused on Astan. They had never been careful when making love. She had assumed. She had assumed because she was human, not elf, that nothing would happen. It had never been her intention to—what had she done?

"O-M-G," Iris exclaimed. She leaned on the foot of the bed, her eyes wide and amazed.

Astan's forehead wrinkled as he wrestled with the mysterious exchange. "What?"

Jelani tried to sit taller in the bed and knocked the finger pincher loose, which set off an alarm. "Hellfire," she muttered. She got it back on, but the alarm continued.

"Jelani, what are you talking about?" Astan persisted.

"A baby?" Iris gasped and then clapped her hand over her mouth.

"A baby?" The color drained from Astan's face. He wavered on his feet and might have fallen if Iris had not grabbed his shoulders and guided him back into a chair.

Jelani did not know which disconcerted her more, Astan's shock or her own queasy rush of denial. "No," she said. "No way. I can hardly take care of myself, much less a helpless child."

Even as the words of protest left her throat she felt something new. Something bubbled up, something warm, something she could not stop. Could it be true? Had she and Astan created a child who was part of them, body and soul? That would be wonderful, wouldn't it? She glanced over at her partner whose face displayed waves of emotion. Disbelief, wonder, even a little fear, but nothing like joy.

She couldn't stand it if he was unhappy about this. If it was real. Or she could be getting all worked up about nothing. Maybe it was just some bizarre strain of flu. Or nerves.

Something heavy trundled past the curtain, pushed by someone wearing soft-soled shoes.

A thin Asian lab tech bustled into the room with her little garden rack of tools clinking like the first toast at a wedding reception. Conversation stopped until Jelani had cursed under her breath at more stabbing of needles. Then the white-coated woman left them alone. The child to their right wailed again and the intercom announced the need for X-ray in curtain three.

"I think I'm stepping out," Iris said, still beaming. "You two have things to talk about. I'll update Lane and Crispy. They're in the waiting room."

She was gone before Jelani could warn her not to tell anyone else until they knew for sure if there was a baby.

A baby?

Trying not to get too excited and thoroughly surprised that she would even be excited, she turned her attention to Astan. His skin still pale, he watched her, his dark eyes incisive as a crow debating what might be good to eat.

"You do not want a child." His tone seemed to accuse her.

She reached for his hand, holding it tight in hers. "Astan, love, I hadn't even considered it. I don't know if I'm ready for a child. If we're ready. Considering our position with the Circle and all the rebuilding we've committed to." Through their touch bond, she felt the indecision in him as well. "Honestly, I didn't think it was an issue. Lane said something about—"

The curtain flew open with a screech of metal rings against a metal rod. Lane stood there, his extra large presence seeming to fill the room. Out of breath, he leaned on the rack at the end of the bed.

"But you're a mule!" Lane said, gasping for breath.

Astan rose again to his feet, clearly taking umbrage with Lane's tone. "And you're an ass."

Lane rolled his eyes. "Lighten up, pal. I mean, she's a hybrid. Half-elf, half-human. Mules are half-horse, half-donkey. Mules can't reproduce. It's their genetic makeup. They've got an odd number of chromosomes or something. So even though a horse has sixty-four and a donkey has sixty-two, a creature with sixty-three can't breed."

So maybe it is just an ulcer.

Disappointment soaked into her. That surprised her even more. How could she be let down by the lack of something she had never even wished for or contemplated? It didn't make sense. She should just be grateful and take whatever thick, stomach-settling potion they gave her.

But now that the idea had materialized in her head, disappointment was indeed what she felt. A baby could be a movement forward in a life situation that often felt like she was mired in mud a foot deep. Something she could look forward to every day as a pregnancy progressed. Some proof to the Circle that she really was trying to make this work.

"Lane, come on," Jelani said. "These are elves. Science doesn't apply, right?"

Lane gaped. "You canna change the laws of physics!"

"Procreation is biology, not physics." She fidgeted on the bed as the finger pincher alarm finally quit beeping. Had her heart stopped? Somehow she didn't think so. But it had certainly been stabbed with the possibility of loss.

"So how many chromosomes do elves have?" Lane demanded.

"I have no idea," Astan said. He turned to Jelani and caressed her cheek. "*Denami*, please, calm down."

Her words came from between gritted teeth. She usually expected the worst. That way she was never disappointed. But how could she have wanted this so much and never even known? Tears filled her eyes in another rush of emotion. "Why do they always take everything from me?"

"Jelani, becoming upset will not help the situation," Astan said, his expression one of concern, clouded with annoyance. "If Rashia were here—"

"It's not fair!"

The lights flickered overhead.

"Jelly Bean, I'm just saying," Lane added, taking a step back after a quick upward glance. The look on his face was odd, too. "I'm no doctor, all right?"

The machine next to her started a rapid beeping and then shut down.

Astan grabbed her shoulder and squeezed hard until she lost the focus on her downward spiraling thoughts and her gaze met his. His eyes were full of love. "Jelani, the doctor will tell us."

Seeing his devotion helped her remember where she was, why she mattered. Her muscles released the tension she had drawn into them, and he eventually let her go.

Lane had not moved. His face was animated as he stared at her. "Did you do that? With the lights? With the equipment?"

She noticed the flickers, but hadn't paid close attention. "I'm sure the place drains power like crazy, Lane. Don't be ridiculous."

"Maybe, but it stopped once your tantrum did."

She tossed the meanest look she could.

"Awesome!" Lane exclaimed with a grin.

Iris appeared behind Lane. "Well?"

"Nothing yet," Jelani said, her emotions still boiling inside. Her frustration faded and the tears that had burned her eyes returned, occasionally running down her cheeks. She wiped them away before anyone could comment on them, shamed by her lack of control.

"Honey, it's all right," Iris said in her best professional voice.

Lane continued to watch the overhead lights. "Did you see what she did? She, like, sparked the hell out of the machinery." Lane was clearly off on another Scooby gang mission. Jelani could see it in his eyes.

"I shouldn't even be here," Jelani said. "I don't have insurance. Or a job. How am I going to pay for this?"

"Oh." Lane looked sheepish for a moment. "I told them you live at 100 Pine Street. The bill will take a while to find your little house in the big woods."

Jelani started to protest but a nurse came in to check the machine, replacing the monitor on Jelani's finger. She took one look at all of them and scowled. "Out!"

Lane pouted, but he let Iris drag him away.

The nurse eyed Astan but he stood his ground. She said nothing else, just set the machine beeping again and left.

Jelani wiped her face with the top edge of the sheet that covered her. The cloth was rough, as though it had been dried outside on a clothesline. Or perhaps she was just oversensitive to it, as she had been to everything else over the past few weeks, including Astan.

"I'm sorry," she said.

"Why should you apologize? If this has happened, we will deal with it."

"I mean, I'm sorry I've been so awful. I don't know what *neris* are like when they're, I mean, if they're pregnant. Human women are crazy." A half smile trembled on her lips. "Hormones, I mean. They get overwhelmed. They cry at everything. They can't eat some foods. They crave others. It's not their fault. Their bodies put the baby first, that's all."

He studied her and didn't reply.

"I just know I've been hard on you. I appreciate you being so very patient." She reached for his jacket collar and pulled him to her for a kiss. "You are the best thing that has ever happened to me, Astan Hawk."

Only after they had been lost in the kiss for several seconds, did the throat clearing of the doctor regain their attention. "Well, I'm going to guess this is the father?"

"Father? Then it's true?" Jelani asked, delighted.

"Very much so. You're going to be parents." The doctor took in Astan's stoic reaction. "No need to buy cigars just yet. You've got some time." He scribbled instructions on his pad and ripped off the top paper for Jelani. "You'd better see an obstetrician soon. Do you have someone in mind?"

"No, but I guess I'll find someone."

"See the front desk on the way out for a referral."

"Sure, we'll do that." Her emotions took a swing in the other direction and she could almost see Astan lurch sideways. She glanced over the paper, the words blurring as more tears filled her eyes.

"To alleviate your immediate problem we're going to hang a second bag to re-hydrate you intravenously."

A nurse appeared behind him with a tray and a clear plastic bag, which she attached on the pole at the head of the bed. She sat down the tray, which held all the tools necessary to establish an I-V setup. Astan took a look at the tray and his face went white again.

The doctor's attitude softened a little and he chuckled. "I know, son, it's always a shock. Come on. Let's go get you some juice." He put an arm around Astan's shoulders. "But just think of all the great ties you'll get over the years for Father's Day."

They walked out and the nurse attended to the business at hand. The pain of another needle faded into insignificance as Jelani laid her other hand on her abdomen. Forget Lane and his crazy theories. A small person, or elf, was in there waiting to meet her, someone who would change her world and maybe everyone else's, too.

Two more hours passed before the doctor felt confident enough to release her into the world again, but only after appointments were made for her follow up care and noted on her chart. The nurse insisted on taking the expectant mother to the curb in a wheelchair while Iris and Lane bickered about which of them would be able to drive her home. The argument continued into the parking lot as both of them went to their cars, still insistent, and Crispy drifted pathetically between them.

"You gotta have friends," the nurse said, her voice underlined with wry humor.

"They're not so bad," Jelani said. She looked behind her for Astan, who had been detained by the doctor for last minute instructions. A woman in a colorful blue scrub uniform came running after her, jabbing a clipboard in her direction.

"Wait! You've got to sign this. Intake form."

"I'm not staying," Jelani said, her hands not leaving her lap. "Not staying at all."

"Doesn't matter." The chunky woman stopped to catch her breath. Jelani could only think it was odd that someone who worked in a hospital would be so overweight. And chewing a thick wad of gum. "Your friend gave us most of your information. You're not working now? And you're pregnant, right? Honey, you're gonna have a basketful of bills. You sign here and we'll get you in the state program. It'll all be covered." The woman studied her, still chewing. "Now wouldn't that be nice?"

Jelani had a random impulse to explain how hard it might be to collect any hospital past-dues when her elven tree didn't even have a cookie bakery inside, but broke down giggling before she could get it out. Instead she reached for the clipboard and scribbled her name on the lines that awaited her signature. "There you go. Thanks so much."

The social worker hardly looked at the paper, just ripped off the bottom copy and shoved it into Jelani's hand. "Good luck with your baby, Miss Marsh." She waddled off down the hall, just as Astan came out of the emergency room, looking flustered.

The nurse waited for Astan, then pushed the chair out through the automatic doors. "You'll get used to it, Dad," she said with an understanding expression.

"Dad," Jelani said. She giggled again, feeling a little giddy.

Iris pulled up to the curb with a triumphant smile on her face. She got out of the car and came over to the wheelchair. "Lane had too much of your crap in his truck, so I get to drive you two home."

"Thank you," Astan said. He held back as the nurse helped Jelani out of the wheelchair, flipping footrests and folding metal parts to make it easier for her, then he took her arm, giving her the support she very much needed.

The nurse gave them cheery best wishes and rolled the wheelchair back inside.

Jelani let them help her into the right front seat of the car, but the thoughts in her head just kept spinning as she considered all the changes her life was about to run into. Tomorrow she would be a different person. At least half a person. Half an elf, too. With a very special package inside.

CHAPTER 8

IF there was one thing Lane Donatelli could not resist, it was a mystery.

Well, Creamy Cupcakes come in a real close second. Maybe even first, some days.

Lane peeled off the cellophane from his third pack of the day. Creamy Cupcakes always loved him, unlike abusive mothers and a cold child welfare system. Some guys, like his roommate Crispy, turned to drugs and wild behavior. Lane had his cupcakes, and his Cave.

After he had left the hospital lot with his overstuffed pickup truck and a wildly nervous Crispy Mendell, he had come back to their apartment and his electronic retreat. His curiosity was piqued by what he had seen and heard.

He rolled his office chair square into the middle of the Cave, an eight foot high horseshoe shaped stack of old cupcake cartons and other crates. Inside the horseshoe sat two narrow tables on which he kept his other true friends, his computers. Four of them, slaved into one power coil, each luminous screen filled with information.

Just like the robot who found himself suddenly alive, Lane thrived on input.

What marvels he had to search out now!

Fascination number one: His friend Jelly Bean was pregnant. It should not have happened. Elves and humans were different species. Crossbreeding should be impossible.

Fascination number two: What was up with the machinery in the room when Jelani lost her cool? She had almost shorted out the lights. In the five years that he had known her, he had never seen even a hint of any such ability.

Of course, a lot had changed since she found those damned elves.

Lane cracked his knuckles then began to type, first on one keyboard and then another, pausing just long enough to lick thick cupcake filling off his chubby fingers.

The unmistakable sweet odor of a clove cigarette came from the apartment's small kitchen. Lane growled. "Crisp, you know those are illegal in the States. They'll only send those brown paper wrappers so long, you know?"

His scrawny roommate leaned forward, peering around the door frame just enough that half of his face could be seen. He seldom ventured near the Cave itself, wary of the webcam.

Once Lane had installed the device, Crispy insisted that the government was using it to spy on them, as if they had so much to hide.

Besides the clove cigarettes.

"What do you mean?" A thrill of real fear ran through Crispy's voice.

Lane shook his head. No use feeding Crispy's paranoia. "Nothing, man. But can't you go out back and do that?"

"It's thirty degrees," Crispy said, indignant.

"It sure is," Lane said. "That's why I'm not going to open the window. We'll just asphyxiate right here."

He started to toss Crispy a harsh glare, but couldn't bring himself to do it. The two had grown up together in the foster care system of Flathead County, Montana, each of them often the only person the other could truly count on. It was likely they knew each other as well as any two people in the world could. Crispy only smoked those things when he was thoroughly rattled. It had certainly been that kind of day.

Lane sighed and wheeled his chair away from the computer bank. "What's up?"

Crispy retreated around the corner of the wall again, but a few seconds later a puff of smoke appeared. "She could have died."

"Crisp, man, she isn't dying. She's pregnant. That would be the opposite, you know? Bringing life into the world?"

"What was that black stuff she threw up? Liquid death."

Lane's lips pursed as he considered the question. He had wondered the same thing. He wondered a lot about Jelani Marsh since she had gone to live in the woods with the clan. "I'm sure she told the doctor about it, Crisp."

Even as he said the words, he wagered internally that she had not mentioned it at all. Their Jelly Bean was many things, but she was not forthcoming with information that revealed anything about herself. She had grown up as damaged as either he or Crispy, albeit in a very different way. While Lane had resented the elves' little charade of using the glass slipper to snag her into their scheme, he ultimately hoped they would find a way to heal her.

If they had, he hadn't seen the results yet.

Iris had gone with the ambulance driver when he had wheeled Jelani inside of the emergency room, so maybe she reported it. She had witnessed what happened. Hopefully Iris had explained what happened in detail, since she was allegedly the most level headed one of them. Or so she thought.

"Jelly's stuff's still in the truck, right?" Lane asked.

Crispy's face appeared again from around the corner. "Why?"

"Maybe she's got a thermos with whatever she's been drinking up there in the woods. Didn't she say they sent some tea with her?"

"I think so."

Lane waited, hoping Crispy would get the hint that he should go get it, especially if he was going to smoke that damned smelly cigarette. Instead, Crispy retreated into his bedroom and closed the door.

Not only was Jelani screwing up her own life, she was going to take his down, too. The last thing he needed was for Crispy to have a relapse into his painfully restricting agoraphobia. And it would not take much to put him there, no matter how far he had come in the last few months.

Growling in frustration, Lane returned to the keyboards sending a different web search off from each. Two of them were on the genetic possibilities of mating different species. One was to a medical site for symptoms of dark vomit.

The last was yet another search about the evils and legal prohibitions of clove cigarettes and their resulting secondhand smoke, for him to print out and leave on Crispy's pillow.

The worst impact Crispy would suffer by Lane's addiction to gooey goodness was the possibility that Lane would have a massive coronary and Crispy would have to find another person to chauffeur him around town. Lane, on the other hand, had no intention of dying from lung cancer, emphysema, or any other lung disorder, when he had never pressed a cigarette to his lips in his twenty-seven years.

Lane shoved himself away from the tables and went down to the truck to see what he could find.

* * *

LANE returned half an hour later from the frigid outdoors with a backpack full of small items he had taken from under the blue plastic tarpaulin he and Crispy had used to cover Jelani's belongings after the ambulance left.

Crispy had been obsessive about the tarp, babbling on about how they had to do it right for Jelani, as if they allowed her ottoman to get wet she wouldn't survive the ride to the hospital. They had worked on it for twenty minutes with Crispy moving up and down across the pile like a spider weaving a secure web to cage the furnishings and boxes. Working alone in the cold, the much less agile Lane had taken just as long to pry these few items out from under the cover, leaving him gasping and nursing a strained elbow.

He dropped the backpack on the table and put on a teakettle of water for tea. He was an Earl Grey fan, just like his favorite starship captain. Besides, a hot cup of tea was the best beverage to serve with a package of Creamy Cupcakes.

While the water heated, Lane emptied the black backpack onto the table. Iris must have grabbed Jelani's purse, because he had not found it anywhere in the front or in the back of the pickup, though Jelani had been carrying it when they went to the apartment. But he did find a box of salty crackers, a bottle of water, several perfume bottles, and a striped zippered bag with assorted cosmetics inside, as well as an aluminum thermos.

He unzipped the bag and checked each of the used cosmetics inside. Other than a hideous shade of red lipstick, nothing seemed remarkable to him. "Good thing I never saw her wear that. So not her color."

The crackers were store brand standard issue square saltines. Nothing there in the single stack box. He sniffed the package but knew he had cupcakes waiting. Dry crackers could not compete.

The kettle whistle screeched and Lane stepped back to pour steaming water into his cup, a tall black mug with orange letters that looked like flame, reading: "Need before greed." He tossed in two tea bags and inhaled the strong aroma of bergamot released by the leaves as the water soaked into them. His stomach growled.

"I'll be with you in a moment my dear," he said with a wink and a nod to the remaining cupcake, sitting naked next to his computers.

The bedroom door opened. Crispy made a beeline for the kitchen, circling from the door to the cupboard where he took out the only mug he would use, a Montana state souvenir cup with a hawk painted on it. He slipped behind Lane, poured hot water into his cup, tossed a tea bag into it, and continued on to the refrigerator where he poured half-and-half into his cup. Without saying a word, he walked out of the kitchen and back to the bedroom.

Lane groaned. "Real mature, Crisp. You know it hurts when you don't talk to me! I might get a hangnail or something." He waited for several seconds to see if his comment sparked a reply. When it didn't, he reached for the sugar bowl, spooning out half a teaspoon into his mug, and adding another spoonful just for good measure.

The bedroom door opened again. Crispy spoke without coming out. "If it didn't bother you, you wouldn't act childish about it. You big baby. Wait till the government sees that." He closed the door.

Lane snickered and went back to examining Jelani's belongings as his tea steeped. The water bottle had not been opened. Since it was commercially prepared and sold he would have to assume whatever was in it had not caused her sudden illness.

"So, not the perfume. Not the makeup. Not the crackers. Or the water."

He eyed the thermos. Feeling like a television detective, except without the gloves and the cool shades, he picked up the canteen and shook it. Liquid sloshed around inside the metal container.

"Well, here goes nothing."

He unscrewed the circle shaped top and took a whiff. The smell nearly knocked him over.

"What the hell is that?"

Coughing, he held the thermos away from his face for a moment until his sinuses cleared, and then brought it close to his nose again. Sniffing more carefully this time, he caught several odors at once. It was definitely something berry-like with a hint of mint and a lot of other herbs. Maybe even some plain cut yard grass. Or if she was lucky, the good kind.

"Uh-huh. What do you think this is?"

He poured half an inch of the liquid into a clear glass and held it up to the light. The substance did not look a lot different from the various commercial green teas he had seen in the grocery store, except that it was full of bits of plant matter.

"This would seem like the prime suspect, Watson."

He debated tasting it to see if that gave him any further clues, but the memory of what he had seen earlier in the day made him decide against it. No vomiting for him, thank you. He had better options.

Replacing the lid once again, he set the thermos in the refrigerator for safekeeping. His own tea, he carried to the Cave. Seating himself in the chair as if it were a throne, he surveyed the kingdom of knowledge at his fingertips.

First, the genetics. He skimmed several Web pages and sharpened his queries, but didn't find an easy answer. The bottom line was it seemed to be that in the very few exceptions to the mule rule, scientists had determined that occasionally female mules could breed with purebred horses or donkeys.

Did this apply to people, too?

As a half-breed, Jelani would then be able to mother a child with either a human or an elf.

But horse stock and mule stock were genetically similar and neither bred with cows, dogs, or giraffes.

Lane's finger idly tapped the side of his mug as his brain considered the puzzle. This meant something. He just wasn't sure what.

"Stay tuned for further updates," he muttered, switching to his third screen.

Causes for black vomit seemed to include yellow fever, alcohol poisoning, and blood in the stomach, most often from a bleeding ulcer. But what he had seen did not fit the standard description of the 'coffee grounds' appearance of the ulcerous bleeding at all.

Yellow fever? Lane had yet to see the mosquito that could stand the Montana winter.

That left poisoning. Damn. It was annoying when Crispy's paranoia proved correct. Fortunately, those circumstances did not come around often. But that theory truly spurred his curiosity. Now he knew he had to discover the reason for Jelani's illness.

He printed the cigarette information off the fourth browser for Crispy, so he could devote that screen to an email plea for help to several of his fellow gamers who had working knowledge of chemistry. Surely it wouldn't be hard to get information on a lab to perform a formal analysis of whatever those witches were feeding his Jelly Bean.

He found it difficult to believe Crispy's assumption that a toxin caused Jelani's problem. If nothing else, Lane knew the elves valued his friend above all else. So if they were not trying to hurt her, what were they doing?

Something mysterious was going on and he intended to find out what that was.

CHAPTER 9

GRIGOR sat atop his makeshift shelter of branches and leaned against the base tree, looking up at the night sky. It was clear and cold. Nothing in the atmosphere obscured his vision of the moon, nearly full and round and sharply white against the November sky.

A blanket covered his legs and torso, an elven blanket Fontine had brought him. He resented having to use the blanket to stop the shivering that he had done nearly nonstop after the snows began.

When he had been with the Circle—no. He was not going to think about that.

Grigor remembered during his time at the human school reading stories of boys in foreign nations who performed a ritual period of solitude in the wild, taking nothing with them, forced to depend only on themselves and their own wits. The challenge honed them, sharpened them, from children into men. The journey to discover what one truly was and what one was truly meant to be should be a revelation, and he was finding that to be true.

Hungry, freezing, and worn to the bone, he had endured the elements since midsummer, the heat, the wind and now the frost. He now knew he could survive alone. But alone was not how he chose to live.

Before the false queen had come, Bartolomey had extended Grigor's leadership abilities. Grigor had brought several of the youngers to Bartolomey's group, the remnants of the mountain clan, eager young elves who were not favored by the Circle. Under Bartolomey's tutelage, he had learned how to assess others, their strengths, their weaknesses, and how to use each to his advantage.

Like Fontine.

The winsome *neris* had redoubled her efforts to convince him to return with her to the bosom of the clan. To entice him, she visited several times each seven-day, bringing packs of food, warm clothing, and useful stories of the progress of the reunification of the clan.

To their credit, Astan Hawk and his mate had managed to gather in most of the elven families who had scattered when the clan had divided a quarter of a century before. Their seldom seen numbers totaled nearly four hundred. A pittance compared to the human population, but Bartolomey had barely held on to a small fraction of that number when he had split the group. A figure closer to seven hundred would be enough over the next few years to build a viable growing community, to reestablish the elves as a force in the Bitterroot Mountains once again.

Once the clan had recovered, what was next? Whispers among the remnants of Bartolomey's group had revealed the possible existence of other enclaves of elves in the world, struggling as they all were against human intrusion. If he could not reconnect with his own clan, the possibility might exist that he could find another one looking for strong male leadership and diversity of bloodlines. This was certainly a possibility.

Fontine did not report any talk about interest in outside groups from the Circle and its minions. That didn't surprise Grigor. Those old women were amazingly self-absorbed. Perhaps that would be his entry.

His ears perked as he heard faint steps coming his way. Even with his diminished powers, if he focused he could often detect the familiar sound of the light tread of his brethren. The false queen had not taken everything, despite her cold heart.

Fontine.

Knowing his former lover might come at any time, Grigor now made a constant effort to maintain himself in a condition she would find appealing. He bathed every day in the river, even though in his weakened condition the water was so cold it made his skin ache and his muscles burn. He wore the clothing she brought him. The food she had carried to his small shelter had filled out his gaunt form to the point that his bones were no longer visible through wasted skin.

She hadn't completely fallen to his charms yet but he hoped that she would. He was sure that he could convince her he was sincere, especially since she wanted to believe in him.

"Grigor?" came her familiar velvety whisper.

He imagined that whisper close to his ear, her fingers exploring his body. The reality of his imagined picture nearly knocked him off the branch where he was sitting.

"Here," he said with a choked voice.

Her head popped around the base of the rough barked tree, a coquettish smile on her face. "You look better!"

"And you look wonderful." He eased off the rough branches of his shelter to catch her hand in his, his feet sinking ankle deep into the snow. "All is well with the clan?"

Her smile broadened. "Yes, more than well." Her fingers caressed his. She was practically trembling with excitement. Something had changed. Had the false queen stepped down at last?

"What is it, Fontine?"

"Jelani is with child. Surely this means the forest has blessed her union with Astan."

Grigor fought to keep the smile on his face, while disgust and anger boiled inside. First, the false queen took what was his and then she stole the birthright of their clan to have a full-bred elf carry on the leadership. Just as her mother before her. Traitors, all.

"How fortunate she is," he said, thinking more of the few remaining days the impostor had left if he had his way, rather than any supposed blessing.

"How fortunate are we all." Fontine's enthusiasm hinted that she was now one of the queen's new converts. "So have you decided? I spoke to Daven about you, and your wish to return to the clan."

Grigor's body reacted before he could control it, stiffening. "You did?"

She pulled her hand away. "You said I should." She watched him with narrowed, suspicious eyes.

He nodded and looked away, stalling until he could steel his face into bland compliance. He had indeed suggested it to her, but still had some trepidation about Astan and his father knowing that he had survived. Either one of them might take revenge on him for his betrayal in the glade. But if he was to get back in long enough to put his plan in motion, he would have to nourish any opportunity. Even this one.

He took a deep breath, the scent of snow on the air. Looking over Fontine's shoulder, he could see the heavy gray clouds that would bring his winter nemesis along before the sun faded below the horizon. "No, you're right, of course. I know I told you to broach the subject on my behalf. I just worry."

"Worry? About what?"

He chose the nearest lie. "That they'll use you to get to me, Fontine. Astan Hawk and the others hold me in contempt. Even think of me with hatred in their hearts. They might follow you so that they can exact revenge for what they judge that I've done wrong, even though I've only done what I believe is right for the clan as a whole."

She looked over her shoulder, then back to him. "That wouldn't be justice, not as the clan sees it."

"But even you believe they would. Look at your reaction. You wondered whether they would have followed you. Your concern shows it is true." He held out his hands to her. "I have no friend in this world, Fontine. Except you."

She hesitated before rushing to him and wrapping him in her arms. "I would never do anything to hurt you."

Her earthy smell filled his nose. He slipped fingers through her loose hair. The tendrils were soft and yielding, like her body pressed against his. The reminder of times past was overwhelming, as his lips sought hers.

Tentative at first, he tasted her lightly, trying to connect with the old closeness, the silent merge, that *nian* had with *neris*, making them one in time. Her fingers dug into his arms as he shuddered, the emotion and need to connect with another of his kind so compelling that his intent to proceed with caution abandoned him.

"Fontine, I must have you," he growled in guttural voice. He backed her against the rugged tree trunk and covered her face with kisses, pulling aside her draped poncho to gently move down her neck, his hot breath and teeth teasing her skin.

She yielded to his searching mouth holding him close, then at last reaching for his hand she linked her fingers with his, holding their hands together at shoulder level. "I love you," she said. Her eyes fluttered closed as she surrendered to the merge.

For the first time in months, he felt the warmth of another life force joining with his and he gloried in it. He became stronger by the second, and for a moment wondered if he had the power to take more than the merge allowed. He quickly squelched that thought before Fontine could read it, knowing he was not yet strong enough. He relaxed and basked in the merge, almost like bathing in the warm and welcoming sunlight. If he could only hold onto this feeling and be whole again.

"You could, Grigor, if only you'd return with me to the clan," she whispered reading his last thought through their touch.

He knew that was true. If he would return, tail between his legs like a shamed wolf to the pack, no doubt having to beg forgiveness, he would be sentenced to the lowliest tasks the clan could find for him until Daven Talvi and the false queen agreed to hold Astan Hawk's sense of revenge in check. Eventually he would regain a sense of status, a sharing of the life forces, but they would never fully accept him. Or trust him.

But he would never give them the satisfaction of seeing him brought low before them. He deserved better than that.

Before she could discern his denial of her plans, he pulled her inside his shelter. Better she believe his need for her was what drove him out of control, than that she discover the dark truth of his long-term intentions. When she finally came to see what he intended, he wasn't sure she would stand by his side any longer.

Unless he had her firmly in hand.

For now, he would make sure her hands, lips, and mind were otherwise occupied.

CHAPTER 10

THE female elders chattered and grumbled, their interminable arguments driving even the birds and small animals away from the glade.

Astan leaned against a tree trunk, endeavoring to remain focused while he half-listened, his thoughts with his beloved. He had come in her place when she nearly fainted while getting dressed. She was determined to drag herself to her duty. He was more determined that she would take care of herself and their child. Nothing the Circle had to say would be more important than that. He had believed it then, and now that he had arrived, he knew it to be a fact.

Knowing why she felt so unlike her usual self had made it easier for him to live with her, even on the rockiest of days. The emotional, needy state was not her fault, but caused instead by hormones running wild. Iris had assured him that the ups and downs were perfectly normal in the first trimester. Along with the need to sleep a lot.

"She's carrying another life inside her," Iris reminded him.

As if I need to be told. This is my child, too.

"Some time will pass before her body adjusts."

Armed with that information, Astan felt justified in insisting that he take on some of Jelani's more routine duties with the clan, like this one, to allow her to rest and save her happier moments for himself.

Beckley's mother Rashia complained about limited access to the queen, echoing similar querulous whines from the others. "How will the queen learn to ameliorate these symptoms that keep her from her duties if she will not allow us to attend her?"

"She has a doctor," Astan explained for the fifth time,

wondering what it would take to get through the Circle's preconceived mindset. Outside the misty walls of the charmed chamber, snow fell, flakes twirling down in the gentle wind. He wished for a moment that he and Jelani were as free as those frozen geometric bits of ice, instead of being bound by duty to the clan.

"She doesn't need a human doctor. She needs an elven midwife," Djana said in a tone that made it clear she considered that the end of the discussion.

Astan eyed his dark-haired grandmother across the open space between them. The gulf felt wider every day. She had been the worst complainant of all. She acted as if she were personally responsible for this conception, almost as if she owned the child to be born.

Astan noticed Djana had warmed toward him again. Had that been all she wanted, that he should father a child with Jelani, the daughter that the Circle wanted her to produce?

But Jelani had made it clear for the moment that she wanted nothing to do with Djana's Circle. She spent her days either out in the forests by herself or curled up in her papasan chair sleeping. Despite Iris's reassurance, Jelani often acted so unlike her usual spicy sharp self that Astan worried about her. When she left their home, he followed her, out of the range of her perception. What he observed did not reassure him much.

Jelani often paused during her long walks to listen to something Astan could not detect. She even spoke aloud, but not to the plants and vegetation her hands and thoughts were guiding back to wellness. It seemed to him that she spoke to another living being, human or elf. The snippets of words he caught did not make much sense to him. She appeared to be in loose conversation with a revered figure of some sort, someone she listened to for advice. He thought it might be Daven, but he never saw his father near during these exchanges.

Was she hallucinating? In her current fragile state he hesitated to ask her. He also could not bring his concern to the Circle without jeopardizing his relationship with Jelani. She would toss him out in half a minute if he broke her confidence, particularly as mistrustful as she was of the Circle now. He would not violate her wishes. Not until the stakes left him no choice.

Astan glanced over at his father, sitting aside in intent conference with several of the Circle members. Perhaps the time would come when he could speak to Daven of these matters. If he could catch Daven in the right mood, he would discuss a situation as equals, not as an inexperienced son coming to his father with a begging hand held out for a crumb. For now, he chose to keep his own counsel.

Another one of the elders started on Astan about some shortcoming of Jelani, but he'd had enough and stood up, calling debate to a halt. "Is she not the queen?" he asked.

A murmur of assent assured him she was. He stared hard, at each of them until he made eye contact. "Then accept her wishes and leave her alone!"

Shock greeted him on a dozen faces. Djana began to speak but Astan silenced her with a sharp wave of his hand. He would put her in her place, even if it was just this once. He could see her surprise at being dismissed, watched as she gathered a retort, and interrupted before she could say a word.

"You searched for her many years and nearly missed her. Despite your incompetence, we were blessed to find her and bring her here, close to our hearts. Trust that in her deepest soul she knows what she must do for the benefit of the clan. She is the queen, by blood and by birth. Also know that when she needs your help, she will ask."

Astan walked out of the glade, knowing in his heart she would never ask for their assistance. But his intimate knowledge of her guided him to defend her in a way that hopefully would leave her in a better space with the old elf women when she was well enough to return.

A small branch fell in front of him, just missing him and landing at his feet. A smothered laugh overhead drew his gaze up to the lowest thick branch of a hefty fir tree. Amid the spiky green needles of the fir, he spied ungainly Beckley and slight built Max smiling and waving at him.

"Listen to the little lion roar!" Beckley called down to him.

Astan grinned, resenting the slight mocking tone, but feeling vindicated, not criticized by their jibes. Beckley was all right. He certainly didn't mind someone criticizing his mother. He would do it himself with any sort of provocation.

Pale, white-haired Max was also Astan's friend, albino skin tight over his child-sized frame even though he had almost seventeen years. Max used his compact body's light weight to move through the air in the way of the flying squirrel, gliding with the wind. In the city Max had shown an affinity for human machinery of all kinds, an unusual trait in a wood elf. His broad range of interests and affable nature made him a favorite among the clan.

"Watch yourself," Astan warned them, his grin firmly in place. "You may be next."

Beckley chuckled and made a little salute. He and Max watched Astan for a few more seconds and then turned their attention back to spying on the *neris* of the Circle.

Astan continued to walk, intending to take a southerly route along the side of the mountain, checking the borders of the elf land coexisting with the human world. Since they had returned to the woods, and since their elf clan had doubled in number, they only occasionally encountered humans on the slopes. Engaged in their own pursuits, humans seldom noticed the elves. The life force power of full blood elves allowed them to conceal themselves from the notice of other species.

Jelani found it more difficult, being half elven, but Daven had helped retune her body's resonance with the earth, to those compatible with the elves' source of energy in the soil.

While Jelani believed that it would be possible to access elements and agencies of the human world to help build up the forests and the local ecology, leading to healthier living for the clan, Astan tended to disagree. Their encounters with the Earth Liberation Front, otherwise known as ELF, and the law enforcement agencies that pursued the group, left Astan with a nagging fear the elves might not be safe from man, even on their own lands. After Linnea's release from the fir tree where she had been confined, the clan members had less contact with ELF, which seemed to suit both groups just fine.

In late September the local newspaper reported an altercation between the eco-terrorists and the police that had resulted in a large number of arrests. Though the elves had nothing to do with the incident, Astan could see the ELF members blaming them since the last altercation had come during a joint mission to save the trees. It was better to avoid them. Humans manifested a powerful ability to carry grudges and to act on them with violence.

"Astan, may I have a word?"

His father's voice behind him, Astan smothered a groan. The last thing he wanted was a lecture about his respect for the elders and the Circle.

Astan composed himself, firm in his persona as the first servant of the queen, and turned to face Daven who was running lightly along the path to catch up. "They needed to hear that," he said without even a hint of defensiveness in his voice. This time, fueled by Jelani's need, he knew he was right. "They're being ridiculous."

Daven sized him up and then smiled. "You protect your chosen mate in many ways."

Astan nodded, still irritated by the niggling grievances of the elder females. "She is not well. She needs some time."

"Of course."

"Of course?" Finding his victory too easy, Astan studied his father to see if he was playing him in some way, trying to 'teach him a lesson,' but he didn't seem to be. The emotion Astan read in Daven's eyes was paternal fondness, and respect.

"I trust you to know her, Astan. None of us understand her better I am sure." He reached his side and started along the trail Astan had intended to take. Astan continued with him matching his sturdy steps.

"So you do not dispute my stand with the Circle?"

"I think you were greatly disrespectful to them." Daven smirked as Astan's eyes rolled with annoyance. "But perhaps they needed to be taught a lesson."

"Perhaps."

Both pleased with each other for the moment, they continued in silence for several kilometers, as the humans measured. Astan caught a whiff of danger on the air and held up a hand. The two faded into the forest behind a thick tree trunk as a black bear, enormous in her pre-hibernation state, lumbered across the path, stopping to sniff the air in search of more food, before moving on to find her winter cave.

"That one will bear two strong young over the months to come," Daven said softly.

"You can see this?" Astan asked.

If Daven had such powers, was he able to 'see' Jelani's 'cub to be' as well? Astan knew little about the state of the pregnancy despite his intimate involvement. He worried about the child, upon waking in the morning, under the bright sun of midday, and well after dark when the owls flew on the night breeze. Not because of Lane Donatelli's rambling about mules and impossibilities, but because of the changes in Jelani. Her good humor had faded. She did not share her feelings as she had before, at least not with him. He couldn't stand being cut out of her confidence. But would Daven tell him the truth or turn this into yet another learning experience?

Daven studied him and laid a hand on his shoulder. *I have detected nothing unusual in Jelani's child. In your child.*

"Nothing unusual? So the child is healthy and well?" Astan's lips twitched into a frown at his father's coy answer.

"The future remains to be discovered. Even I cannot see all that will come to pass. Patience, my son. Patience."

Astan growled.

Daven let go of him and gave a belly laugh that irritated Astan even more. "Since the day we met her, we have known our Jelani was a force to be contained and managed. A most valuable characteristic. You are well matched with her, my son."

Astan flashed back to their conversation about Veraena. "As you were well matched with my mother?"

Daven shoved his hands in the pockets of his jacket. "We were evenly gifted. Each of us tapped into a source of magic different than the rest of the clan. We had just begun to discover the extent of our talents, beyond the reach of the others, when the queen was taken."

Astan's mind went over the familiar story he had been told since he was a young boy. When Queen Linnea had chosen a human mate, her brother Bartolomey rebelled and sent elves to kill her. Her body died, but her life force had been saved by healers of the clan and placed in a tall tree. Daven and many of the other elves had gone into a magic state of suspended animation, waiting until the time was right to rescue her.

"How did you leave my mother if you loved her so much?"

"I believed with all my heart it was my duty. I believed she'd appreciate my choice. She loved the clan, as did I. So I understand exactly how you are torn between your love for your mate and your love for our clan."

The wistful note in Daven's voice was one Astan had not heard before, one that surprised and touched him. Astan's mouth worked as he struggled for a response, but he could not come up with one. He had never seen his father this vulnerable, even when Grigor had shot him. Daven Talvi had always appeared larger than life.

Astan stopped walking and crossed his arms. From the ridge where they stood, the horizon was obscured by dull clouds stacked in layers halfway up the gray skies. Hearing the tautness of underlying stress in Daven's tone, Astan felt like his future was equally buried in weighty mystery.

Movement below caught his eye. It was an elf in a hooded cloak. As the hood blew back in the cold wind a burst of blonde hair flowed free. Fontine. She looked behind her, as if she were worried that she would be seen or followed, before hurrying on. His analytical ability flicked through probabilities. What was she doing walking into the mountains alone?

With what he knew of her past and all the other bits of information he had available, the answer flicked into his mind.

Grigor.

His throat closed in a tumult of anger, resentment. and fear.

Daven came up behind him, seeing the *neris* below them before she vanished from sight. He didn't comment.

Astan turned to study his father's face and saw, with yet another flick, that Daven was not in the least surprised.

"Grigor?" Astan asked in a strained voice. "You knew she's going to him?"

"It's true. Grigor has surfaced in the forests. Fontine has set her heart on rehabilitating him, bringing him back into the fold."

"No!" Astan's fury burst from him like the heat of a flare gun as it spit out its load, fueled by the realization that Grigor lived, but even more since Daven had known and had kept the information from him. "Someone should have killed the traitor when Bartolomey died. He cannot—"

"I don't believe he can, no. But Fontine believes she loves him. She believes he loves her. The power of love is strong. We both know that. As the Vincent said, many things are possible if one believes."

"Grigor will never change his treacherous heart."

"Perhaps not." Daven shrugged. "But perhaps it is also better to be aware of Grigor's intentions and movements. Fontine will tell us more than she realizes." His knowing look told Astan they would be secret partners in this knowledge.

"You knew this and did not tell me?"

"What purpose would it have served to tell you, Astan? You have so much on your mind with Jelani's erratic pregnancy and the work of healing the forest."

Astan stared at his father in disbelief. "We cannot discount this situation! Grigor always demonstrated great intelligence and great ability to deceive and destroy. If he has plans—"

"We have no idea whether Grigor will ever brave the actual return to the clan, Astan. Fontine says he is quite weak and debilitated, nearly starving."

"Let him starve, then!" Astan's blood boiled at the threat. How could Daven accept this possibility so calmly? "He may be preparing to take revenge for Bartolomey's punishment. He may be ready to strike at any time. He may be watching us from the forest even now!" Astan turned to face the dark woods, feeling the itch of an imaginary target between his shoulder blades.

"We will definitely monitor the situation. I promise you."

Daven crouched down onto his haunches and drew his cloth bag of runes from his pocket. Closing his eyes, he reached inside and drew out three runes, which he then laid side-by-side on the frozen ground.

Astan hunkered down with him to study the marked stones. He did not know all the nuances of interpreting runes, but he was familiar with the basics.

"Ha! Treachery! I told you!" Astan pointed to the leftmost stone, *ulin*, the sign of betrayal and duplicity.

Daven nodded slowly, studying the layout. "As you know, Astan, the three stone formation shows us past, present, and future. Treachery is not disputed in the past. Look to the center." He gestured toward the middle rune. "*Eykon*. A moment of clarity and setting goals. All must focus on what truly matters."

"I can't imagine that Grigor will focus on any more than his own wants and needs," Astan growled again with frustration and eyed the last rune. *Semnon,* the unknown force. The mysterious. The unexpected. "And again, your rocks provide us with no answers."

"The future is clouded." Daven's jaw was set and his expression was troubled. He scooped up the runes and slid them back into the bag, not meeting Astan's eyes.

Astan's reaction was condensed into a terse grunt as he straightened and prepared to move on. He would grab the first opportunity that arose to neutralize the threat Grigor posed. If Daven wanted to work with him, Astan could live with that. But he did not need to wait for Daven's help in order to secure his family.

This time he intended to make sure that if any more lives were lost in the battle between the clan and Grigor Biren, that it would be Grigor alone, who paid the ultimate price for his sedition.

CHAPTER 11

WHEN Jelani awoke, she found herself on the bed with Astan sleeping next to her.

Their various responsibilities dictated that this situation presented itself very seldom these days. It was a moment to be cherished, she noted sleepily as she scooted next to him. She was just enough smaller to exactly fit inside the curve of his body.

His sleeping form adjusted, aligning itself against her, and his arm slipped around her middle, cuddling her close.

She sighed, content.

To make the picture perfect, Azrael jumped up onto the bed and lay on her feet. She could feel the vibration of him purring right through the bones in her ankles.

Astan had explained how he had chastised the Circle and kept them away from the tree house door and Jelani was grateful. She had left her stepmother's house at sixteen and had managed fine since then, for the most part, without a nagging parent telling her what to do every minute of her day, much less two dozen of them.

She had been to a couple of appointments at the Fort Missoula medical park and Dr. Pitt had not shared anything unusual in her test results. But no doctor in her history had ever found that anything about her registered out of the ordinary during an exam. She could apparently pass for full human.

She had taken Iris with her the first time, so he would suspect she was a single mother nervous about her pregnancy and not tell her anything he believed would worry her unnecessarily. Jelani had definitely not shared anything that might worry him. Like the circumstances of her own birth. Or that her child's father was an elf.

Or the possibility existed, though Jelani found it hard to believe as she did about most things that might cut in her favor, that the pregnancy was just fine, despite being a blend of elf and human. At least she hoped that was it.

If Djana and the others had been less pushy, or less critical, she might have been more disposed to listen to them. They had all had elf babies, after all. They had also reminded her of the sketchy stories told of her own birth 'in the elven way,' before her father had left the area with her, his heart broken by the loss of Linnea. No one had ever explained exactly what that meant, but she deemed it pretty important.

Hopefully there was plenty of time for that. By human calculation she might be as much as four months along, leaving her five more. That should be plenty of time.

Astan's warmth along her spine brought her muscles into a relaxed state. No one had ever had such a cozy effect on her. Over the months as companions, their separate selves had somehow adapted, their resonance becoming closer in synch. Often they shared common thoughts, though they did not have the sort of telepathy Daven seemed to share with any elf he chose. When they were quiet together they would even begin to breathe at the same rate. This was a little spooky to her at first, but after all these weeks their synchronicity had finally become a comfort.

She lay still with her eyes closed and listened to Astan's even breathing that was thick with a hint of a snore. But after several minutes, it became clear that her brain cogs had caught onto the wheel of her thoughts, setting her mind in motion. As comfortable as she might be, she could not go back to sleep now. Rather than toss and turn, and possibly deprive Astan of much-needed sleep, Jelani carefully slipped out from under his protective arm and left him to rest.

An early walk through the trees would calm her. She quickly dressed in a thick pink sweater and some elastic waist brown slacks that barely stretched to accommodate her expanding belly, and then drank some of the raspberry leaf tea that the Circle had left for her. Of the varied herbal mixtures the *neris* brought her, she tolerated the red raspberry best. The Circle never left any commercially flavored tea, just leafy combinations of bland or bitter tisanes that did not improve much even with honey.

They had brought her the teas from the time she first moved into the woods, citing their pleasure in serving her as queen. After the initial weeks of the pregnancy, she tired of the constant battle with the elders, so she drank them. It was less hassle. And her body felt better when she did, despite how they tasted. So she choked them down and let her hormones sort them out.

As she placed her fingers on the magical spots that opened the door, she felt it release and swing outward. She stepped outside, pausing a moment to take measure of the sensory feast in the sharply chilled air.

Birds called to one another from the safety of the pine branches overhead, a *pip-pip-pip* to the west and shrill whistle of caution to the east. High above the trees floated a pair of eagles, soaring on the wind in intertwining circles.

Jelani could not see as far as the eagles so she couldn't know for sure, but she liked to think that the pair she often saw flying together were the birds that she had tended at the Wildlife Rehabilitation Center, the one with the broken wing that she dubbed Romeo and the female who had tried so hard to get into the Center after her injured mate. She wanted to think of them as both flying free again.

She could also hear the stream running, bubbling under its icy cover, though it had to be at least a hundred yards away.

Jelani had finally learned in recent weeks that her sensitivity to the sensory world, the roar of car engines that never before bothered her, the depth of sensation of taste and smell, the clarity of her vision, were all due to her growing hormone imbalance. Or so Rashia and the other medical whizzes of the Circle told her. She had run that theory by Dr. Pitt and he had not condemned the herbals but he gave her prenatal vitamins anyway. Along with a look that implied she might be a little crazy.

So she dealt with it. It was not like there was an expert, local or otherwise, on cross species births. Even Lane had come up dry in his research, which was saying something.

Frowning, she studied the bulge that was her abdomen. It looked bigger than it had the day before. It seemed to have grown each day of the last two weeks. She looked significantly further long than four months. Her appetite had been almost nothing, so it was not simply added fat. What was going on?

A grumble escaped her as she supposed she would likely have to consult the Circle for the truth. Soon.

Jelani moved away from the tree house following an animal scent she did not know, something female, and from the frequency of the scent deposits, the she-animal had been moving fast.

Glancing over her shoulder to make sure she had not been followed, Jelani hurried through the snow, now some six inches deep. In elven boots she hardly left a print on the snow, even in her awkward shape. Within the first fifteen yards she found the animal prints that corresponded with the scent markings, too small to be a mountain lion or cougar. A badger perhaps, or a large raccoon, based on the five pointed toes and claw marks. The fourth foot dragged as the animal walked. She must be injured, though no blood marked her trail.

Curious, Jelani followed the markings for some time, much farther than she had intended to stray from her home. She stopped when the trail suddenly ended in a smear of blood and a spray of hawk feathers on the otherwise unmarked snow. Instinctively she glanced up, half expecting the raptor to come after her for discovering his dirty work.

She studied the sector of woods around her. At first it was unfamiliar. Much of the Bitterroot forest looked like every other stand of tall firs and pines when she first moved there, but as she had become more familiar with the area, she now recognized many of them as individual places.

Daven's history lessons had taught her that in years past, when the clan was healthy, their range of dominion extended to Glacier National Park on the north, south to the Bitterroots of Idaho, east nearly to the beginnings of the Missouri River and as far west as the point where the Clark Fork of the Columbia River emptied into Lake Pend Oreille.

Where was she now?

She climbed up a nearby outcropping of granite, her new belly making her a bit awkward, to see if she could identify any landmarks to give herself a clue. The sight that greeted her took her breath away.

Bright blue painted X's marked half a dozen large trees in the closest row to where she stood. Others had blue and red ribbons tied around them.

She walked down from the outcropping to the glade below. Now she could see the dirt road that led west. She knew exactly where this particular road ended, in junction with Route 93 north of Missoula. She had been here before, helped paint and spike the trees in front of her, when Daven had persuaded her to help the eco terrorist group, the Earth Liberation Front. They had spiked the trees to prevent them from being logged. Apparently their work had paid off.

No vehicles were parked along the lane, awaiting the return of their occupants. When she listened, she heard no indication that ELF was here. Driven by memories that dropped into her head like heavy hailstones, shaking her confidence, she started to run into the woods past the marked trees. She and Astan had once come here in a mad rush to meet the others, the day Grigor had taken her. The day she had met her mother for the first time. The day Astan had nearly died in her defense.

Here.

She closed her eyes, and she could almost feel tension thicken in the air, echoing through time. She had felt so lost, bewildered at the betrayal of the human who called himself Legolas and then the treachery of the clan's own Grigor.

Richard lying there, dead.

Astan shot, dying as far as she knew.

Daven, willing to sacrifice himself for her safety as well.

The emotions of that day, long suppressed, surfaced again and she found herself on her knees, sobbing. Loss, then fear, then joy, then loss again.

My poor darling.

The words whispered into her head, the voice neither male

nor female. Jelani looked up sharply.

"Who's there?"

No one but the wind.

Suspicion dried her tears and drove her to her feet. "Who's there?" she asked again.

Her sharper eyes could detect no one in the shadows of the trees, though she found a whiff of smoke in the air, very faint. Could it be pipe smoke? Had the spirit of her father survived? She took several steps in the direction of that fateful confrontation and then hesitated. Many spirits had existed here, others not as benevolent as her father.

Lately, she had felt a presence with her in the forests, a warm presence that listened to her as she carried on a spoken monologue, working out issues she did not feel that she could talk to anyone about.

But the presence had not really carried on any conversation. Just silent support. This was odd.

I have always cared for you.

"Always? That's a long time," she said aloud. Where was the voice coming from? She cocked her head to listen but the words seemed to be coming to her from everywhere, no specific place.

When you need counsel, I will be here, child. Come to find me.

"Sure you don't have a business card? Phone number? 1-800-crazyguy?" She placed her hands square on her hips. "Come on out and let's chat, shall we?"

As soon as she had said it, she mentally kicked herself. What if it was a bad guy and he actually showed up? Then what would she do?

How far had she come following that injured animal? Obviously, too far. Astan often followed her. Did he really think she didn't notice, as sensitive as her hearing had become? But this time she knew she was alone.

She should go.

Unsure, she waited. The wind picked up. Suddenly snow began to fall in thick white flakes that increased in intensity, swirling in the wind around her. Several flew into her mouth and nose, causing her breath to catch uncomfortably. She coughed and stumbled backwards away from the marked trees and toward the ridge.

The snow came down harder and collected on the ground, accumulating very quickly. Wind whistled around her ears. She covered her head and ran along the top of the ridge, tripping several times and falling to the ground. Her hands sank into the new snow scraping on the rock below the soft whiteness. Trying not to panic, she hurried down the far side of the ridge toward the valley where Missoula lay, miles away.

The mini-blizzard seemed to follow her, continually knocking her off balance. She fell down so many times she considered the possibility that she had hurt the child. Covering her face with her arms to keep herself from being blinded, Jelani avoided most trees but hit several with her elbows as she passed too close.

This was crazy. Some small part of her mind not focused on staying upright and undamaged kept up an internal monologue about the impossibility of such an occurrence. A blizzard that followed someone? Voices from the air? She must be losing her mind.

On the other hand, neither was more improbable than a glass slipper on a city sidewalk. Look where that had gotten her.

Her boot caught on a fallen branch and she went down hard, into an ice-crusted pile of old leaves. Whimpering, she cradled her bruised knee.

"Please, please, stop," she begged the cloud overhead. "I don't want to hurt the baby, please!"

All you had to do was ask for my help.

The snowfall immediately came to an end and the winds were silent.

She cocked her head and looked around her, waiting for the second half of the prank. Blizzards didn't have a central section where all was calm, like the eye of a hurricane or the inner column of a tornado. Confusion set in. Did she know an elf who could control weather? She couldn't think of any, though there must be one, somewhere.

She brushed herself off and tested her knee. Sore, but functional. Other pains evidenced themselves as she started walking, shins and ankle and elbows, but she did not stop to assess them. Before the snow began again, she needed to be far from here.

Her limping walk broke into an awkward jog and finally into a full run, and she did not stop until she was in territory she knew was safe, back under the fir trees south of the Swan.

Out of breath and exhausted, she leaned against the trunk of a fat old pine, sliding down the bark to sit at its foot. Her heart pounded in her chest, and even her skin tingled with the rush of blood through her veins. She hardly noticed the cold snow, an inch or two deep here with a little crust on its top from a day's sun.

What had happened up there at the tree spiking site? Had she really heard voices? Had something malevolent attacked her?

She had not been pursued and she hadn't really seen anything either. No *person* had been there. Now that she had escaped, she wondered if she had really heard anything at all, or if her ghosts had just taken advantage of her current condition and hypersensitivity to roost for a bit on the edge of her mind. A lot had happened in the past six months and she had moved on so quickly to what had been shoved onto her shoulders that she might not have worked through everything.

As her breathing finally slowed and she began to feel safe and in control again, she noticed a little flutter in her abdomen.

Could it be?

She shifted her weight a little to be more comfortable and closed her eyes, focusing on the place where that movement had occurred. *Come on, little one. Don't be shy.*

Sure enough, another little flicker inside.

Reassured that despite her bruises, everything must still be all right now that the baby was moving, Jelani pushed herself to her feet.

She would return to the clan lands and find Rashia. The elder had been begging to examine Jelani and the child. She could have Rashia check her injuries, explain them away as clumsiness, and perhaps avoid telling Astan at all. He would only get worked up and forbid her to go anywhere alone.

Focusing on the joy of life within her, Jelani set her course toward the elf equivalent of the apothecary, where she knew she would find the old *neris* tending her leaves. Astan already worried about too many things. Jelani's ghosts could remain her own.

CHAPTER 12

ONCE Lane spotted the bundled up postal carrier delivering mail across the street, he had been unable to focus on anything else.

His report on the chemistry of Jelani's tea had to arrive today. It had to, before that pregnancy got much farther along. He had never trusted those elves, not for a minute. Not even the so-called 'good guys'. Since the elves had appeared, Jelani's world and that of her friends had been turned topsy-turvy.

Through the partially frosted window, he observed the progress of the mailman. Maybe he could score his mail early if he caught the guy on the street.

Grumbling, Lane slipped his big feet into cheap black sneakers but didn't bother to tie the laces since that would have required bending over. Not worth the effort for a short jaunt.

"Crisp, I'm going to get the mail!" he called, shrugging on his well-worn brown pea coat.

Crispy peeked out of the bedroom, where he was reading yet another book on government conspiracies. "If we get any large manila envelopes, dispose of them immediately."

"Not unless they're ticking," Lane said with a tolerant grin.

"Or if they have anthrax." Crispy's intent gaze insisted that danger remained inevitable.

"Right. No anthrax today." Lane shook his head and headed down the stairs, clumping awkwardly as his loose shoes threatened to slip off.

Their apartment was one of three on the second floor of the old building, but he and Crispy did not know their neighbors well, other than to exchange occasional murmured greetings as they passed in the doorway. They preferred to keep to themselves, and the neighbors apparently did, too. It was a win-

win in Lane's book.

The interior stairway was unheated and a little chilly, but Lane was not prepared for the blast of cold air that hit him when he opened the door to the outside.

"Oy! Next year in the Promised Land!"

Only he didn't mean the deserts of Israel but the paradise of Seattle, home of computer culture and a thousand coffee shops. And much less snow and ice.

Grateful the snow had stopped and that the new business in the storefront on the first floor had shoveled the path in front of it, he trudged onto the sidewalk and scanned the street for the hapless mailman.

There. Half a block down.

He started off to meet the man before the large WoW poster in the new storefront window caught his eye. He swiveled to a stop, his attention refocused.

What was this? How long had it been since he had been outside? An office supply and computer sales store? Practically within arm's reach? And was that the laptop he had recently read about, bells and whistles galore, with the twenty-inch monitor, the 920A video card with quad core, eight gigabytes of RAM, and a terabyte hard-drive?

He belatedly noticed his slack bottom jaw and closed his mouth, trying to retain a little dignity before the store clerk noticed. Glancing in through the glass he saw the young black man grin and realized it was too late. He gave a sheepish half wave, and the clerk beckoned him inside.

Lane looked down the street and saw his target negotiating the signature for a package with one of the nosy neighbors, the woman who always looked down on Lane's rattletrap pickup as though it were a giant contagious cockroach. He knew her. The postman would be awhile.

He entered the store, blessed warmth welcoming him. "Hey, nice poster," Lane said, gesturing to the window. "Can't wait till the expansion pack comes out."

"Me either," the young man agreed. His athletic build hinted at a high school career on the football field. "I'm Kevin Briscoll.

You're the guy upstairs, right?"

Since he had just lumbered down the flight of stairs next to the shop, sounding a lot like a wounded elephant, it was a pretty obvious guess. "Yeah. Lane Donatelli."

"Nice to meet you, Lane." Kevin came out from behind the counter, a heavy brace on his left knee, and crossed to shake Lane's hand.

"How long have you been here, man?"

"A couple of weeks now. I wanted to get up and running in time for Christmas sales, so I cut a few corners. I hope to get a little better settled after the holidays."

Lane stared a moment at the brace, curious.

Kevin didn't seem to mind. "National Guard. Just got back from a tour in Afghanistan and two months of rehab after a wall fell on me." He shrugged, a faint smile fading quickly from his face.

"Sorry to hear about that." Lane gestured to Kevin's leg. He nearly commented on the lack of need for the government to become involved with others' struggles, but was not sure of Kevin's politics. Better to stick to the stuff he understood.

"So, the 920A?" he said, turning back to the window.

"It's prime. Two gigs DDR3 V-RAM. Video card has 1660 streaming processors." Kevin walked over and turned on the device. It booted fairly quickly and Lane's acquisitive eyes studied every blip and flash.

"Liquid cooling?"

"Oh, yeah. Totally built to avoid overheating. Basically a compressed desktop, man."

"What about the game?"

Kevin's grin broadened. "I knew you were in. Let me guess." He looked Lane up and down. "Definitely a Hordie."

"For the win!" Lane chuckled. Was he so obviously a troublemaker?

"Wait till you see."

Kevin tapped on the keyboard bringing up his WoW sign in page. Once he filled in the blanks, the screen changed to the cityscape where his toon was last located. "Check the graphics."

Lane had never seen the City of Dal move so smoothly. Usually the screen lagged because so many gamers in the MMORPG played there at once. But this changed scenes as though Kevin might be the only player on the screen. "Sweet!"

"You bet. Your city frames per second is gonna blow your mind. This machine can do more frames than Andretti does laps at the Indy."

Kevin entered more data and maneuvered his toon into interaction with some others. "And with these ultra graphics you can practically Pinocchio your elves into real boys."

Lane laughed out loud. That was all he needed. More elves becoming real.

"Well, definitely awesome." He sighed. "Now for the reality check. What's the cost?"

Kevin accessed his user interface and scanned his current standings before turning back to Lane. "About five grand."

"That's what I thought. Way out of my range."

"You could put it on your Christmas list. Have you been a good zombie this year?"

Lane snickered. "It's been an interesting year, that's for sure. Elves and all." He thought a minute, never taking his eyes off that shiny bauble on the table in front of them. "Do you ever get anyone who needs computer repair, or maybe wants a custom build? Maybe we could do a trade."

"That could be. I dabble myself, but who knows? I might get more work than I can handle." Kevin left the machine running and went to the door as the mailman entered. Lane fiddled with the keys, manipulating the pixelated characters for himself.

"How are you?" Kevin said as the uniformed man handed him a rubber banded stack of envelopes and catalogs.

"Freezing my ass off." The mailman gave a good-natured smile. "But it beats being unemployed."

"Sure does, sure does," Kevin agreed.

Lane tore his attention from the computer to focus on his original task. "I'll take our mail so you don't have to go up," he said, holding out his hand.

The man dug in his satchel for a large manila envelope. "Got a certified. Sign the green card."

Kevin pulled a pen from his front pocket for Lane to use. Lane scribbled his name in the designated space and the mailman gave him the envelope along with the rest of their mail.

"Is it ticking?" Lane quipped.

Both men gave Lane an odd look, and he chuckled. "Never mind. Thanks."

The mailman left to deal with the rest of his appointed rounds and Lane fidgeted, anxious now to read the report he had waited for. "So I'll stop back in a couple of days and see if you have work for me?" he said with a last regretful look at the laptop in the window.

"You do that. We'll compare game servers. I've been looking to switch."

"Deal." Feeling a little more special now that he knew someone who understood and even encouraged his particular addiction, he shook Kevin's hand and returned to the apartment.

* * *

IN the kitchen, Crispy waited with two plates, his face screwed up with annoyance. "Where were you?"

Lane stashed the big envelope inside his coat. "Sorry. I had to wait for the mailman to get here. What's for lunch?"

"Leftover stir fry from HuHot's. Black Thai peanut sauce."

"Yum. Let me hang up my coat."

Lane kicked off his shoes into the pile behind the door and hung his coat on the back of his chair. Turning his body so it would block Crispy's view, he slipped the report from the manila envelope and shoved the envelope inside one of the boxes that made up the Cave. Crispy would never look there.

His report in hand, Lane joined his roommate at the small table that served as their dining area. Crispy's mail consisted mostly of advertisements, but two gilt-edged envelopes were addressed to both of them, indicating the rare occurrence of something more personal. Lane watched surreptitiously as Crispy opened them.

"Iris sent us a Christmas card!" Crispy chortled as he

displayed the holiday card with the little bunnies and birds decorating a tree, very pleased with himself and the world.

"Already? Is it even Thanksgiving yet?"

Lane could care less about the whole commercial holiday process, including the exchange of greeting cards, but his heart warmed to see his closest friend so thrilled. The change in attitude was a great improvement over his recent doldrums.

His hands shaking with excitement, Crispy tore open the other one. "The Sierra Club!"

Lane frowned. "The Sierra Club? Why would they be sending you a card?"

Crispy eyed him. "Why wouldn't they? They love trees. I like trees. I love trees."

"But you hardly go outside."

"I do too! I've been to the woods with Daven every week, since, you know."

"Oh." Lane's brow scrunched up until it felt like it carried the weight of deep trenches. "I thought Iris was just taking you to the store."

"Hmmph. Shows what you know then, huh?" With an emotional chip on his shoulder nearly big enough to be visible, Crispy settled in to eat his steaming pork and noodles.

"It's all good," Lane said, turning to his own mail. The report he had been expecting was from one of his online contacts, a fellow gamer who lived out in Portland who had analyzed the liquid from Jelani's thermos to see just what was in it. Lane perused the list thoughtfully.

Red clover. Red raspberry leaves. Chaste berry, whatever that was. A trace of nettle.

He turned to the next page where his friend had made some hand written notations.

As far as I can tell, this mixture is designed for only one purpose. To increase fertility. I'd say your friend is trying to get pregnant. There's plenty of medical routes to this, so I don't know why she's dosing herself with such high concentrations of these herbs. Seriously, Lane, we're talking mega doses here fit for an elephant or a T-Rex. Especially if she's got any kind of allergy, this stuff could very well be what's making her sick. TTY Saturday night at the raid. IM me if you've got more questions!

Lane let the information sink in, the implications of it burning him. Finally he could contain it no longer. "It's a conspiracy!"

Crispy didn't even look up from his plate. "I told you so."

CHAPTER 13

GRIGOR Biren sat in a small circle of light, the bare remains of the fire Fontine had left him when she had returned to the bosom of the clan earlier that day.

He knew he should be grateful that he had fire at all in the bleak winter. He had done without for the first several months. All the same, it rankled him to be dependent on someone else for the basics to which he was surely entitled.

Night settled in while he stared at the dying flames. Only after the harsh call of the snowy owl from a tree overhead did he glance at the stars above. Billions of fires, set there in the sky, none of them any more useful to Grigor than the embers in front of him.

It wasn't fair. He deserved better.

As he sat hunched over with hands tucked beneath his arms for warmth, a sound came to him, but not from behind and not from ahead. It seemed to be all around. A rolling laugh, first a mere whisper, and then growing until it echoed from the trees around him. Grigor brushed his hair back from his shoulders and stood up, stepping out of the firelight, wondering which of the clan felt brave enough to perform such a joke on him.

That movement was likely all that saved him from instant cremation.

A moment later his fire leapt up, twelve feet high, burning with mad fury. Sparks flew from the tops of the flames and floated skyward until he could no longer see them. The snow all around his feet began to melt away.

The laughter faded after a moment, as if with an air of anticipation.

Grigor, amazed, walked slowly around the fire studying it.

Magic, it definitely was, but whose? Why would any of the clan take an interest in his welfare?

"Why indeed?"

The voice came directly from the flames, which flickered as the words passed from them. Grigor recognized the speaker, though he did not understand how he could be here.

"Master Bartolomey?"

"Good boy. You always were the brightest one." The voice, almost affectionate, seemed pleased.

"But, Master, I do not understand." Grigor thought back to the confrontation in the forest, the day the old queen had been freed from her tree, the day Lorenz had punished his rebel son Bartolomey by sending him off somewhere in that accursed vessel.

"You thought I was gone?" Again, Bartolomey's deep laughter echoed around the glade. "Sidetracked, perhaps, but not departed. Even Lorenz is no match for me when we are on equal ground. My power comes from a place much older than his, much more malleable and protected. I have taken steps, my boy, exercised options that Lorenz could never have imagined. As if a mere bauble could contain all that is my essence."

Grigor knew that laugh, and the voice sounded right, but he was still not convinced. If Bartolomey had been stronger than the old king, then why had he simply not deposed them all and disposed of the false queen on the spot? "If that's so, how did the king send you away?"

"If you were so strong, how did that weakling Astan Hawk follow you to the place of meeting? If, if, if! I was caught off guard. That was all. That despicable human, Vincent Marsh, playing at magic with that vessel."

That phrasing certainly sounded familiar. Perhaps it really was Bartolomey.

"Of course it is." The voice took on a hint of scorn. "Now my question to you, boy. Are you intending to live under a bundle of sticks like a discarded piece of garbage, alone the rest of your life? Or are you going to set things right?"

Grigor was stung, shamed in front of all those points of light staring down at him. "How can I do that with the whole clan against me?"

The laugh washed over him again and the fire shot up even higher.

"You don't need the clan, boy. Not when you have access to the power of a mage."

Grigor stiffened. "Mages don't exist in this world," he said, unconsciously parroting the teachings of the Circle.

"Your outdated group of witches would like to believe that is so. They are right to fear our power."

The fire containing Bartolomey broke suddenly into five smaller fires, spreading over thirty square feet. The light flickered and flashed off the snow tipped trees around the space where Grigor had been sitting. He jumped back to avoid being burned.

"Come into the center, my boy. Feel my energy. Though I now reside on another plane, I control magic beyond your comprehension."

Hesitant, but desperate to prove his courage, Grigor sloughed off his blanket and thin coat to avoid burning them and stepped cautiously into the center of the circle. Heat surrounded him, warmed him, and he felt his old strength returning, transferring from the soil into his body, from his feet to his ankles, from his hip through his spine and out to his fingertips, into his head, so that even his hair rippled and grew with power.

"Yes!" he cried. "Yes, master!" The fires crackled around him. He soaked in the feeling, the power, as much as he could, hungry for even more.

"Does she bring you this feeling, your little strumpet, selling her soul to save you?"

Grigor's conscience pricked at such a description of his lovely Fontine, but he didn't speak up to defend her, not in the face of this potential. He did not want to risk Bartolomey's anger and possible retribution. The warmth he received from Fontine was a faint ray of winter sunshine compared to this. This was what he wanted. He shook his head. "No, Master."

"The clan has nothing for you, Grigor. Do not return to them."

If he could have his power all for himself again, he had no intention of dealing with the clan. Why would he ever degrade himself to beg their forgiveness? "What shall I do, master, to serve you?"

"What serves those of the Council of Mages is the disharmony of the elven clans and of men," Bartolomey said speaking through the bright heat of five flames. "Men do not overmuch concern us, as they fight their wars and hate each other, effectively wiping themselves off the surface of the land. Let them destroy their cultures with their strife and their chemicals. The mages have no need of them, or their lands.

"But the elf clan serves us best when chaos reigns."

"What? That makes no sense. The elf clan is strongest when it is united."

"You presuppose that the mages and the Lelan work together for the greatest good. That may have been so before the clan broke at Linnea's passing. But when that opportunity arose, the mages discovered how their individual powers increased when they separated themselves from the clan."

Bartolomey's lecture paused for several long moments while Grigor absorbed the full implication of what he had said. The mages had broken off from the clan to increase their power? At the expense of the clan?

All of his life, Grigor had been taught by the elders that only when elves united could their power grow. Now he was faced with the opposite premise. An elf alone could not only survive, as he had, but could actually thrive, even grow powerful, without the clan.

"While the clan is in disarray, they waste their vitality, the strength they receive from their connection to the soil. Only then can the mages siphon off those energies, to save them for a time when the clan is on the true path. We can hold, even grow that strength, to share it once again with the clan. These energies make us powerful. The energies that would make you powerful, my boy. You yourself have the makings of a fine mage."

"Me? A mage?" Grigor could not believe his good fortune. He did not need the others.

He could continue to live and with persistence perhaps become a mage. A mage more powerful than any one of the elves of the Bitterroot clan. More powerful than Astan and his pathetic grandmother Djana. More powerful than the hated queen.

"What must I do?" Grigor asked.

"Continue as you have been, keeping yourself separate from those who would harm you, and yet increase your effort to stir the pot of discord with the clan. You shall be our delegated warrior."

"A warrior." Now that sounded like something Grigor could believe was his true fate. "And if I do?"

"You will have your gifts restored and more. You will free me from this plane to return to my rightful place among the forests."

"I swear I will do these things!" Belatedly wondering about the plan, Grigor's midsection grew a little queasy. How was he to accomplish this task as he had promised? "Am I to do this alone, without aid?"

The fires rippled. "Of course not. There is one in the clan, a female."

"Fontine?"

A sharp reply and burst of flame. "Not that insipid waste of elf flesh!"

Grigor cowered a moment and then forced himself to relax and listen.

"A female hiding among the clan, as you once were. Concealing her true nature from her fellows. She will come to you on the fifth day from this one, at sunset at the point where the big river passes over the rock of the ages. Do you know the place?"

Grigor's memory searched to locate a mental picture of the small diversion of the running waters, where as a young elf he and the other youngers had tested their courage by swimming out to the huge boulder, trying to remain standing on it for the count of ten before being swept off by the currents. "I do."

"I am asking you to defend what you know is right, Grigor. The fight will be difficult, but the rewards will be great. Do you understand?"

Grigor nodded, assimilating the information along with the restorative heat of his life force running through his muscles, his blood. "Master, how long will I retain what is mine? What you have returned to me?" He hated that his voice held a pathetic, desperate tremble.

"What you have is temporary, my boy, but your strength will pass slowly. Once your task is complete, I will be able to give you all the power you had and more for you to keep forever."

Disappointed that Bartolomey had not made him whole all at once, Grigor fixed on the promise. Even he was not rash enough to challenge Bartolomey, demanding rewards not yet earned. He knew the Master. If he followed through on the tasks set for him, the prize would be his.

Patience was not one of Grigor's strongest qualities. Even he would admit that. But for all he had lost, the chance to regain it was worth a wait. "I shall do as you ask."

"Remember, stay away from the clan, except to foment dissension among them." There was that laugh again. "They are well on their way to breaking apart now, thanks to their embrace of that imposter. Only a small bit of pressure in the right places will destroy their tentative union. I have faith in you, my boy. I have faith."

The fires flared up sending Grigor, trapped in their midst, crouching to the ground in a rush of fear. Just as quickly they were snuffed out. Lost for several seconds in the sudden pitch blackness, Grigor's nerve wavered.

But soon the stars came into focus again, and the moon lifted over the horizon, reflecting off the snow that surrounded his location, though his immediate area was bare ground, the snow having melted in the heat from the fires.

That proof the encounter had truly happened, along with the vitality rushing through his body, firmed his resolve. As he left the ashes of Fontine's fire to retire to his makeshift shelter, Grigor considered what had been given to him.

Five days, Bartolomey had said. In five days Grigor would meet the *neris* who would change his life.

CHAPTER 14

AFTER several attempts to jump-start his seldom-used battery, Lane managed to bring his old red pickup to life.

He headed out to the woods alone, a man on a mission. A man who barely fit behind the truck's fixed steering wheel. A man ignoring the rusting muffler's roar. He prayed that any passing law enforcement officer would have the courtesy to do the same.

The discovery that the elves had dosed his closest female friend with enough fertility herbs to deliver a whole litter of little squirming elf babies infuriated him. He was sure that they had not told Jelani. She would have said something on the day the ambulance had taken her to the hospital. So she truly did not know.

And the elves were evil.

His head rumbled with plans for revenge, all of which he knew would be as useless as water guns at a drug-gang firefight. Jelani would not hear any criticism of her dear elves. Astan would glare and bristle. Then Daven would come over and put some kind of whammy on Lane, brainwashing him into soporific Love and Peace themes, pushing aside his anger.

And it was anger, he decided.

As he shifted the truck into fourth to drive up Highway 93, the rough grinding of the gears echoed the harsh clash of feelings inside him. During his years in the foster child system, therapists he mostly ignored had given him permission to own his feelings, to be irate about what one person did to another person against his will, especially without his knowledge and cooperation.

Similar to what had happened to their foster mate Sammie, who had been murdered by a mother's paramour when she had failed to protect him. And what had happened to Crispy, when his mother neglected him in favor of the bottle, leaving him to be abused by a series of others.

What had happened to himself. But Lane didn't think about that any more.

The issue here was not Lane, it was Jelani and her free will to get pregnant if and when she wanted to, not at the behest of a cluster of old elf witches.

He didn't know Astan well, but of the group Astan seemed like the most honorable. Lane knew where he stood with Astan. He dealt straight. Lane imagined he would be a little hot when he shared what he knew with them.

Caught in traffic, Lane smacked the steering wheel with the heel of his hand. Thirty minutes to go, if the damned construction cleared. Even on sunny days like this, how the state crews could continue to work in the winter weather was beyond him. Even if the job was half done, one would think they could find a good place to stop and pick up again after the thaw, instead of subjecting themselves to the cold. It was bad enough that summer was construction season. Now Montana had extended the joy throughout the holidays as well.

Lane sighed and slipped in a compact disk that lay on the seat next to him. A ripple of piano arpeggios poured from the music player, followed by a symphony of kettledrums and violins.

"What the hell?"

Lane scrambled for a case to see what he had put in the slot instead of the greatest hits of Queen, which was what he thought he had grabbed. His hand came up with a couple of cupcake wrappers and an old milkshake cup, but no case. With a guttural curse, he popped out the disk and read the printed information.

New Age? When had someone been in his truck listening to New Age? *Hellfire.*

At least the flagman still held them at a dead stop. He tossed the disk back over the seat and reached across to the basket on the floor in front of the passenger seat for the music he wanted. Breathing hard with the effort of leaning forward, he pushed himself upright, slid in the disk, and then pushed the button to click through the selections until rock music began to play. Now that was more like it.

The delightful falsetto of Freddie Mercury distracted him from the report, from the anger, from the world. Like the game.

His online games gave him the chance to be someone else, someone who had clout or power, someone with an interesting life story. He controlled his own fate. He was not dependent on others to define his future.

Not just in the context of the games either, but also in the extended relationships he had with the people on his server. Just as he had tapped into his network to find someone who knew chemical analysis, he was available to provide information about computer systems and the history of fantasy literature. Their little band worked together in the virtual world as well as the real world. It was almost like the family Lane always wanted but would never have.

The next step of his plan was even more daring. He intended to snare some elf DNA to help test out his theories about how the cross breeding of species could have taken place. One of his gamer buddies taught in the genetics department at the University of British Columbia across the border in Canada. Lane had not figured out how he was going to explain to John the reason for the investigation that he wanted. But something would come to him.

As his bird-like old grandmother Nunzia used to say: *"Quel che non ammazza, ingrassa." What does not kill one will feed him, make him stronger.* Of course, Nunzia had been beaten to death by her drunken husband, so apparently she was right. And she was an idiot for not leaving the abusive bastard.

Once the traffic started moving, Lane let Queen move him along the road. It wasn't long until he drove into the nearest trail to the place Jelani now lived. There was no way to drive up to the front door, unfortunately. Damned inconsiderate of her. He hefted himself out of the truck, his worn sneakers nearly up to their tops in snow. He muttered at the incipient wetness, annoyed by it, although he had made the choice not to make the effort to put on his old leather boots.

"Never get wet in the Cave," he muttered.

Lane hauled his large computer case from behind the seat. Inside was his laptop, even though he did not think he would use it, a couple of Linux manuals, and a copy of the report for Jelani. He also checked the bag to make sure his big thermos and two packs of Creamy Cupcakes were in there. Jelani had gone substantially nuts and granola since she had moved to the woods. She would never have anything that would sustain him.

And he sure as hell was not drinking any tea the old ladies made.

He could not remember exactly how long it took to get to her place from the trail. Fifteen or twenty minutes maybe. Definitely longer than he walked most days. But it probably wouldn't hurt him. Much.

He would just distract his mind by thinking about that new computer in the window of the storefront and what he could do with it.

With the strap of the heavy case slung across his chest, he blundered along the path. The crisp cold air burned his lungs, as his breaths came shorter and faster. He knew he spent too much time hiding in his apartment, living through his keyboard and a bunch of disks and drives. So much safer than the real—

Something heavy hit him from behind and he yelled as he stumbled forward.

"Lane!"

A delighted squeal and a pair of arms pulling him upright told him exactly where he could find Jelani. He swallowed any protest he was about to make. "Hey, Jelly Bean!"

"What are you doing here? I didn't know you were coming!"

He twisted around so he could hug her and found her belly pushing against his, even through her thick coat. He frowned and reached for her shoulders, distanced her a little so he could get a better look. "You're showing already."

She looked down at her stomach with a mock gasp. "Oh, no!"

"Serious, Jelly Bean. What's up with that?"

To his annoyance, she diverted him with a smile and slipped

her arm through his. "Come on. Let's go back to the house. It's cold out here! I'm so glad you came." She leaned close. "Did you bring me coffee?"

"You wanted coffee?" he asked, plugging an innocent note into his words.

"You forgot!" Her resulting pout was a familiar sight, and one that reassured him that she had not changed too much in her time away.

He grinned. "Of course, I didn't." He patted his case. "Brought you a whole thermos, brewed and ready to go."

"Lane, you're the best! How's Crispy?"

"Seems good. He said he's been out here often. Have you seen him?"

"A couple of times, when Daven's brought him by." She looked at him, nose wrinkled in consternation. "But it's a big forest, you know. Acres and acres of vegetation."

Her answer ratcheted up his grumpy attitude. "Right. And what is it you do out here again? Hug trees all day?"

"Make them grow." Her smile became something quite contented as she reached out a hand to pat the trunk of a sapling on the edge of the path. "Like what I used to do for your plants at the apartment? Somehow they like to listen to me, to do what I ask them to do. Like this, look!"

She dragged him aside to a small area where huge trees had been snapped in half, their decapitated upper parts lying on the ground like a child's pick up sticks game.

"You break all the trees?"

"No, stupid. A lightning strike got them." She punched him in the left arm. "Look closer."

Lane surveyed the area, about the size of half a city block, and after a moment noticed that between the fallen trees, a myriad of young trees had pushed up through the snow, perhaps a foot to eighteen inches tall. Extrapolating that a few years out, the little glade would repopulate itself in fine form.

"You did that?"

"Yep." Her face glowed with pride. Lane could not remember seeing her look so happy in all the time that he had known her. "Come on!"

She dragged him, stumbling, through the snow, that seemed to get deeper as they went into the wood. At that point, all the trees looked the same to him and he was glad she had found him. He would never have been able to pick the right one on his own. It wasn't as if it had windows and sat thirty feet across at the base. Or had a mailbox. Or even a welcome mat.

She stopped suddenly and reached out to one of the tree trunks, placing her fingers on it. With a crack and a creak, the trunk slowly opened. He closed his eyes, still reluctant to believe this bit of magic, and she pulled him inside.

"It won't collapse," she said.

It was the same 'I've told you this a thousand times already' tone he used so often with Crispy.

"I don't believe you," Lane said, as he always did when she reassured him. He just had to find some way to turn off his mind. Then he could believe any silly crap that the elves wanted to feed him. People inside trees? Sure. Houses in trees? Sure. Flying dragons? Whatever.

Once he had crossed the threshold the door swung closed again.

Inside, Astan sprang to his feet, a quickly erased expression of alarm crossing his face. "Hello, Lane."

Astan came no closer and didn't offer his hand to shake as Daven would. But then Daven always seemed a little phony to Lane. He preferred Astan's guarded, even paranoid style. It felt real and definitely familiar.

"Do you want some tea, Lane?" Jelani asked.

"As long as it comes out of a city-sealed package." Lane nodded to Jelani's partner. "Astan, how's it going, dude?"

Lane took off his coat, hanging it on a hook near the door and sat his case on the floor next to the table. A piqued yowl issued from the bedroom and Jelani's cat bounded out, looking fat and happy. Like her mistress.

"Hey, Az, what's new?" Lane scratched behind the cat's ears in the old familiar way. Azrael apparently liked it too, because he rubbed up against Lane's leg with fondness.

Several balls of soft white, creamy yellow, and pastel green yarn lay on the table along with a crochet hook and a small stack of little booties, some of them more irregularly shaped than others. Now there was a domestic side of his friend he had never seen.

"Baby booties?" Lane asked. "Really?"

Jelani blushed. She looked back at him over her shoulder while she filled a kettle with water from a pitcher on the counter. "We wouldn't want Juniorette's feet to get cold now, would we?"

"Guess not."

This evidence of motherly tendencies shocked him, but not as much as Jelani's physical appearance. With her coat off, Lane got a good look at a body that seemed much more like seven months pregnant than four. He did not understand it. Any of it. Not how she could become pregnant by an elf, not how it happened so fast, not how she seemed to be so happy here in the trees and animals and bugs and snow, when before she had been hysterical at the sudden appearance of a spider in a room.

Astan filled the awkward silence that followed with the scrape of his chair against the dirt floor and a faint smile for the thoughts in Lane's head.

"It is going well, I think." Astan retook his seat in the handcrafted wooden rocking chair, a book in his hand. "The child thrives."

Lane cleared his throat and chose one of the chairs at the table, wondering if it was too rickety to hold his bulk. Hopefully someone had put a spell on it, making it stronger than it appeared. "Yeah. About that."

"About that what?" Jelani frowned as she brought him a steaming cup and a spoon.

"I, ah...." He stalled, lifting the cup to his nose for a precautionary whiff. But he need not have worried. It was definitely Earl Grey. "You remembered."

"About what?" Jelani persisted, the edge in her voice attracting a hard look from Astan.

"Well, Jelly, I kind of went out on a limb the day you went to the hospital, and we didn't know what was wrong."

"That was weeks ago." She put her hands on her hips. "What are you up to?"

Astan got up and came to join them, putting a possessive hand on Jelani's shoulder. Her fingers came up to touch his, and linked tightly onto them.

Lane took a deep breath and rummaged in his bag, taking out a copy of the report. "You know how I am. I couldn't let go of the mule thing."

"Oh, for Pete's sake!" Irritated, Jelani pulled away from Astan and went back to tea brewing.

Astan, on the other hand, fastened onto the mystery of the envelope. "If Lane left the safety of his home and came all the way out to us, he has something important to share, Jelani. We should listen."

Surprised by support from that quarter, Lane squirmed in his chair. He really wanted a cupcake. Really wanted one. But he held off. "I, um, had that tea analyzed. The tea in your thermos that day?"

She stood up from her squat at the hearth with a cup in her hand that she gave to Astan. "Tea? Oh. Raspberry leaves, right? One of the *neris* of the Circle made it for me."

"That was in there. But here. You read it." He handed her the envelope.

She opened it and slid the report out to study it. Astan read over her shoulder. Lane sipped his still hot tea, thinking about the cupcakes in his bag, listening to the fire crackle and snap, wishing just a little that he was far away, in a house that did not have the potential to squish him flat.

As they read through the second page, Astan nearly spit, his mouth twisted in anger. "Those meddling old bats!"

Jelani's face went white. "How could they?"

Astan stared into space for a moment, his speech stilted, as if thoughts were being handed to him on a platter. "That's why they kept after me. That's what they kept expecting me to do. They wanted a princess. Someone they could groom and teach from birth, as you should have been taught. Someone who will—"

"Be their little puppet!" Jelani finished her voice catching. She tossed the papers on the table with a flash of anger in her eyes.

Observing them, Lane was almost sorry he had brought the report. The contentment he had earlier seen on Jelani's face had vanished. Maybe she and Astan would have been better off not knowing. Ignorance was bliss, isn't that what the folk said?

She had turned to stare at Astan, her thoughts even clear to Lane, who was half-distracted in obsessing about his cupcakes.

Astan, too, must have read her thoughts, because he set down his cup and grabbed her when she would have turned away from him. He waited until she turned to him again, and he never let go of her gaze, with such intensity that even watching was nearly painful to Lane.

"*Denami*, I would not have consciously let this happen. You know my heart where you are concerned. I would give my life for you at any starry moment. We will make sure it does not happen again. I swear this to you."

They stood locked in each other's contemplation so long that Lane suspected telepathy. Uncomfortable at the depth of emotion that seemed to fill the room until it echoed, Lane's hand slipped into his case and he slowly drew out the top set of cupcakes, trying hard not to crinkle the cellophane, which of course meant it made enough noise to startle the other two into remembering they were not alone.

"Sorry," Lane muttered.

Jelani's hand went to her abdomen and she gave a faint laugh, an odd sound without mirth. "I guess our little bun isn't any happier than we are. Ouch! Don't kick me! It's not my fault." She observed the place where her hand was for several long seconds. "What are we going to do, Astan?"

"I don't know." He squeezed her hand. "I need time to think."

She nodded slowly, still absorbed with her internal movements.

"There's coffee," Lane reminded her. He took the thermos out of his case and set it next to Astan's cup on the table. "I promise nothing's bad in there. Well, except the coffee."

Jelani, a faint smile showing her willingness to be distracted, picked up the thermos and twisted off the cap, taking a long moment to commune with the rich aroma that wafted from the top. She drank right from the thermos, shivering with the first couple of sips and then she put the thermos on the table, an odd expression on her face.

"Coffee never made me—oh!" She ducked behind a curtain. Unpleasant noises followed.

Eying Astan, Lane frowned. "Something's not right here. That pregnancy is moving way too fast, at least by human standards. And she's been a coffee addict forever. That." He pointed to the curtain. "That is not normal. If she's still been drinking whatever crap they're feeding her, who knows what else is going on inside her?"

Astan nodded, reluctance magnified in the tight set of his jaw. "If I find they have harmed her in any way they won't escape my wrath."

The darkness in his voice chilled Lane to the core. More confident now that his worry for Jelani was shared by someone who could do something about it, he shoved the cupcakes back into his case.

Jelani came out, even more pale. "Is something wrong with me? Have they, I don't know, changed something? Made me someone else? Astan, please."

"Come lie down, Jelani." Astan helped her curl up into the papasan chair, and tenderly covered her with a blanket, smoothing her hair back from her pale forehead. "We'll discover what has come to pass, *denami,*" he promised her. "You should rest now."

Lane did not need the pointed look Astan gave him to drive him to his feet, poised to escape. Things were beginning to get a little weird. "Look, guys, I'm sorry to be the one to tell you about this. Really."

"Not your fault," Jelani murmured, lying back in the chair. She did not look well.

Lane was reminded of an old sci-fi mini series when a young woman was impregnated by an alien lizard, and how the child within threatened her life. It couldn't happen to Jelani. He would do what he could to stop it. "Astan, I want to talk to this Circle. I want to find out what they think. What they plan." Lane gestured to his case. "I'll get them on webcam, whatever it takes. I'll tell them it's for the book."

Astan eyed him blankly.

"The book I'm writing about the elf queen," Lane said. "Not Jelani. Her mother. The quest. You know."

"Perhaps," Astan said. "I cannot imagine they will speak freely to you. To a human," he added with a small apologetic nod. "Even if they did, I cannot say whether that would help."

"What if we leave the clan?" Jelani said, trying to get out of the chair. "What if we go before they can do anything else?"

Astan rested a calming hand on her shoulder. "Shhh. Love, we shouldn't make any rash decisions. I'm not even sure how far you could go in your condition, and now that you are a child of the soil," he said. He turned to Lane. "But I suppose we should keep as many options as possible available to us. Is there anything you could do?"

Lane nodded, his brain racing. Was he really ready to get knee deep in a supernatural conspiracy? Half of his mind was reluctant to consider the disruption in his life, but the other half saw the chance to fulfill a secret desire, to live his exciting online life of quests and battles. He could take on any elf. A cartoon one, anyway. As long as he had his usual weapons of choice, his dragon's head staff and magic dagger.

But he had real life skills and resources, too. "Sure, man. I've got connections all over. You let me know."

"I shall." Astan waved at the doorway, his fingers doing something Lane could not detect. The door opened without him touching it. "Farewell, Lane."

"Um, yeah. See you." He snatched up his case and his coat and hurried out through the expanding crack. His last glance was of his dear friend curled in the half circle of her chair, and the elf she loved tending to her as any man ought to do. The vision settled his purpose.

Astan had asked for his help, and Lane would give it. Even if it meant war.

CHAPTER 15

GRIGOR waited the five long days, stretching out the last of the food Fontine had brought until he was almost desperate again. The vigor gained during his meeting with Bartolomey's spirit had strengthened his body against the elements. But as Bartolomey had warned, that vigor slowly trickled away.

By the time he had traveled across the several leagues that took him to the appointed place at the head of the river, he was weary to the point of exhaustion.

Thanks to a few days of sunshine, the snow had melted in spots. His elven power weak, he sloshed through the mud and lingering icy piles of slush like a human, his feet becoming soaked and frozen in short order. The rugged contrast between this and the days when his passage over any natural surface was light and free, almost like flying, spurred him on. If his life did not change he would wither and die.

The rocks climbed gently higher until he reached the place where the river met the trail, just as the sun neared the horizon. The river was partially crusted over with ice in shades from pure white to a dirty gray, but the water still burbled over the rocks underneath, sending musical notes into the atmosphere, counterpoint to the wind high above whispering through the pine needles.

He considered finding a thick piece of bark to ride down the open part of the river, as they had done when they were younger, but decided that the possibility of falling into the freezing waters without the protection of elven power was not worth the risk. Instead, he walked along the edge of the bank, his feet crunching on chunks of frost and sticks that had fallen under their crystal-coated weight. Finally, he drew even with the large boulder to which Bartolomey had referred.

He stepped behind the thick trunk of a fir tree, an old one, its bark split and cracked so that his fingers slipped between the loose sections as he held onto it, watching for a glimpse of his contact from a safe place. Just in case.

He saw no one.

He listened, a faint trace of something coming to him on the breeze. There. Was that singing?

As he listened closer, a tune came to him. In the half-light as evening fell, he surveyed the area around the tree for the source of that repeated refrain, a melancholy melody that spoke to him of a lover who was lost.

Movement on the far bank caught his eye.

As light faded around him, it grew across the river. A tiny light at first, above the ground, like it was held in someone's hand, a bright sparkle of radiance that reflected off the rock wall behind it. Then it spread, illuminating the ground for several arm lengths. Grigor stared in wonderment.

When the bright light had reached the size of a large brown bear, a shadow formed in the center of it. A moment later a female elf stepped from the shadow, a perfectly proportioned vision in a deep blue doublet and leggings, her boots of black leather. But he could not take his eyes from her face. Her eyes were the color of the midnight sky, her skin a warm brown, and her hair was like silvery strands of fine thread. She was a creature of beauty such as he had never seen in all his years.

Even after she appeared, the light stayed all around her. It was as if it were both generated by and feeding off her presence, so bright that he wondered how far away it might be seen. He racked his brain trying to remember any of the elves of the clan who had demonstrated such an ability. He could think of no one.

She spoke in an alto voice, rich and melodious. Amused, too. "Seems folly to come so far only to hide, doesn't it?"

Her gaze snapped around and focused right on him, those jewel like eyes pulling on his weakened body, almost dragging it from behind the tree to face her. He tried to remain upright, not wanting to give in to the fatigue that sapped his will.

She walked right across the top of the rolling water as if it were solid ground. When she came close, the scent of baking sweets, vanilla, cinnamon, and other spices he couldn't name, along with the smell of fresh cut cedar swirled around and enticed him. She looked with those midnight eyes into his soul.

"Poor Grigor. Such a dull version of one who used to be a strong elf. One of the most promising." She walked around him, studying him as if he was under one of the human scopes from the science classes. She was not his age at all, but older. Her air was of one self-assured and experienced. Her skin though, was still as smooth as Fontine's. One slender finger reached out and caressed his cheek as she leaned close to his ear. "Oh, but the possibilities within," she breathed, hardly above a whisper.

As the air left her lips and entered his ear, Grigor felt a dizzying rush of emotion, warmth, strength, sexual energy, and power jolt through his body. He would have stumbled if some unknown force had not held him on his feet. Seconds later, he felt like himself again and he knew somehow this time it would not fade away.

"Who are you?" he asked, turning to face her, surprised to find she stood eye to eye in height, surprising, since most *neris* had to look up to him. An elf could be lost in those eyes, eyes he was sure now that he had never seen before among the clan. She must have been one of those scattered loyalists who had returned when the false queen had appeared.

"Who would you want me to be?"

The question seemed to hold many meanings. He could not think straight while she was looking at him. What he wanted at that moment was to name her his lover and to take her right there on the cold ground, to make her his. But he would not admit it.

Her laugh, like velvety soft cloth on the ear, soaked through him.

You're a bold one, you are. Do you fancy yourself strong enough to conquer me?

His gaze fell to the cold ground as he flushed with shame. He had no idea she could read his thoughts. Even as he thought those words, he knew she could see his humiliation as well, and he would lose any chance he had of ever winning the exotic creature.

Nonsense. But what we need to concentrate on now is our common enemy. When we have defeated the clan there will be plenty of time to get to know one another as well as you would like.

Her finger caressed his cheek again and he felt a heated response in his loins. "Command me," he said.

She reached inside her doublet and pulled out a small item wrapped in a piece of green elven cloth, soft as baby rabbits' fur. "Take this talisman. The mages' protection charms it for you only."

Grigor held out his hand, more excited by the moment their fingers touched than by the receipt of her gift, but he dragged his attention away from her eyes to unwrap what she had given him. A grizzly bear's claw, black and polished, nearly as long as his index finger. The tip was very sharp, nicking his skin as he picked it up. The thing practically vibrated in his hand.

"A very powerful charm," he noted.

"For one who is very important to us," she purred. "You must keep this talisman with you always. Through this contact, the mages who watch over us shall be able to protect and guide you."

He studied the smooth object for several moments, then wrapped it up again and tucked it into an inside pocket of his jacket for safekeeping. "You are truly of the clan?" he asked.

"I am an elf, like you," she said with a girlish smile. "Born to the soil of the Bitterroot, like you. Concerned about the future of our clan, like you."

"The false queen."

Her expression changed, her anger so concrete that he actually took a step back to protect himself. "The false queen destroys the clan even as we speak. She has spread dissension within the Circle. She does not follow the teachings of the soil. How could she? She is an outsider!"

Grigor considered what Fontine had told him. "So it is not true that she has healed the forests? That she is with child, which brings the Circle together?"

A flash of fury in the other's eyes nearly struck out at him. The light around her sparked and then subsided. Perhaps he should not have questioned her. He opened his mouth to apologize but she stopped him with her finger across his lips.

"These are only further evidence of her intent to deceive," she said. "Jelani set out to trick the Circle into accepting her, drawing away the support for the true ruler of the clan."

"Bartolomey," Grigor said.

She nodded. "You will see these tricks start to fade as the clan falls apart. Already the magic she has used to support living things is deteriorating. Soon the forest will be less than it was before she came."

"And the child?"

The other's eyes blazed. "Yes, the child. The Circle desires above all things a female to be the next in ruling line, one they may teach and coddle and control. But their magic is weakened by the false queen's presence. Djana and the others no longer govern."

"If the hopes of the clan are pinned on the child and something were to happen to the child...."

No more than thinking aloud, Grigor was startled by the sudden, warm approval in the other's eyes. She even enfolded him in her arms, leaving him awash in her spicy scent and hardly able to catch his breath in the rush of acceptance and love that surrounded him.

"Truly you are the insightful one! Master Bartolomey is wise to recommend you. Indeed, this would be the solution to bring power back to the forests, back to the mages, until the clan is ready for the Master's return."

"But I am banned from the clan's soil."

She stepped back and paced on the riverbank. "Others in the clan would follow you. You were the leader of the youngers before the sleepers returned, were you not? You were a fine and strong leader denied your rights to participate in the clan council."

"Yes, it is true," he said, wondering how she knew. She must have been part of the old clan in some way. How else would she have this information?

"The others who were disaffected by the rigidity of the Circle, of the favoritism always shown to the sainted Daven Talvi and his son. They would listen to you, Grigor. You must convince as many of them as possible that what has happened is wrong and that you can lead them to a better, stronger path for the clan."

She stopped and looked into his eyes. "Can you do this? Can you save your clan in a time of nearing disaster?"

He hesitated, not wanting to promise something he was not sure he could deliver. She stepped close again and took his hands. Her voice nestled close to him, a soft embrace, and an encouragement he could hardly resist.

"Please, Grigor. I am not too proud to beg you."

His pride needled him into agreement. "Yes. I will save my clan."

Her smile radiated warmth and love. "I knew you would. You will save us all."

She let go of his hands and stepped back onto the water. "Keep the talisman with you at all times. It will make you strong and protect you."

"Wait! You have not told me your name!" He started after her, empowered enough to cross the snow drifts lightly, but the water still soaked his shoes and he had to stop at the river's edge.

"Call me Firefly." She looked down at his feet, still smiling, and then waved her hand. A flash of light filled the air. She was gone.

Grigor pulled back from the water, afraid for a moment that the dark would swallow him again, but he found his hands held a trace of her sparkle. He removed the talisman from his pocket and ran his finger along the length of the claw again. He would be like the bear, an enemy with no mercy. He would retake his place and restore the others to the true path. The false queen would lose all she had invested in her traitorous plan.

He realized now that he did not have to kill Jelani at all. He could take away something much dearer than her life. All he had to do was figure out how to get his hands on this most vulnerable target, and the mages' reward was a promise given.

His heart lighter by far than when he had arrived, Grigor headed back to his usual shelter, noticing with delight that he no longer left prints in the snow.

CHAPTER 16

IN the days following Lane's shocking disclosure, Astan watched Jelani retreat into a silent sorrow.

Pale and listless, she withdrew into a paranoid place where she whispered constantly to someone, but it was not him. She would eat nothing that she did not prepare with her own hands. She would not sleep unless he guarded the door. She would not even go out into the forests, something he knew had always soothed her.

For the first time Astan was afraid.

The child within her continued to grow. He could see that by her size. Lane claimed that the pace of growth was wrong for a human, but Astan knew elf babies came in a few months with the help of the clan's midwife. This child was a blending of the two. Who would know the answers?

Rashia, who had birthed Jelani herself, came several times to the door but Jelani turned her away. She reminded them she had a human doctor, but she refused to go see him, as well. She insisted that she was no helpless *neris*, that she did not need the Circle's interference. Her circumstances were different than her mother's, she had said. Linnea had been fully elf, with a half breed baby. Jelani was part human. Mostly human, she insisted through torrents of tears and recriminations. Sometimes she hardly sounded sane.

Astan had to do something. Take action before he lost his mind as well.

When he could no longer remain inside the tree house, he promised to guard the door from outside. "I've got to have some fresh air. *Denami*, why don't you come, too? The walk would do you good."

"I won't give them the chance to get their hands on me," she said, retreating to the bedroom.

Helpless to argue he left their private space and stepped out into the forest. Deep breaths of the sharp, cold air cleared his lungs and his head, but his heart remained troubled. He began to walk in a small square around the tree, always keeping the door in sight, in case she should mistrust him and check. What was he to do?

Outside, away from her flurry of negativity, his mind began to clear. He did not need his odd mental flicking to know why she was upset. But it might help him decide what to do.

He concentrated on a memory from the tree house, the woven twig basket from the Circle with its bounty of hand tied cloth bags of herbal mixtures. His outrage added the description of 'poison' to his mental picture, but his anger only clouded the process. He erased that thought and started to concentrate again.

Tea. *Flick.* Jelani, her abdomen round, their child within.

Flick. Lane and the possibility of escape into the city or beyond.

Flick. Rashia, the midwife, the baby in her hands, hurrying away into the old forest.

Mid-flick, his vision went dark as a heavy hand fell on his shoulder. He pulled away with a start.

Daven stood there, studying Astan with deep-set eyes which read more than was on the surface. He glanced toward the tree. "When was the last time she came out?"

Astan shrugged. "Five days, perhaps? A week?"

"So I feared. I want you to see what has happened." Daven started to walk away but Astan didn't follow, still haunted by his visions. "Come," Daven prompted.

"I can't. I can't leave her. She's in such a state." Astan's voice broke, weary from the exhaustion of no sleep, his burden of worry, and the agony of watching Jelani's pain.

Astan felt his father's empathy, as Daven returned to his side. "Then see in this way."

He placed his hand once again on Astan's shoulder, but this time Astan was prepared. His mental vista changed to an open space he knew along the ridge, a place Jelani had healed several months before. New trees had sprung up and a rush of undergrowth had spread across the area, even a burst of golden fall wildflowers just before the snow had set in.

But now it appeared different, and not because of winter conditions. The young trees lay flat on the ground, their needles dried and brown.

"What does this mean?"

A deep breath filled Daven's chest, then eased out through his nose as he selected his words. "It could be as simple as Jelani's hormonal adjustments."

Astan considered the tone of Daven's statement and shook his head. "But you don't believe that."

"No. Other signs indicate the blight is wider than just the plants of the forest. Rumblings of the Circle—"

Astan held up a hand to cut him off. "Do not tell me about those old women. After what they have done, they have no say in my home any longer!"

Eyes wide with surprise, Daven crossed his arms. "What have they done Astan?"

Frustration flaring again in the telling of the tale, Astan shared with his father the information Lane had brought them. His body shook with emotion by the time he was done, release sinking through him like warm water, relief at being able to let some of his righteous fury loose. "They had no right. Look what their meddling has brought about!"

Breathing hard from his agitation, he waited for his father to produce one of his usual smooth replies about the Circle, some syrupy explanation that would make everything right again, but the stunned look never left Daven's face.

Finally Daven shook himself loose and rubbed his forehead. "This is very serious."

"By the snake's tooth, it is. And just as poisonous." Enervated as the adrenaline faded, Astan leaned against a thick fir trunk, his eyelids growing heavy. He felt more exhausted than ever.

"When did you last rest, my son?" Daven asked, brow

furrowed with concern.

"I don't know. Days ago. If I don't watch, she—"

"Let me help," Daven said. "Come, let's go inside."

"She may not allow you in."

"She'll let me in," Daven said. His customary grin evidenced, though clouded like a ghost of itself.

Astan wasn't so sure, but the firm arm around his shoulders steered him to the door. Daven opened it and stepped inside. Jelani was asleep in her chair. Astan automatically went to cover her with a blanket, the elven blanket that was so light it didn't disturb her.

Daven pointed to the bedroom. *Now you lie down and rest yourself. I'll handle Jelani if she wakes. I will let no one in.*

Astan studied his father's face and wondered if he could be trusted. With this new change in attitude, he thought so. He hoped so.

Go.

His father pushed him toward the bed. Too tired to argue, Astan stumbled the rest of the way, almost asleep before he even hit the pillow. Then blessed nothingness.

* * *

ASTAN awoke to soft voices from the direction of the little table. So sluggish he could hardly open his eyes, he crawled forward on the soft mattress until he could see who was talking.

Jelani, still wrapped in her blanket but out of her chair, waved a fork at Daven as she made a point Astan could not clearly hear. At least she had a fork in her hand.

Daven got up and went to the counter, bringing back a couple of apples and what appeared to be some kind of grain. Jelani protested at first, but he laid his hand over hers, looking intently at her, the way he always did, and she eventually surrendered and let him slice the apples for her. Astan focused on not moving a muscle, torn between being pleased at his father's success and jealous that Jelani would respond to Daven and not to him.

Magic be damned.

After he had watched for several minutes, his thoughts coalescing a little as he woke up a bit more, he was surprised when Daven turned and smiled at him.

"You might as well get up. We've been waiting for you."

"You've slept all day and all night!" Jelani dropped her blanket. She hurried over to cuddle Astan a little, much to his surprise. Days had passed since she had tolerated any sort of physical affection. He sat up cautiously, letting her slide into his arms, embracing her with fond warmth.

"I didn't mean to sleep so long," he said retreating into instinctive apology.

She kissed his cheek. "You needed it. I'm sorry I've been so difficult."

Astan eyed his father. Something had changed since he had been asleep. Something major.

"What's going on?"

"Jelani and I have talked. She's agreed to see Rashia later tonight. Then we're going into town to fetch her friend Iris."

Astan stiffened, not liking the sound of all this. When he had gone to sleep, he had believed Daven understood his position about the Circle. This was not an imagined fuss that could just be smoothed over. What happened to Jelani was Astan's territory, not Daven's, not the Circle's. He was her chosen.

"*Denami,* is this true?"

"Come hear what Daven has to say," she said.

Taking his hand, Jelani pulled him toward the edge of the bed. A tight note underlay her voice. He looked into her eyes and saw doubt reflected there, too. All was not sunshine and rainbows. Daven had not solved the problem, then. Perhaps Daven truly meant to help them and not the Circle. This time.

Astan went to the hollowed out gourd bowl on the side counter and scooped a handful of water to wash his face. The cool liquid brought a shock to his skin and kicked him thoroughly awake. With one deep breath under his figurative belt he was ready to face the truth, bad news or good. He joined them and then started with the least harmful bit of what he had heard.

"So Iris is coming to visit?" Astan asked.

"Iris is coming to stay," Daven said.

"Stay? For how long?"

"Until the baby is born," Jelani said. Her jaw set in the way he knew so well that meant argument was futile.

A human ally could be a good thing under their current circumstances, so Astan nodded. The most they risked was a few new pairs of boots and a potential redecoration effort. He surveyed their small living area. "Where do you propose to put her, *denami*? On a limb above us?"

"Don't worry about that, Astan. I'll take care of it." Daven parceled out several bites of the grain on a plate in front of Jelani, and she ate them almost absent mindedly. Astan raised a curious eyebrow. Daven's knee brushed his under the table.

She is severely undernourished. Yes, I charmed her, but she must eat, Astan. Otherwise, your child will not live.

Astan didn't respond. Again, Daven was handling them both. But she did have to feed herself and the child. Swallowing a sharp retort, he shifted in his chair, his next comment directed to the prior subject. "I think you'll be happier with her here."

Jelani gave a faint smile and continued to eat the grain.

The true sticking point, as far as Astan was concerned, was Rashia. He trusted none of the Circle any more, not even his grandmother. The dreams he had experienced even today while he slept had clearly come from her, allegories in various forms that all washed out to the same bottom line: *do your duty by the clan.* Maybe he would. After they began to deal fairly with him and with his beloved.

"And Rashia?" Astan asked.

Daven's expression was vague, one Astan had not seen him wear often. "Jelani and I have come to an agreement on this. I cannot tend her, as it is not within my skills. It is clear she cannot be treated by the human doctor in the city, as Lane has said. What occurs in her body is something he will not understand and will treat as an abnormality. He might even recommend the removal of the child in a premature manner, which could be a disaster."

Jelani shuddered and Astan could almost sense her fear, even in her distracted state. He slid a hand onto hers and squeezed it to reassure her.

"The only source to whom she can turn is an elven midwife," Daven continued. "No one else will understand what changes are occurring."

"But they've brought on these changes with their accursed potions!" Astan spat.

Jelani twitched at Astan's outburst and seemed to realize where she was. She looked down at the plate and pushed it away.

Azrael eyed them from his perch at the end of the counter and hissed, his fur standing all on end.

Daven's lips pressed together in irritation.

Astan got up to search for something to assuage his own rumbling stomach.

"So," Daven said, speaking with exaggerated patience, "who better to explain what is happening, hmm?"

Perturbed, Astan had to admit that surely the Circle knew more about the birthing process than he did. What choice did they have but to cooperate?

He held out for the last bit of control they could grasp. He would force Daven's support, even if it meant contradicting the old women. "Very well. But I want you to watch them every step, Daven."

Daven's quick look let Astan know that he had heard and understood the change in status indicated by the use of his proper name. "You'll be in good hands, Astan." Daven turned his smile on Jelani. "You'll see. When Rashia comes, we'll all know where things stand."

Daven tried to jolly the young woman into eating a little more, but Jelani would drink only pure water that Astan carried in from the stream. The silence grew thick in the room until the midwife arrived. Daven let her in.

Jelani retreated behind the table to stand next to Astan, her trembling fingers clutching his. She stood close enough that their legs touched all the way down to their bare feet, which stood on the well worn soil. He looked over at her, his eyes drawn to that prominent swelling of her belly that contained their child. The three of them, baby included, stood together. As long as they remained that way, they would stand strong.

"Yes," she whispered, reading his thoughts, as was inevitable in such close contact.

He squeezed her fingers and turned his attention to Rashia.

The gray haired elf limped awkwardly into the space, taking a good look around her. Astan suspected she gathered intelligence that she would later share with the other members of the Circle. Most of them had not been inside the queen's residence, as he and Jelani tended to be very private. Under current circumstances, none would get within a walking stick's length of the door, if Astan had his way.

Rashia's ill fitting gray garments threatened to make her fade into mist, no scrap of color to make her seem vital. As she passed Astan he caught the scent of unwashed body and old rags. It seemed odd. The Circle members, when they had lived in the human city, had always taught that elves should be fastidious about cleanliness, priding themselves as more particular than the humans.

What was happening to them? Was this in any way connected to the relapse of nature Daven had showed him before? Had the decay spread to individuals as well?

"Astan," Rashia said in greeting with a little bob of her head. She did not look him in the eye. Daven must have told them that Jelani and Astan knew the truth. That was just as well. It was hard enough for Astan to stand in the same room with one who had nearly poisoned his mate without striking out at her.

Jelani stiffened. Astan felt the rush of emotion that came through their touch. It was not fear, as he had expected, but pride. She stood just a little taller and pinned Rashia in her incisive stare like a rabbit in twin headlights.

"You are here at my sufferance, Rashia," Jelani said. "You will do your duty and then you are dismissed."

The tremble that remained in her fingertips did not extend to her voice, and only Astan knew the depth of control it took Jelani to manage that. *Good girl.* A smile curved his lips as his fingers tightened on hers.

Rashia was not as adept at hiding her surprise at Jelani's tone. Her eyes widened and her mouth opened and closed a couple of times before she chose the words she wanted to use. "Yes, my Lady."

Daven, standing between them like the referee at a wrestling match, wary of both sides, nodded once to Jelani. "Now the examination," he said. "Rashia, what do you suggest? The bed? The chair?"

Rashia eyed both alternatives and then gestured to the bed. Astan wondered if her choice really mattered or if she just wanted to get a look at the queen's bedroom.

Jelani didn't move.

Daven reached for her hand. "Please, Jelani, as we agreed."

Astan released her with reluctance, his parting thought to Jelani that the sooner they began, the sooner Rashia would be gone. Once Daven had her, Jelani walked as if in a dream to the bed and lay down on the side closest to the rest of them.

As Astan had suspected, Rashia's nondescript eyes studied every part of the room as she waited for Jelani to get settled. Her hand flashed in and out of her pocket. Astan cleared his throat in warning. Whatever she had been about to do, she eyed him a moment, then returned her hand to her pocket.

"Just the examination," Astan said, the edge in his voice short of the blade he wished he held in his hand. Realizing the depth of his anger surprised him. He actually wished for that blade. Not because he did not want a child. He always expected a child would come to them. But not like this. Not engineered by outsiders with their own agenda. The deed was done. All he could do was wait and hope that the pregnancy turned out well. If he lost Jelani....

He could not think about that now.

His initial impulse had been to walk around to the bed's far side to hold Jelani's hand, but after what he had seen, he remained where he could watch Rashia's every moment. Daven stood at the head of the bed, his concentration on the young woman. Astan imagined it commandeered most of Daven's ability to keep Jelani calm in the same room with one who had fed her the fertility tea.

Rashia stood, eyes closed, next to the bed, arms extended to the east, gathering her strength. Would she be honest? Astan had always been taught that lies and deceit were not the elves' way, but she and the others, hypocrites all, had certainly been guilty. He crossed his arms, nerves burning with the urge to strike her. He would leave her alone, until she did something she was not supposed to.

"My Lady, I must touch you," Rashia said in a humbled tone. "All will be well. I will not hurt you in any way. This child is of great significance to us. We honor this child and you, as well."

Jelani lay still and stiff on the bed. "Proceed," she said through clenched teeth.

Not hesitating a moment once she had permission, the old midwife gently laid her hands on Jelani's abdomen, drawing some strength from each of them to complete her study. Astan managed to hold his tongue, also his breath, as Rashia's scrutiny proceeded.

The midwife grew agitated as minutes passed and finally pulled away, her hands flopping in the air like fish out of water. Daven released Jelani and grabbed Rashia's shoulders, helping her to a chair, where she mumbled to herself, disturbed about something.

"Astan, some tea for Rashia, please?" Daven asked.

Resentment bubbling in him at allowing the old *neris* to spend one second longer in his home than necessary, Astan resisted the urge to refuse outright. "If it will speed the result," he groused, going to the hearth.

Slow to get up from the bed, her distended abdomen seeming even bigger than Astan remembered from that morning, Jelani shuffled over to the table to join them. "Tell me," she said, dark eyes big in her pale face.

"I don't understand what's happened," Rashia said.

"That makes several of us," Astan snapped.

Daven shot Astan a pointed look and he tried to sublimate his anger, focusing on tea for all of them, one of the human blends, since that is what Jelani would trust.

"Start with what you did to get me knocked up," Jelani said. "You couldn't wait to have a little girl to make your new queen, could you? Since I'm such a disappointment!"

Rashia continued to fidget.

Astan brought a tray to the table with the teapot and cups and set it down with a clatter. "She asked you a question," he said, temper barely under control. Daven rose to his feet, drawing Astan's attention, reminding him of the necessity of restraint.

The old woman tapped the edge of the table, distraught. "But it's not a girl!"

Astan and Jelani exchanged startled looks.

"It's not?" Jelani asked.

"It's gone wrong. It's gone wrong. What did you do?" Rashia's vein covered hand reached out and grabbed Jelani's. "What have you done?"

Startled, Jelani pulled away.

As Astan moved to block the midwife from further contact with Jelani, Daven put a hand on Rashia's shoulder.

"Tell us, Rashia," Daven said in his usual smooth and calming tone, that voice that commanded compliance. "What was the plan? Perhaps then we can decide what's to be done."

Rashia rocked in her chair, fighting with the words that spilled from between her lips. "It was for the best, only for the best. We wanted to solidify the queen's bond with her partner and the Lelan, and a child, a daughter. The herbs were carefully balanced. They would not have hurt her. We would never harm you, Jelani." She turned to Jelani, a supplicant on a mission to convert the lost. "We only have love in our hearts for you."

"You cheated and tricked me. I don't think that's what love's about," Jelani said, folding her hands safely in her lap out of the old elf's reach. "Besides, that tea tasted like raw sticks and mowed grass. Give me a double shot of espresso in my coffee any day."

"Coffee? The human drink?" Rashia looked horrified.

"Well, yeah." Jelani let Daven pour her some tea, and she sipped it slowly.

"Did you drink it?"

"Of course." Jelani frowned. "Coffee's got to make up at

least a quarter of my bloodstream by this time."

"By the Lady, we had not anticipated. Such a different brew with significant toxic qualities. Human interference." Eyes wide with confusion, Rashia bolted to her feet. "We must consider the implications."

"The pregnancy, Rashia." Astan stepped closer. "I haven't heard what you have to say about her health. The health of the child." Her manner did nothing to reassure him, so he took a wild stab at the truth. "It's moving too fast, isn't it?"

The old elf's head snapped around to eye him. "How do you know?"

That was answer enough for him. He didn't reply. "What are we going to do about it?"

"She will have to be delivered in the next few days. If the child is too frail to remain with her, the Circle shall take him to a safe place."

Astan's vision returned to him, drenching him with fear as if soaked with a bucket of ice water.

But Jelani laid down the law. "Like hell you will." Jelani stood, shoving Astan aside and going toe-to-toe with the midwife. "*If* I let you deliver the child, you will not take him. Under any circumstances. Let me make that clear. You've already tried to poison me and my child. If there are any more shenanigans, any at all, I swear to you I will take this child and run as far away from you as I can. You will never see either of us again. Is that clear enough? You take that little bit of news back to your damned Circle. Hear me?"

Rashia jerked and stared as if she had been slapped. "We'll see about that." She limped as quickly as she could toward the door, escaping before Jelani or Astan could say anything else.

Daven opened his mouth to say something, and then closed it, putting his head in his hands.

"Well said, *denami*," Astan whispered, taking his trembling partner into his arms. She dissolved into tears once Rashia disappeared. "Everything will be fine," he told her, rubbing her back, comforting her as best he could in light of what he had seen, reassuring her of what he was not sure he believed himself.

Daven finally straightened and Astan watched him over Jelani's shoulder.

"So, you see what your Circle has done?" Astan asked his father. "Now it's in the open. She's admitted it. Don't tell me we can trust anything they do."

Daven didn't flinch, his hand going to the bag of runes on his belt, fingering it from the outside. "I believe her when she says they meant well, Astan. The clan suffered too much through those seasons when we had no queen to risk Jelani's life. If they harmed her intentionally, they would be no better than Bartolomey. I can't believe they meant her harm. I cannot believe it." He closed his eyes. "I must ponder these developments. The future is cloudy, hidden, and I can't see why. Some force of magic interferes."

"I will tolerate no further interference," Astan said, determination soaking into him from the earth itself, from the air he breathed, from the beloved *neris* in his arms. "Even if it means leaving."

Daven looked from one to the other. "Be cautious, Astan. Remember, you did not go far when your grandmother took you into the city. None of us can leave our soil for long, live beyond the proximity of the clan without a physical impact."

Daven walked over to cup Jelani's chin in his hand and look into her eyes. His tone was fond, as he spoke, almost caressing. Astan kept a firm grip on her, wanting nothing more than to pull her away from that all too familiar touch. But he would allow her to choose who could lay a hand on her and who could not.

"You are already in jeopardy, as is your child. Your son," Daven emphasized with a little smile. "This is not a time to be impulsive, to take a risk, in your weakened state. I beg you to let this pregnancy run its course, holding any rash decision until the child is born and the two of you are healthy and well."

"Then what?" she whispered through her tears.

"Then I hope I know how best to advise you. Once we are through this, the end of whatever mists of deception the Circle may have brought upon us, perhaps the way will open for the runes to tell the right path."

His father sounded sincere but all Astan could think was that he had chosen the side of the Circle once again. He did pull her away now, a possessive arm around Jelani's waist. He held on a little tighter. "We shall see," he said.

Daven smiled at them both, but something distracted lived in that friendly expression and threatened to let uncertainty escape. "Thank you for allowing me into your home," he said and then left the tree house.

Astan pulled Jelani into a full embrace in the center of their small house. He held on as if he would never let go, taking in her scent, feeling the cool surface of her skin, the baby protesting with muffled kicks from inside. He was the Guardian. He was responsible for the safety of his mate, the queen, and their son. He was trained in battle techniques against outside enemies, as he had been taught all his life, but he had never expected that the real battle would be against those who claimed to love him, his own family.

He could well imagine how the dead queen Linnea must have felt all those years ago, learning that her own brother led the conspiracy to kill her.

His heart torn, he latched onto the one truth he knew for sure. He would let all else burn, save his love for Jelani. Not because of his duty as the Guardian, but because without her he knew he would have nothing left in this world.

CHAPTER 17

AFTER Rashia left the house, Jelani let Astan comfort her

The midwife's confession and Jelani's own impassioned speech had started something boiling inside her. Ever since she had been associated with the elves, she had faced an enemy. First Richard. Then Bartolomey. Now it appeared her own clan had turned on her, pretending only the best of intentions.

The one good item in all the day's events was the thought of Iris coming to stay. Daven promised to handle all of the arrangements with Iris, who always had unused sick days and vacation time at the end of each year. She never took a day off if she believed her clients needed her more. Jelani knew Daven would be able to persuade her that Jelani needed her more. Knowing how Iris felt about Daven, it seemed like a perfect setup.

Jelani hoped Iris could stay two weeks or longer, to make sure she survived this experience. Just until the birth. The birth of her son.

A son. The thought gave her a little tingle of joy, the first she had felt in awhile.

Dr. Pitt had not given her insight on the sex of the child because he had not run an ultrasound test. Six weeks earlier when she had seen the doctor, his only comments were that the child seemed to be growing at a quick pace, and that Jelani was a young, healthy woman and no complications were expected as far as he was concerned.

Ha! If he only knew the whammy Mother Nature had applied to this baby.

Paranoia aside, she had expected the child to be a female. Probably because that was what the Circle expected, too.

Daven didn't remain long after Rashia left. Jelani forced herself not to believe he had followed the old witch back for a convocation of the Circle. He had promised to help Astan and Jelani, and he had seemed genuinely shaken by what he had heard from Rashia. That was what she had to focus on.

"Come join me, *denami*?" Astan asked her, seeming to click into a different gear. He sprinkled a bit more of the elven dust onto the stones of the fireplace. The fire flared up, warmth spreading through the room. He held out a hand to help her lower her pregnant bulk onto the multi colored, hand braided rug, then curled himself around the curve of her body, pulling a blanket over the two of them.

Now that Rashia was gone, he couldn't stop smiling. He practically radiated contentment, an emotion she knew had been absent in both of them while she had been so sick. She guessed the reason without much trouble.

"You're terribly pleased with yourself, aren't you?" She teased him.

He snuggled closer. "Not at all. I'm pleased with you."

She leaned back against him, the warmth of his body warming her even more than the fire in front of her. He ran his fingers lightly down her forearm, letting his hand settle onto her wrist. Where their skin touched an almost chemical reaction occurred, instilling a sense of well being in her. She took a deep breath and felt through their shared sense of ease that he did the same. One with her.

"Apparently you didn't pay attention in biology class then. The male determines the sex of a baby. Chromosomes and DNA or something."

"Yet Rashia believed she could force the child to be female. How is that so?"

Jelani shrugged. "Perhaps those herbs favor the motility of one kind of sperm or another. Who knows? The bottom line is that we will shortly have a son. You and I, together, in our home."

He pulled her close and kissed the back of her neck. "Then our troubles are only beginning."

"Beginning? What do you mean?" His warm touch offset what could have been a warning. Was there more to be concerned about from the Circle?

"Midnight feedings? Diapers? If he is at all demanding like his mother, we shall live in an earthly hell."

He couldn't keep a straight face and finally tickled her to show he was teasing. She squirmed, laughing, trying to escape his probing fingers. The struggle ended with them face to face, his lips on hers, and they soon transformed the peaceful moment of togetherness into a full evening to rediscover all they loved about one another.

* * *

WHEN she awakened the next morning back in her own bed, Jelani at first thought her world had turned on its side.

The house was different. Bigger, with two new rooms. Rooms with doors, another novelty in their home.

"Astan," she whispered, digging her elbow into the ribs of the *nian* sleeping next to her.

"What?" he mumbled. He rolled toward her, up on one elbow to see past her stomach, and then snapped awake. His feet hit the floor, already on guard status at the mystery. "What now? Who has been in our house?"

Jelani pushed herself upright and then off the bed, feeling even heavier than when she had lain down the night before. She could not see her feet past her stomach, which she knew was always a joke associated with pregnant women, but it did not seem so funny to her.

She waddled awkwardly to the first door. Inside she found empty space about eight feet across. "This must be for Iris," she said delighted. "We need to find her a bed. And a desk." She frowned at the other door. "Then what is—"

She touched the second door, and it opened onto a room about the same size, as full as the other was empty, holding everything complete for a nursery. Inside, she found a baby's cradle carved out of a thick log, elven blankets, and even some regular quilted coverlets. Someone had even handcrafted a swing of sorts with wooden poles for supports. Stacks of tiny clothing piled onto a table caught her eye, hand-sewn little shirts and pajamas in a variety of colors, soft as goose down.

Speechless, she stared, piecing through, one item to the next, in wonder. Astan must have thought something happened to her because he popped through the door a few seconds later, still pulling on some pants, skidding to a halt as he saw what was there.

"Daven?" Jelani asked.

Astan nodded. "Most likely. And this bounty, all the gifts the Circle has been creating these months through."

"For me? I mean, for him?" Jelani held up a tiny gown, hand sewn in green and so finely crafted that the seams were nearly invisible. She struggled to hold her hostility and rejection of the Circle in the forefront of her mind in light of these delicate wonders. "Look at this. Do you think they all helped? How else could they complete all these in such a short time?"

Astan slipped an arm around her from behind. "They mean well, as Daven said." She felt in the taut muscles of his protective arm no bending of his skepticism. "But we don't have to trust them."

"Good." She laid the baby clothes back on their pile. "What should we call him, Astan?"

Astan's hand slipped to her arm, and turned her to face him. "We cannot choose, *denami*. When the child is born, he will tell us his name."

She eyed him like he was speaking gibberish. "Right. Babies learn to talk when they're like a year old. They don't talk when they're born."

Astan smiled. "Believe, Jelani. Have faith."

Really? Throwing my father's words at me again? She did not believe in much any more, except watching out for herself. But a small nagging voice reminded her that belief had brought her this far. What a change she had made in her worldview! Life had turned around to a place she would never have anticipated. More wonders surely waited ahead.

If she and Astan could just hold on, together.

While she continued to sort through the gifts, a familiar voice squealed from the other room.

"Hello? Jellie? Are you here? O-M-G. This is just the cutest house ever!"

Astan's face molded itself into a tolerant smile, and he handed Jelani the robe she had forgotten when she had gone exploring. She slipped it on and tied the belt as best she could over her protuberant belly. "If I get much larger I'm going to explode," she complained as she went out to greet her guest.

Daven waited with Iris, a duffel bag over his shoulder. "I told her she didn't have to pack so much," he said.

"Of course she did." Jelani laughed and hugged her friend.

"Holy sea-biscuits, honey, you're huge!" Iris stepped back, holding Jelani at arm's length. "Daven said you were about to deliver, but I didn't think he meant in five minutes!"

"Not five minutes. I'm fine." Jelani avoided Daven's sudden look of interest. "Why don't you boys go on out and play, hmm?"

A glance over her shoulder showed her that Astan actually looked relieved. Guilt trickled through her midsection. She had been hard on Astan these last weeks. She knew that. Once this baby came, she would make it up to him. Pregnancy was just harder than she had ever imagined, and this pregnancy had been the hardest of them all.

Astan went to dress in a more appropriate manner for the outside, and she shuffled to a chair at the table. Her belly hung out so far that she had no lap at all any more. Azrael tried to jump up on her and slid back down, thankfully not engaging his claws.

She groaned. "This is ridiculous."

"Daven said you've been feeling blue. I knew something was up. I'm proud you chose me to help." Iris scooped up the disappointed cat, cuddling him, and then settled in on the chair next to Jelani. "And you sent Daven to ask me to come out." She winked.

Jelani knew exactly what she meant. "Mmm. I'm sure that didn't put you out very much."

Meanwhile, Daven rummaged in the cupboard and appeared

with a bowl and some cereal, a dried fruit and seed laden creation Astan had made for her. "You should eat," he told Jelani.

She did not want to eat, but when she opened her mouth to tell him so nothing came out. Frowning, she tried again. Still nothing. She eyed Daven, who smiled sweetly.

"You should eat." He handed her a spoon.

Iris studied the room curiously. "So, no refrigerator, right? No electricity?"

"Nope." Jelani took the spoon, feeling put upon.

"Where do you keep the milk?"

"We don't have any," Jelani said with a shrug.

"How can you eat cereal without milk?" Iris sat back in her chair, stunned. "What about cheese? Meat? Frozen food?"

"Iris, have you looked outside lately? It's freezing. There's a box." Prodded by Daven's stern eye, Jelani shoved a spoonful of cereal in her mouth.

"Where?"

Jelani knew that Iris was not going to give up. She wagged a finger at the bottom of the cupboard while she chewed. Daven graciously opened the wooden door, letting a small blast of winter into the small room before he closed it back tight again.

"Oh." Iris' hand fluttered at her chest in surprise. "I never would have guessed."

"Dear Iris," Daven said, "there is much about magic you have yet to learn."

"I hope you're going to teach me," the blonde replied, a definite coquettish note in her voice.

Instead of panicking, which Jelani thought would be his best bet, Daven merely smiled and took Iris' hand. "I'd be honored."

Astan hurried out of their room, which Jelani noticed had a newly-installed door, too. "I think I'm getting out of here just in time," he whispered in Jelani's ear and then hugged her. "If you need me—"

"I'll know if something happens," Daven interrupted. "We'll be here."

The defensive growl of protest was low in Astan's chest, so soft that Jelani wondered if Daven had heard it. She patted the arm that held her, to reassure Astan he was the only one she wanted. "We'll be fine, love. Don't worry, all right?"

"Of course I will," he said. He jerked his head toward the door and Daven released Iris' hand with reluctance.

"Eat that cereal," Daven ordered, pointing to Jelani's bowl.

"Whatever."

The two left the house, and Iris popped up to explore the different rooms. Jelani found that the cereal became more appealing as she dug it from her bowl and before long she had emptied it.

Little coos and squeals let her know Iris had found the nursery. Jelani left her dish on the table and made her way into the room with all the baby items. Iris knelt on the floor, rocking the wooden cradle with several blankets strategically folded within. Her eyes shone with unshed tears. "We're going to do this, Jellie. You'll see. Everything will be just fine."

Her friend's confidence helped to boost Jelani's mood. "I'm glad you're here, Iris. Thank you for coming."

"I wouldn't have missed it, honey. Daven's invitation was just so sweet. He's so worried about you." Iris got up and pushed the swing into motion, admiring it as it rocked and slowed. Then she pushed it into action again.

"I'll bet he is. He and all his dried up prune buddies."

Iris turned a piercing look on her. Jelani imagined that Lane had filled Iris in by now on what his chemist friend had discovered, so she had to understand their concerns. "To hear Daven speak about it, honey, he is one hundred and ten percent in your corner."

"Maybe he is, Iris. But I'm worried, too. Especially when Rashia confessed they were trying to make me have a girl. And what? Coffee changed my chemistry enough to flip the sex of the child? How are we supposed to know who we can trust?"

"Well, now you won't have to worry alone. I'm here." Iris slipped an arm around Jelani's shoulders. "First order of business is to get you dressed and outside for a walk. A sharp body brings a sharp mind."

Jelani eyed her. "You're not talking to Crispy here."

"I know. But Daven said…."

The explanation went on but Jelani tuned it out. She knew when she was being manipulated. So far the meddling of Astan's father had been tolerated because she believed her cared about her. But 'Daven said' was going to become an issue if it continued for long, especially if it came through Iris' lips.

On the other hand, the way her friend's cheeks pinked up just a little whenever she said Daven's name satisfied Jelani. At least the dream Iris had held for more than half a year would come true. She would get the chance to be up close and personal with Daven Talvi. It was the least Jelani could do for her best friend.

Hardly taking a breath, Iris moved on to her next question.

"So where did he put the bathroom?"

CHAPTER 18

LANE bristled, as Iris told him over the phone how she had been summoned to the woods by Daven and, ostensibly, by the Circle.

"What we should have done," Lane complained, "was drag Jelani's ass out of the woods and back into town, where we could keep an eye on her!"

Curled up with a book in the corner of the couch farthest from the webcam, Crispy looked over and added an emphatic nod to Lane's statement. "She needs friends. Sometimes trees just aren't enough."

Lane snorted. "Trees are never enough." He leaned back in his chair feeling helpless. "So what are we going to do, Iris?"

"I don't know," Iris said. "I had to trek out to a convenience store on the highway just to get cell-phone service. At least I'll be here to keep an eye on things. She's the size of a city bus, Lane. Honestly."

Lane did not like the note of worry in Iris' voice but she had a point. At least one of them was there with her. "So Pretty Boy Daven arranged all this, did he?"

"It's not his fault. He's looking out for Jellie the best he can. She's pretty stubborn."

"Don't I know it." A parallel track in Lane's mind ticked into action, plotting how he could use this turn of events to his own advantage. That mule thing was still stuck in his mind. He needed some elf genetic material, though, if he was ever going to learn the truth. "Look, do you think you could get him to set me up a meeting with this Circle of theirs? Tell them something, like that it's for the book? Or at least for public relations? You know, that any friend of the queen's is a friend of theirs?"

"What for?"

"Just like that tea, Iris. I feel better double-checking everything they're doing when it comes to Jelly Bean. Don't you?"

There, he had put it on her. One thing he knew about Iris was that her social work background almost always made her bend in favor of the client. It was why she had continued to work with Crispy for five years, even when he seemed doomed to failing to overcome his agoraphobia, despite her working with him above and beyond the assigned hours through the agency. It was why she carried her work phone 24-7, so that her people could call her for advice, even in the middle of the night. She would recognize that he was right.

"All right. I'll see what I can do. But don't you plan to come here and stir things up any more than they are already! Everyone's a little touchy. Something's not going right, even outside this pregnancy. No one wants to talk about it, though."

"Oh, really?" Lane's smirk seemed to permeate his whole body. "We'll just have to do something about that."

"Lane."

She was miles away from him, calling. He could ignore her scold. "Hey, well, it's been great talking, Iris. You tell him we'll be up Friday, all right? Might as well use those new snow tires for something. See you." He hung up before she could say anything else.

"We?" Crispy said without looking up from the page he was reading.

"Sure. We. You need to get out, right? Crisp clean air. Fresh snow. Mountain views." Lane grinned.

"I'm not the one with computer withdrawal, duh. I like the woods."

Annoyed, Lane bustled over to the Cave for a Creamy Cupcake. "Who said I'd get computer withdrawal? I'm taking the laptop. I've got batteries you know. I'll get those old witches with their own words."

A little smile twitched at Crispy's lips. "You best be careful. They'll whammy you."

"They will do no such thing," Lane growled.

"Mmm." Crispy turned the page and continued reading.

Lane tore the cellophane off his treat and took a large bite, tapping each of the keyboards of his four computers, watching with satisfaction as the fantasy comic art screensavers disappeared.

Whammy me, indeed. As if they could.

"I've got a plan," Lane said.

"I know. You told me." Crispy's forehead wrinkled in consternation. "But even if you prove that elves and people are the same, what can you do with that information besides make the government come after Daven and the others? And Jellie."

"The government?" Lane rolled out far enough to cast a curious eye at his friend. "What would they care? Not like they're on the grid. They don't take money from the feds. They're like the Amish in a way."

"Elves don't pay taxes."

"Exactly. The bottom line is that most of those elves think they're something special," Lane said, returning to the computer. "Better than us humans. Just like whites thought they were better than blacks for so long. Or all the kids who thought since we were fosters, that we were scum. If I can prove we're the same, then they don't get to look down on us any more. It's a matter of pride."

Crispy, frown in place, returned to his reading.

Lane reached for his first keyboard and tapped in an email to his genetics expert buddy, asking exactly what he would need to get in order to have a full analysis of chromosomal material done.

At the second, he opened up a browser to the future weather predictions and checked the likelihood of snow and ice both Friday morning and afternoon. So far, the forecast was clear. *Excellent.*

At the third, he opened a popular search engine and typed in 'Tuesday free food' to see if he could score any local bargains on dinner by delivery. Nothing but a free kids' meal. He considered Crispy speculatively.

Nah. No matter how I tried, I couldn't pass him off as under twelve.

Those guys won't deliver anyway. Damn.

At the fourth, he hesitated, thoughtfully consuming the rest of the sweet cake and licking his fingers before he entered a query for protection against evil spells. Unsure what he would find, he was amazed to find page after page of sites that could keep anyone safe from evil at a range of prices from ninety-nine cents to two-hundred dollars. A couple of freebies caught his eye. One in particular seemed basic, needing only a black pen for the drawing of a pentagram, some simple natural elements, crystal and lead, and some fresh herbals. He hit the 'print' key and waited for the paper to chug out of his inkjet.

No whammies here, thank you very much.

"Hey, Crisp, where can we buy some wormwood?"

* * *

WHEN Friday came, Iris confirmed that Daven had wangled permission for Lane's meeting.

Bundled up to protect themselves against the ancient pickup's faltering heater, Lane and Crispy headed for the forest.

On arrival Lane bailed out of the driver's door with his computer case, patting his pocket to make sure he had his little bag of protection tucked into the pocket of his jeans. Oddly enough, the coffee shop where Jelani used to work carried the herbs he needed to craft the talisman, though their warning was clear. Wormwood was not to be taken internally, as it was the stuff from which absinthe was made. Everyone knew how bad that was. As long as it was evil enough to scare away elf juju, Lane would be satisfied.

He trudged up the path as Crispy milled around in the six-inch snow like a puppy, his gloved hands touching everything as they passed.

"You're like a damned kid," Lane said, thinking maybe that free meal could have applied after all.

Crispy just grinned and kept going, checking out small trees, snow banks and other features of the landscape around them. He was brought up short, though, by the discovery of a dead hawk in the snow.

Lane, several steps behind him, did not see what he cradled in his hands until he pulled even. He could not believe what he was seeing from a man so afraid of germs that he wouldn't touch a used bar of soap.

"Crispy! That's dirty! Put it down!"

"It's dead," Crispy said petting the hawk.

"Obviously." Lane looked around the clearing where they stood to make sure no other animal was waiting to pounce on them for stealing its lunch. "We don't seem to have a defibrillator handy, you know?"

"We don't need one. Astan saved his father," Crispy said quietly. "He brought Daven back to life after he got shot up there in the woods. You remember? The day that Jelani's mother came out of the tree?"

Lane rolled his eyes. "Of course I remember. You know, Crisp, that's different. I mean, this is—It's an—" He realized argument was probably fruitless. Besides, this situation was not all that different from what had happened with Daven. He had been pretty lifeless when Astan had dragged him into Jelani's cabin. Hours later, Astan, with some 'healing hands of the king' thing, had been able to revive him like any other miracle worker. "What the hell. Bring it along. Just keep it away from me."

He stumped onward to Jelani's tree, feeling like an idiot knocking on the bark outside. Crispy murmured behind him, continuing to cuddle the limp bird.

The door opened with a loud crack, followed by the commotion of Iris effusively welcoming them in, hugs all around, although the bird did slow her down a bit.

"Crispy, it's good to see you in the woods," Iris finally said with an odd glance at Lane.

"Hey, that is so not my idea," Lane protested as he bustled inside, tracking snow in his wake.

"Where's Astan?" Crispy's voice pitched softly, as if he was afraid to disturb the bird's rest.

"He'll be here soon, honey, but don't you think maybe you should leave that outside? Jellie's here, and she's about to have a baby, you know? We're trying to keep the place extra clean."

Lane thought Iris' smile was a little forced. His attention was captured by the referenced pregnant woman who moved slowly from the back room to see them, her face thin, dark circles under her eyes. Iris was right. She was huge.

"Hey, Lane," she said, smiling, but without her usual enthusiasm. "Crispy, you made it. Come in."

Iris pulled out a chair for Jelani to sit in, and she lowered herself in a way that looked extremely uncomfortable. Lane wondered how much of that was because of what the witches had done to her and how much was due to being the size of a small weather balloon.

No disrespect intended.

"Yeah, Crisp. Leave the zombies outside, hmm? There aren't enough brains in here to go around." Lane dragged a chair over to sit beside Jelani, his leg pressed up against hers companionably. He pulled a small thermos from his case that was filled with her favorite coffee. "You okay, chickie?"

Iris finally persuaded Crispy to leave the hawk outside until Astan returned. She pulled wet antiseptic cloths from her pocket for him to wash his hands as they came back in and then put the kettle on the fire. "Better safe than sorry."

"Jelly Bean?" Lane persisted.

Jelani looked at the thermos blankly and then set it on the table next to her. "Fine. Fine, all right? I mean, do I look fine? I look like hell. I know that. Thank you for reminding me!"

Lane pulled back a little. "You been living with wild animals so long you caught rabies or something? Don't bite my head off."

Hunkered down by the fire, Iris spoke over her shoulder. "She's been like that since I came. Better when Daven is here. Sorry."

"Don't you apologize," Lane said. "She needs to take some responsibility. She got knocked up, whether she intended to or not. You do the crime, you do the time."

Jelani elbowed him so hard he almost fell off his chair. "Shut up."

Iris poured some hot water into a bowl and made Crispy wash his hands. "Now you kids play nice."

Lane winced and rubbed his ribs. "Where is Daven?"

As if on cue the door swung open, and Astan and his father entered.

With evident surprise Daven eyed Lane and Crispy, but his expression quickly changed to his usual affable smile. "You're early!"

Lane studied Daven, suspicious of his motives, but noticed that Jelani seemed to calm down. "So when's that baby coming? Soon, I hope?"

"Any day now," Daven said.

"Mmm-hmm." Lane fiddled with the clasp on his laptop bag. "Are we ready to interview?"

"I think so. Astan?"

The other elf shook his head. "I'll stay."

"Had enough of the female element meddling, huh?" Lane cackled and got to his feet.

Astan eyed Lane. It was not exactly a hostile glance, but friendliness was certainly lacking. "I'll stay," he repeated and walked past them all into one of the side rooms.

Crispy hesitantly followed him in and Lane heard him ask about the hawk, complaining that he'd had to leave it outdoors in the cold. Raising the dead seemed like a good chore for the afternoon, Lane thought.

Less dangerous than dealing with the witches.

"You been redecorating, Jelly Bean? Seems to me you only had one bedroom last time we were here. Beats the hell out of me how you do that without the tree getting any bigger."

"The power of magic," Daven said with a warm smile.

"Yeah, yeah. Abracadabra. A la peanut butter sandwiches. Sure is amazing."

Lane checked his case for the sample collecting materials, making sure that he would be ready for any of several possibilities. He had a buccal swab kit that his friend had sent him, but he did not imagine any of this mysterious Circle would just let him invade the inside of their cheek. He sure wouldn't if the circumstances were reversed. He had also brought a stash of cotton balls just in case he had the opportunity to gather any blood samples, in the event of a random paper cut, or a spider bite. Also, several plastic zipper bags to hold his prizes.

If everything else failed, he intended to exercise the 'clumsy' card and trip and fall. If he could arrange that, he could yank a hank of hair off someone's head, or even better use the UZI Tactical Pen he had ordered off the Internet. The gadget looked just like a pen, but the crown of it was a sharp device that could collect DNA when jabbed into skin. The tactical pen was designed for use by law enforcement officers under attack, so that they could identify someone who had assaulted them and then left the scene. But it served Lane's needs just as well.

Whatever it took.

He and Daven bid goodbye to the others and left the tree, Daven taking him in a direction Lane had never gone.

Noise aloft caused Lane to look up and he realized with a start that elves lived all around them, mostly in the open. He ducked aside, seeing several overhead on a gossamer canopy of seemingly nothing at all.

With a curious look on his face, Daven pulled Lane back onto the path and then stopped. "For what purpose?"

Disoriented by the weird elf living arrangements, Lane stepped away nervously. "Huh?"

"For what purpose do you want to take our blood and hair?"

Stunned, Lane just stared for a moment before he remembered Daven had just touched him and could read minds in that manner. Remembering that ability, he backed up several steps. "You really need to stay out of my head, pal."

Daven did not move. "We intend you no harm, Lane Donatelli. Neither do we have any evil designs against Jelani. She is very precious to all of us."

Boy, this guy sure knows how to schmooze, doesn't he?

Lane imagined little tendrils of 'I don't care if you eat my brain' oozing all through his head. "So if you're not plotting against us, you'll do the tests? Just so I can sleep better at night knowing how Jelani became mother of the year?"

Daven frowned a moment and then nodded slowly. "If you will come to understand that we all seek to live in peace."

"Cool. Let's do this thing."

* * *

ASTAN tried to shut out the conversation from the other room.

He knew Lane had the best of intentions, but the *neris* of the Circle were not a group of human women in a quilting bee or coffee klatch. They were powerful and they were dangerous. Better to leave them alone, not stir them up.

But maybe Lane's little project would put Jelani at ease. As agitated as she had been, Astan was for anything that might bring her some peace.

Good luck, Lane. Just watch your back.

Jelani's friend Crispy followed him into the bedroom, babbling something about a hawk. He spoke so fast Astan could hardly understand him.

"Whoa, whoa," Astan said. "Slow down. Calm yourself."

What he wanted to say was 'go away and leave us alone'. Now that Daven had arranged for Iris to live with them they had even less privacy than before. Less than what Daven gave them. Less than what the Circle gave them.

But in light of their situation, Astan's attitude was the same. He would willingly make the sacrifice if Jelani felt more like herself.

Crispy nodded and took several slow breaths, inhaling deeply, his eyes closed. His hands hung mid-air in front of him, as if he was not really sure what to do with them.

Curious. But then Crispy had always conducted himself differently from any human Astan had ever known.

"Now, again, please?" Astan asked.

"Astan, I found a hawk. I think he's dead. But there is something about him. He needs help. He needs me." The thin little man's narrow hands reached for each other, his fingers clasping awkwardly, like strangers.

"A dead hawk?" Astan stared a moment, not sure what he had heard. "Where did you find it?"

"In the woods. On the way from where Lane parked the truck."

Astan watched Crispy twitch, finding him more like a child than a grown man. A dead hawk. He sighed. What was next?

"He's a red tailed hawk," Crispy added.

The detail focused Astan's attention. Hawks carried a certain magic, seen by the elves as messengers from the spirits of the forests. The red tail showed that the hawk was mature, one who had survived the dangers of the world and come to adulthood. Perhaps this was a sign.

"Where is it?" Astan asked. "In here?"

"No." Crispy pouted. "Iris wouldn't let me bring it in."

"Understandable. Come. Let us see this hawk of yours."

Astan and Crispy passed through the main room, where Iris and Jelani worked together on some yarn project. "I'll be right back," Astan said in response to Jelani's anxious look. "I'll be outside. I won't leave the area. Promise."

Jelani's faint smile was reassuring.

A frown creased Iris' brows. "Don't let him bring that nasty thing in here," Iris said.

"Of course, not." Astan opened the door and allowed Crispy to exit first.

Crispy hurried off to the left, leaving deep footprints in the snow. Soon he bent down to retrieve a small bundle wrapped in a blue wool scarf. He studied the bundle with birdlike dark eyes, his black coat and pants a stark contrast to the snow around them. The air was crisp, silent.

"Here it is. Now, do like you did for Daven." Crispy held out the bundle. "Please."

Astan took a deep breath. "You understand the bird may have been dead too long for magic to reanimate it."

"I know."

"And that for some animals, their time on this land is short," Astan explained. "And they are not meant to live longer."

"I know."

"And that my connection with Daven was already strong, so it was easier to call him back from the next plane."

"I know."

Astan soaked in the innocent look on Crispy's face. How long had it been since Astan had felt so simply hopeful, so convinced that others around him would do the right thing? Surrounded by the schemes of the Circle and so much uncertainty about the rest of his life, Astan had fastened onto Jelani and their child as the only reality he could trust.

But Crispy still believed. In him.

"Let me hold it," Astan said.

Crispy carried the bundle across the few feet between them and placed it in Astan's hands. "The hands of the king have power to heal," Crispy said. "It's a rule. Period. No changing."

Astan felt his lips curve into a smile. "We'll see."

He turned his attention to the limp pile of feathers, gently pulling back the scarf from the bird's body, which was the length of his forearm all the way to his fingertips. The bird's eyes were closed. Its head lolled sideways. Astan could sense no heat from its body. In fact, it was even colder from being out in the snow.

Impossible.

He looked up. Crispy still wore that confident expression.

Unbelievable.

Astan closed his eyes and concentrated on his hands. "Brother hawk, you belong to the sky." He pictured the hawk flying free, its wings spread, its beady eyes searching the ground below for movement. He could almost feel the freedom of floating on the wind. The rush of emotion channeled itself into his fingers, almost like a jolt of energy that moved between his skin and the feathers of the hawk.

"Hurry," Crispy said. "Before someone sees."

"It will be fine, Crispy. Do not worry." Astan didn't open his eyes. He noted a change in temperature of the body in his hands. It had started to warm. "Come on, then. Rejoin us in the world, my friend."

He held tightly to the bird as it continued to warm, holding its wings close to his body. These birds were strong. Once it came to life, he might not be able to hold on to it.

"You're doing it." Crispy's response was breathless, excited.

Astan reached for a bit of that animated energy to help boost the life force of the hawk, taking Crispy's hand and laying it on the bird's breast. Before Astan could warn him that the bird would be wild and dangerous, the hawk's beak closed on Crispy's finger.

Expecting blood, Astan let the bird slip in his hands as he tried to block further damage. But moments of the scene came to him in flashes. Crispy's hand was held by the hawk, but not with any attempt to harm him. It was more the way a baby reaches for an adult's finger for comfort. The bird rose out of Astan's hands, wings flapping. Crispy's face broadened with a delighted childlike grin as the bird came to life in front of him. Then the bird faltered, the wings coming to rest, its talons tangled in the scarf.

"What's wrong?" Crispy asked.

Astan placed a hand onto the bird's back, assessing the space between its wings. "It's still tired. He's come a long way back from the other plane, you know."

"Yes, I know." Crispy cradled the hawk in his arms, cooing to it. "I'll take it home."

Astan frowned. "What will you do with it in the human city? It belongs in the open. In the wild."

"Sometimes being where you belong can be more dangerous." He took a deep breath. "I belonged with my mother, but she couldn't protect me. Then I belonged with my foster parents, and that wasn't right, either. I'm hiding from my real life, living with Lane. And there I'm safe."

"Hiding from your real life. An odd way to describe your existence." Puzzled, Astan braced his feet apart, feeling washed out after resurrecting the hawk.

"I have an odd existence," Crispy said softly. He looked down at the hawk. "I'll take care of him until it's time for him to come home. Don't worry about him, Astan. Thank you."

"You're welcome."

Crispy was lost in the glory of the hawk. "I'll go back to the truck and wait for Lane." He stumbled away in the direction of the path, talking to the hawk.

Astan stood there for a few minutes reaffirming his connection to the earth. Hiding from one's real life? Did that really serve a purpose? Surely one should deal with the life given to him.

But then everyone knew Crispy was a little off. Right?

Astan took several breaths of cold air, in and out, until he came back to himself. He listened for Daven and Lane, but they were nowhere near. Better he stayed with Jelani, protecting her and their child. It was all he could do, for now.

* * *

LANE dropped the case to the ground, digging inside for his kit. Taking one of the cotton swabs in hand, he asked Daven to open his mouth. The swab itself was easy. He put the swab carefully inside the glass tube provided for the sample and eyed the second one in his pack. "You know what, let's do two. Just in case."

Daven seemed to suffer the minor inconvenience with good humor, waiting while Lane packed everything away. Both of them carefully ignored the amazed attention they received from the elves overhead. "Perhaps now you will refrain from harming the members of the Circle. Many of them would take umbrage at losing any of their hair. Or being stabbed with a writing instrument." He gave Lane a half-amused look from the corner of his eye.

"Yeah. I'd hate for that to happen. They might turn me into a newt." Lane snickered, forcing the sound to cover a sudden rush of nerves. Then he indicated to Daven that he was ready to move on.

Daven did not reply, but pointed ahead in what Lane thought was a westerly direction. Some fifteen minutes later, they approached an open space with a number of fallen trees set into a rough square. No one else in evidence, Lane set his feet solidly into the snow with a smirk.

"Looks like they all went to tea, huh? Maybe we'll have to try another day."

Daven's smirk mirrored Lane's. "No need." He held up his hand, almost in mime mode, and placed it against what looked like a solid surface, even though Lane could only see plain air. Suddenly, a space about the size of a door appeared, within which the scene changed. Even though on the outside the calm winter scene still appeared, inside a group of older women sat around a blazing fire. Heat actually flowed through the open door, welcoming them in.

"After you," Daven said gesturing toward the group.

Guess they fooled me. Epic fail for the old Lanester.

"Damned elves," Lane muttered, as he stepped into what seemed to be a room with opaque walls that kept out the cold and wind. Frowning, he looked out the 'door' and saw snow and ice. Inside there was none. The older women, dressed in muted tone dresses of various shades of brown and gray, had stacked cups near a plate holding some sort of sticky looking cake like substance on a low table nearby. They fell silent as he came in, but none of them stood up.

Daven came in and closed the portal. It must have been with a wave of his hand. Lane saw nothing that resembled a door handle or anything that one could touch at all. He wondered what would happen if he wanted to leave, if there was no handle on the inside. That usually meant being trapped. He hated doors like that, and small spaces. He forced his thoughts off that path. There was no time for that.

Daven stepped forward into the middle of the group, and Lane focused on the elf's movement instead of his own fears. "This is Jelani's friend Lane, from the city. He has some questions for the Circle and I would urge you to tell him what he desires to know. This will please our queen. We trust that once this comes to pass, that her calm will be restored and we may proceed to the birth of the child without further complications."

The collective gaze of the witches swiveled to fix on Lane, who began to feel like a criminal caught in spotlights on some police reality show. He had not realized what the exact *quid pro quo* was for this meeting. Would they force Jelani to be more cooperative now? Could they fry him on the spot? Pinpointed by their cool contemplation, he thought maybe life as a newt would be preferable to being turned into ash.

I would give anything for a Creamy Cupcake.

A sigh escaped him and he set down his case, pulling out his laptop then surreptitiously checking his pocket. He had fully charged the computer battery before he had come, so he knew he would be able to last for a while. Glancing around, he saw nothing he could use to set the machine on, though, and one thing ten years of devouring cupcakes had done for him was remove any possibility of actually using it on his lap.

One woman, her hair mostly black with two severe streaks of gray coming from her temples, touched the table where the tea sat and the table slowly mushroomed to a height of three feet. *Perfect.*

"Thanks," he stammered, a little shy under their solemn regard.

"Of course." The woman smiled at him in a vaguely familiar manner. "We may have met in the city, at the coffee shop. I am Djana." When he didn't react, an irritated expression crossed her face. "Astan's grandmother?"

Now it came back to him. That was Daven's 'pacify the humans' smile, for sure. All of a kind, they were. He fussed with the laptop, booting it up and squirming for some sort of interim light conversation to take up time until he could have his fingers back on the keys.

"Oh, yeah. Jelani mentioned you all the time. You made her that dreamcatcher, the one with the blue jay feathers."

"Exactly." The woman beamed, and then retook her seat on a thick log amidst a low buzz of chatter Lane could not make out. Warmth came from many of the faces and he guessed they might be as curious about him as he was about them.

"You can sit down," Daven said.

"There's, ah, no chairs or—" Lane suddenly noticed that a thick chunk of log had appeared behind his legs. He glanced over at Daven, who just smiled as he helped himself to tea.

Djana studied him with bird bright brown eyes. "What is it you wish to learn of the Lelan, Lane Donatelli?"

"All the secrets." Lane watched the keyboard and fought hard to keep his straight face, wondering if they would see through his flip answer. The silence around him fell so deeply it was like being mummified in bubble wrap and he finally looked up, just to make sure they were still there.

They were. But their faces had lost any cordiality.

"Kidding!" Lane said. "Looks like I need a full battle rez here without much manna."

Their only reactions were blank stares and knitted brows.

"Resurrection without enough energy?" he offered, in an attempt to interpret his gamer slang. Where had his quick wit gone? He knew he had lost them. How could he win them back?

"You know, I'm working on a book," Lane said, typing in his password. "About what's happened to Jelly. I mean, I'm seriously calling it a novel. Who would believe that could really happen, right? Truth is stranger than fiction, and all that."

He surveyed the group. Not a degree warmer. Nervous, he reached in his pocket finding the talisman there. It did not seem to be doing much good. He rubbed it with his fingers. Nothing like wasting perfectly good wormwood. He tried again.

"I just wondered what happened to those guys who were with Black Bart up in the forest there. The king. Well, the old king. You know, the one who looked like a wizard? He said everyone could be friends again, but I didn't know if elves could do that. Humans couldn't do that, probably. No, sirree. People like to hold a grudge."

He didn't dare look at Daven. The old Cheshire Cat grin on his face must be a mile wide. After all, he had fulfilled his side of the bargain. He had brought all the old horses here as Lane had requested, but apparently no one was going to make them drink.

His fingers itched toward the cakes on the plate. "Anyone mind if I have one of these?"

Finally a timid throat cleared. "Help yourself. Would you also like tea?"

Surprised, Lane looked around the group until he tracked down the source of the comment, a thin little woman off to the rear of the gathering. Before he accepted the offer of a hot drink, he remembered what he had learned about their herbal brews. "Ah, no, thanks. But this looks delicious. Did you make it?"

Her cheeks flushed and he was pleased to see the effect. Maybe they were not so different from humans, despite all the razzle-dazzle. Grabbing the cake closest to him, he sniffed it cautiously and then took a bite. Heaven. Spicy and sweet and full of some kind of fruit he could not quite identify.

"Oh," he mumbled, his mouth still full. "Oh, this is good."

One of the other ladies handed him a small cloth to wipe his fingers. After that they seemed to want to bring him more, or get him something to drink. Or just come close to him. He tried not to get too alarmed.

"So, um, what happened to the guys who left the clan to hang with Bart?"

"Some of them have stayed with us, reunited," said the woman who had made the cake.

"Really? That's great." He started typing, taking notes as fast as he could. "So it's just all's forgiven, come home?"

"Not for all." That was Djana. "Some must atone for their acts before they may be welcomed again."

"Only some? Who, like Bart's old lady?"

"Malina." A hush fell on the group as the name was spoken. "She has passed to the air."

"She what? Passed? You mean, like died?" Lane typed in the words, delighted to have this intelligence on the elven community. "That's how you die? You just sparkle off into the atmosphere? That's radical!"

"No sparkling," Daven interjected. "We simply become one with the forces of nature again."

"I see." *Tappety-tap-tap.* "So until these guys atone, what happens to them? They just go all Iron John and live by themselves in the woods, snapping themselves up spiffy rooms like this?"

"Not at all." Djana pressed her lips together, moving into a position that looked more comfortable, if it was possible to be comfortable sitting on a rough barked tree trunk. Lane was already having his doubts.

Daven spoke up again, almost cutting his mother off in a move Lane thought highly suspicious. "Those who harmed others are no longer one with the soil."

"One with the soil? What does that mean?" Lane was reminded of an old television show where the guardians of the planet came right up through the ground as though they were part of it.

"That means for all practical purposes they lose their elven abilities and must live as humans do." The disapproval in Daven's voice was clear. Lane tried hard not to be offended at the way 'humans' seemed to have a seriously negative connotation.

"Oh." Lane looked up at Daven, who stood on the other side of the table. "So the guy who shot you and Astan, who killed Richard, he's lost his powers now?"

A muscle in Daven's jaw twitched as he looked away. "Grigor Biren is condemned to live in such a manner for the remainder of his time in this life. It is the way of the clan."

"Sucks to be him, then." Lane paused out of respect for Daven's deep feelings, and then typed in all that information.

The session continued for another hour, the Circle members sharing tidbits with him, most of which he did not previously know, all of which would add pizzazz to his novel, some of which he hoped would help him sort out this mess with his Jelly Bean. He didn't pause to categorize it now. This would be a task requiring all four of his computers, and at least a six-pack of cupcakes. Maybe more. Right now, all he had to do was collect the information, while he was literally eating out of their hands.

"You can't make up stuff like this," he muttered, his fingers flying. "You just can't make it up."

When he had finally taken down the answers to all the questions that he had conceived of, Daven collected him, with thanks to the ladies, and led him out of the elven shelter. The elf women called farewells after them that faded as the door closed behind them.

"Can I help you carry that?" Daven asked, gesturing to the computer case.

"I've got it," Lane said. His brain was spinning with the depth of new information it had just been fed.

"Watch your step." Daven crossed over a large fallen tree trunk in a movement that wasn't quite a stride or a leap but something between, a floating motion that gracefully propelled him over the obstacle. Lane, nearly hypnotized by the transit, tripped over a thick branch hidden in the snow and fell, hard onto his belly.

Groaning at the sudden painful impact, Lane tried to right himself, bogged down by the heavy computer case hanging from his shoulder.

Damn, those old cliché gods were right. The bigger they were, the harder they did fall.

"Ow," he moaned as Daven helped him to his feet, taking the case from his shoulder.

"Are you all right?" Daven asked his expression solicitous. He leaned down to touch Lane's bruised knees. A heat rushed through the aching places and then the pain disappeared.

At first relieved, Lane suddenly stiffened. "Don't you whammy me!" he cried, jerking back out of Daven's reach. "I've got protection!"

But by then it was too late. Daven's hand slipped into the computer case and paused a moment on the laptop, all the while smiling that politician's smile. "It's for the best, Lane. We must protect the queen and the clan."

"But—"

"I know you wouldn't want Jelani to come to harm. It's okay. Everything will be fine." Daven reached out to tap him on the forehead, just once, lightly. "Come on. Let's go see if Jelani has some tea for us."

Lane fought to hold on to his memories of his session with the old witches, but they fuzzed out into a pleasant glow. He followed Daven, jaw set with disappointment, digging in his pocket for the talisman, which he took out and tossed over his shoulder with a tight mutter. "Nothing like stale wormwood to make your day, right?"

He almost didn't mind it. And somehow that was the most frustrating of all.

When he couldn't even remember why he was out in the woods, Daven reminded him that there was tea and a group of good friends at Jelani's house. Well, that didn't sound too bad. Maybe if he was lucky there would be a cupcake or two.

CHAPTER 19

GRIGOR sat on a tall outcropping of red rock, miles away from the assembly of the Circle, hardly agitated at all by any loss of powers.

Since meeting Firefly, he had used his bear claw talisman every opportunity he had been given to reinforce his growing personal repertoire. He wanted to be able to dazzle those of the youngers he meant to recruit for Bartolomey.

Fontine promised to bring several of them when she returned to see him next. He expected her later this afternoon. She would be pleased to see him looking stronger, and he would let her take credit for the improvement, knowing that would reinforce her own needs. He did not have to reveal the truth. Not to her.

Many truths settled into his field of knowledge these days, especially the truth that as a partner, Fontine was nothing compared to the mysterious and powerful Firefly.

Every time he held the dark bear's claw in his hands, he thought of the mysterious *neris*, older and wiser than he, shadow and light, her warm throaty voice practically caressing him as they spoke by the river. Perhaps one day he would enchant her the same way she had caught him, keeping her energy and gifts for himself, or at least sharing with her as an equal. He needed to convince Bartolomey and the mages that he was worthy. If the winds were lucky he would do just that.

Midwinter was nearly upon them. A month before Grigor would have seen only ice and frozen rock all around him. Now with his powers slowly restored, he was able to sense the life in the soil around him, the energy coming right through the bottoms of his heavy shoes. He could feel the dragging breaths of the pregnant she-bear in the cave below him, the lethargic beating of a heart in hibernation. The wings of a hawk flapped momentarily in a tree overhead and he reveled in the ability to hear the sound.

He was coming back. The elf queen would not beat him.

Now he needed to fulfill his promise to his Master to win his reward, to complete his transformation from a weak elf on the jagged edge of survival to a powerful enemy of the clan. Once he had his converts he would be halfway there.

His newly sharpened eyesight noticed when Fontine came through the trees on the opposite side of the clearing. Her face brightened in a smile as she offered a shy wave. Several figures emerged from the woods after her, surely candidates for his selection. Who had she brought with her to seek glory in the battle for pure bloodlines?

While he had recognized Fontine's blonde locks from some distance away, the other youngers were more difficult. He could see that all were male, but several concealed themselves under hooded brown cloaks. Fair enough. The wind was brisk this high on the mountain, and even capable elves who were a cherished part of their clan could still get cold.

As they came closer, he focused in on them, recognizing several by their projected vibration alone. The first was Terzon, who controlled the very soil with his thoughts. He had been with Bartolomey as well, at the very end, when they had thought to rid themselves of this false princess, but he had realigned himself with the clan when he had seen which group would benefit him most. He had grown strong and tall over the months since Grigor had seen him, his gray eyes sharp and observant. Had he truly been brainwashed back into the bosom of the Circle or had he, like Firefly, been biding his time until the chance to rebel arose?

If he were as deceitful as Grigor imagined, he would be a solid ally.

Second in the troop was Hidal, who had changed so much that Grigor hardly recognized him, now a tall, muscular, dark haired adolescent instead of a pudgy boy. Hidal, the foster son of Jense, a *nian* who had lived just outside the city, had never had much attention from the elders. While they were growing up he had often done Grigor's bidding, vying hard with the others for his attention, wanting so very much to belong, to be important to someone.

Grigor grinned. The hungry ones were always easier.

The third, Yadin, stood at mid-height, his hair a nondescript brown, his eyes a faded blue. Nothing stood out about him. Other than the fact that he had been a childhood friend of Astan Hawk. Grigor's eyes narrowed. What had brought him here? Of the three, he was most likely a spy. They would have to be cautious around this one until his loyalties were established.

Grigor stretched his legs and jumped down, belatedly considering that Astan had better playmates now than when they had been youngers together. Perhaps Yadin had been shoved aside as Astan's new queen and position of honor replaced his childhood friends. Time would tell.

The last, walking boldly with his hood down and pale auburn hair flowing with the wind, was an elf Grigor did not know. Nearly of adult age if his bearing was any indicator, his eyes were bright blue, almost turquoise, and they seemed to penetrate right through Grigor's skin to study whatever they might find within. He did not smile or make any other familiar gesture of greeting. Instead, he walked just behind Fontine as they crossed the open, snow-covered space coming up toward the rock where Grigor waited. He stood close, but behind the others, as Fontine moved to embrace Grigor.

That was when Grigor realized why that one had come. Those turquoise orbs burned with jealousy that flared as the young *neris* smiled, warm in Grigor's arms.

That one wanted Fontine.

Fontine let go of Grigor slowly as she looked into his eyes. "You look very good. Healthy. I'm glad the jacket I brought you fit."

"You're the best," he said, caressing her cheek, just so he could watch the other elf's reaction. Yes, there it was again. A flash of heat, quickly hidden in the depths of the icy glare. Fontine noticed his interest in the newcomer and turned to make the introductions.

"Grigor, this is Vez. He and his foster mother escaped to the western mountains when the clan split. Vez has never felt aligned with the clan since they returned."

Grigor studied the azure-eyed *nian*, looking for a chink, some way they could bond short of his tossing Fontine to Vez like a bone. He was not quite finished with her yet. "Your foster mother is a member of the Circle?"

"No," Vez snapped. "The Circle didn't feel she was qualified. She couldn't demonstrate enough of a gift to impress them."

"And what the Circle says goes." Grigor nodded, lips pressed tight. "Even when it comes to a queen."

"A queen who's hardly strong enough to even produce the Circle's desired representative to the next generation." Vez crossed his arms.

Grigor raised an eyebrow. "There is news of the child?"

Fontine nodded to Terzon. "Tell him."

"First, I would like to know how you have survived," Terzon said as he walked behind Grigor, observing him. "The clan has taught that one who kills another elf or a human shall lose his connection to the soil. That he shall wither and die as the mountain grasses. Yet you seem to thrive on your own. Explain this."

"Yes, explain." Yadin's face indicated his consternation that he had not asked first. As long as Grigor had known Yadin, he had always been a follower, not a leader. Perfect for Grigor's purposes.

Terzon, on the other hand, held challenge in his expression. Grigor shrugged, not ready to disclose his secret just yet.

"How else can I explain it?" Grigor began. "The Circle is simply wrong. They have lied to you for all these years to control your behavior."

The other's brow wrinkled in disbelief. He started to object but choked back his response, showing his uncertainty. Perhaps Terzon had been sucked back into the sheep's mindset. That would be a shame.

Vez, however, spat on the ground. "While the old witches reward the others for their lack of backbone."

The more Grigor heard from Vez, the more he thought they had in common. "Exactly. Those who bow down and worship them are given all the opportunities."

Even Hidal nodded in agreement. "That is not all," he said, leaning closer, as if someone might overhear them. "Rashia told Djana and the other women that the child is male. That somehow the queen defeated every effort they made to produce a daughter."

"Male? Foolish human, has she learned nothing?" Grigor threw his hands in the air going for effect. "She is not fit to rule the clan."

"So who should, Grigor?" Terzon asked, apparently feeling the need to be contrary. "You?"

"I would not be afraid to, if it came to that. Would you?"

"I'm sure no one's offering me that choice. Or you." Terzon leaned against the rock Grigor had been sitting on, arms crossed, a challenging look still on his face. But something in his voice wavered just a bit, showing a gap there, an entry, if Grigor could only answer his questions. Terzon would take his way out of the female run group at its first opportunity. "So who? Who can displace this weak queen?"

"Someone born to the royal family," Grigor said. The yearning for choices on the faces of those youngers before him urged him to reveal what he knew, to demonstrate his potential power. But he had not discussed with Bartolomey whether to share the news that his Master had only been exiled, not destroyed. Could he be so bold? Would the revelation doom his hopes of attaining mage status? Or had Bartolomey chosen him because he was the right one to tell the others? How could Grigor know which was true?

"Royal family?" Hidal laughed without much humor. "No others remain of the bloodline of Lorenz and Ele. Linnea is gone and we have heard what happened to Bartolomey." He glanced at Terzon, who nodded before he spoke.

"Frankly, Grigor, we aren't in a position to abandon the life we have, as much as we might dislike it, without the promise of something better. And I don't mean living out here in the wild, pretending to be the king of nothing."

Terzon's tone mocked Grigor to the core. It was all he could do not to lash out, especially now that he had his powers again. But Firefly had commanded him to win others to the cause. He fought to control himself.

"Terzon, I don't do things by halves," Grigor said. "You know this about me. I tell you that we have the chance to restore the righteous ruling blood to the leadership of our clan. We both served Bartolomey."

That seemed to grab the attention of each one of Grigor's companions.

"Bartolomey?" Yadin breathed.

Terzon and Vez watched with narrowed eyes. Grigor had to be very careful now. He turned to Fontine, whose face radiated adoration. "We need to gather more supporters to our cause. Surely I'm not the only one who's noticed every natural thing deteriorating over the last couple of months, while the so-called queen has wasted everyone's time producing a male heir."

Vez shrugged. "It's no worse than before she came."

"I disagree," Hidal said. He stepped forward, his cloak blowing open showing worn boots that needed replacing. "More of the clan is united in one place, true enough, but we are not 'together.' The infighting is ridiculous. The false queen is self-absorbed."

"Jelani is coming to the end of a very difficult pregnancy, one the likes of which the Lelan have never faced!" Fontine interrupted, her tone a bit self-righteous. "I wouldn't expect any of you to understand, since you are not female."

Grigor frowned, dismissing Fontine's comment. "Either she's a queen or she's not. She can't play at the game only when she's not with child, any more than she should allow any other distraction to keep her from her calling. The Lelan should come first when you rule the clan. So Bartolomey professed."

"Again you mention Bartolomey," Terzon said but he did not ask anything more explicit outright. Grigor exchanged glances with Terzon, and he saw a glimmer of the recognition of the truth therein.

"Bartolomey is dead," Yadin insisted. "The old king sent him away in a magic vessel. Astan said he was there, and he saw it with his own eyes."

"Astan." Grigor nodded thoughtfully. "Now there is a truly unbiased observer."

Vez laughed, a dark and frightening sound. "The lapdog of the Circle. May he perish in flames."

Oh yes, Grigor liked this one indeed. This gathering was a very good beginning. Time to celebrate a little, show the other youngers that Grigor had not spent his time wasting away toward death, but truly had something to offer them.

"Come, my friends. A small feast has been set out for all of us to enjoy, back at my new dwelling. Discover how those live who are expelled from the so called beneficence of the Circle."

He took Fontine's hand, kissing her pout and dissolving it, reassuring her that he appreciated her. He needed her more than Vez, for the moment. The others followed behind as he led them over the top of the ridge and down to his shelter, a proper elven platform in the trees, with all the comforts he had once enjoyed while living with his mother before his expulsion.

At last he was leading again. Now that he had potential followers, he would soon be in a position to exact revenge against the woman who had taken everything from him.

CHAPTER 20

JELANI had fallen asleep in her chair early in the evening of the previous night, so it was dark, all except the remaining embers of the fire burning, when she woke up with pain shooting through her midsection.

"Astan!"

She tried to get her feet untangled from the blankets on her, but the pain overwhelmed her. She pulled in air through her nose in little half breaths. A whimper escaped her. What was happening? Rashia said she would not have a regular human labor. Something was wrong.

"Astan!"

Light footsteps came running from both bedrooms, Iris and Astan reaching her side at nearly the same time.

"What is it, *denami*?"

"Is it time, honey?"

"Please call Rashia," she whispered.

Astan stopped to grab his jacket by the door and was gone.

"What did the midwife say about what to do if you had contractions?" Iris fussed around with the blankets, her fluttering making Jelani crazy.

"She said I wouldn't have them!" Jelani finally untangled her feet. "Help me up."

Iris lifted her with an arm under her shoulder. "Are you sure you should be up? Tell me what you need, honey."

"I need to be far, far away," Jelani said, a hint of humorous sarcasm coming to her through the ache in her belly. "Why don't you hold this for me for the next hour or so and I'll just step out, hmm?"

"Funny." Iris hugged her for a moment. "All right, I saw this on television once. Maybe if you just walk a little the muscles can un-cramp, all right?"

Another wave of pain started at a horizontal line in Jelani's middle and spread in all directions. The child objected, kicking and squirming inside her. Jelani could hardly keep her feet. She leaned on Iris, determined not to let this defeat her. "You think about this before you do the nasty with Daven, all right?"

When Iris did not come back with a snappy reply. Jelani eyed her. "You already did?"

Her friend blushed and bit her lip. "He's been showing me his favorite places in the forest."

"In the *snow*?"

"You know Daven. He can pull magic out of his fingers. Anywhere."

Jelani studied her face, glad for the distraction. She recognized that smile. Whatever they had done must have been mind blowing. Good for Iris.

Astan burst in through the door with Rashia following him, Daven practically carrying the midwife inside. Jelani's knees weakened with relief and she almost fell before Astan grabbed her other arm.

"Where do you want her?" Daven asked, his voice tight with worry.

The old *neris* waddled closer to the expectant mother with one hand extended forward. "I must examine her. Hold her still."

Jelani's first reaction to the order, a colorful objection to being treated like a piece of livestock, was swallowed by more pain. Astan and Iris held her up and Daven stepped behind her, his hands on her waist comforting in their support. She breathed through it as Rashia laid her hands on Jelani's abdomen.

"Is it time to explain the elven way to give birth?" Jelani gasped.

"Shh. We can wait no longer. The time is now." Rashia seemed to explore the cavity that held the baby with her fingers, first up, then down, and then she mumbled some elvish words Jelani did not understand. Daven echoed them and Jelani felt numbness extend from the place where his hands held on to her, downward, blessed relief from the pain. She started to thank him, but then Rashia made a lunge toward her, her face inches away.

"*Kenat figgar!*" she cried.

She pulled back a moment later, a blood covered baby in her hands. The baby, definitely male, made no sound but waved his arms and legs in the free air around him.

Iris gasped. The two elf men said nothing, though Jelani felt Astan waver a little, his face white. Daven's right hand left her side and went to Astan's shoulder, and a few seconds later the baby's father looked a little more solid.

Jelani looked down, expecting to find a gaping hole, expecting Rashia would be making excuses about having to lose the mother to save the child, expecting she had only minutes to live. But her gown hung just as it had when she put it on, except for the large bulge that was now missing. She sneaked a peek underneath, looking down through the open placket. Her skin was unmarred.

"That's it?" she asked, stunned.

"That's it." Daven's voice was warm by her ear. "Rashia will now introduce the child to his world."

As he spoke, Rashia took a light blanket from the bag at her hip and wrapped the baby in it, moving toward the door.

Instantly suspicious, Jelani pulled loose from Iris' arm. "Where's she going?"

"She must connect the child with the soil," Daven said. "It is as it was when you were born. Your connection with the soil brought you back, did it not? When you returned to the forest, your reconnection brought you into our world."

"I don't want her to take the baby. Astan, bring him back."

As Astan moved to follow Rashia, who had disappeared outside, Jelani felt her heart pounding. Her head became light. "What's happening?"

Daven caught her when she would have fallen and sat her in a chair, laying a hand on her forehead. "You need to rest. Astan, stop!"

"He's my son, not yours," Astan snapped. "Rashia, bring back the child."

"Astan." The voice was firm, clearly an order.

Jelani started to speak but Astan shook his head, his face flushed with emotion from the scene they had just endured. "What you need to realize, Daven, is that Jelani is not your woman. You do not command her. Or me. I am the chosen of the Queen, not you!"

Faces paled and eyes stared all around Astan. Even Jelani was surprised at the vehemence with which Astan snapped at his father.

Daven took a step back as if he had been physically punched.

Astan's face changed and he stared at Daven in that distant way Jelani had come to recognize as the time when pieces fell into place in his understanding of his world.

"You wanted to wed Linnea," Astan whispered. "If she had not chosen Vincent, you would have taken her."

"Enough!" Daven barked, eyes blazing with hazel fire, cutting him off. "This is no time to discuss that matter."

Jelani had never seen Daven angry. He had always been the quiet diplomat, the teacher. Whatever Astan's ability had tapped into must be raw and rough to bring such a knee-jerk reaction. She was actually afraid for Astan.

She got awkwardly to her feet and stumbled over to Astan, slipping an arm around his waist and holding tight. Their emotions were perfectly synched following the birth of their child, and she could read his every thought.

Astan turned slightly so he was between Jelani and his father, and she realized he was afraid for her too. She looked across the space of a couple of meters to Daven, and saw recognition in his eyes. Astan had called it correctly.

As Astan's gaze locked with Daven's, the flicks and pictures kept coming, touching both Astan's mind and Jelani's.

Flick.

Daven watching, wanting the queen Linnea, heart breaking as he lost her to the human Vincent Marsh.

Flick.

When he couldn't be king, Djana encouraging him to choose another *neris,* selecting silver-haired Veraena, who had always excelled in the use of magic, as Daven had. But he had never wanted her.

Flick.

When he had the chance to save Linnea, when he had the choice between her and his clan, he had taken it without a second thought for the partner he would leave behind.

Flick.

He had seen the chance to be king again when Linnea's daughter had come along, but he had lost it to Astan. He had never gotten over it. He still had hopes.

Father and son stared at each other, each knowing what the other knew. And Jelani knew, too.

"What's going on?" asked Iris, who wasn't privy to the telepathic communication. She laid a hand on Daven's forearm, her pretty face concerned.

Daven growled and turned away. "Nothing."

Out the still open door, Jelani caught a brief glimpse as the sun's earliest rays lit the scene of Rashia on her knees in the snow, bending down to put the baby on the ground. "Astan, she'll hurt the baby! He'll get frostbite!" She started out, but Astan stopped her.

"I'll handle it," Astan said and then walked out the door.

Daven hesitated. When he spoke, his voice assumed the old strength and authority. "It is our way, Jelani. He must be sealed as a member of the clan."

"He must remain healthy and not get pneumonia," she complained.

Astan came back inside, a blanket wrapped child in his hands.

"Wait!" Iris asked, looking confused. "What about, I mean, the afterbirth and placenta and all that? What happened to that?"

"Rashia says Jelani's elven biology will absorb that. She'll be fine now." Daven did not seem to know what to do with his hands. Not looking Jelani in the eye, he made a gesture toward Astan and the child, but Astan turned away and walked over to Jelani.

Rashia stepped into the room and held a whispered conversation with Daven. Both nodded, as if in agreement.

Crossed the small room, Rashia put her hand on Jelani's forehead, holding her just out of reach of the child.

"It is done," Rashia said. "This child is of the soil. You are now charged with the care of this child. You shall bring him up in the ways of the forest and teach him his responsibilities to the Bitterroot clan. If you fail in these teachings, the child will be given to others who will do what is right."

She stepped back and Jelani could again move, a little horrified at the midwife's words. Maybe those words were part of some ritual and they were said to any new parent of the clan. She had not been present when any other elf children had been born, so she didn't know. But her hormones were on fire. She took it personally.

"Like hell you will," Jelani muttered.

She watched Astan and was reassured by the firm set of his jaw that he did not intend to give an inch when it came to the baby, at least not where the Circle was involved.

Daven's disappointed look did nothing to stem Jelani's growing hostility. His attitude, which had always seemed so kind and pure, held dark corners she had never suspected. That frightened her. Most people she knew had hidden depths, things that they had done which didn't make them proud, and they explained those with the 'I'm only human' excuse. Daven did not have that easy out.

He opened the door once again, escorting Rashia outside. He beckoned to Jelani's friend as well. "Iris, come. Let us allow this family some time to get to know each other. Perhaps Jelani will realize now that she has her child, that her child is part of the clan, and all is well. There remains no reason to nourish a hard heart."

Iris didn't hesitate, but grabbed her hip length turquoise coat and scarf and disappeared with the two of them out the door. Jelani, a bit surprised at Iris' quick defection, took a moment to wonder on whose side Iris might be. Had she traded her status as Jelani's best friend for that of Daven's partner?

Silence settled in as Jelani came close to Astan, finally able to connect with her son. He pulled back the blanket to reveal their son's face. Everything else faded from her mind when she saw him for the first time. He might have the round, chubby face and faint fuzz of dark hair that any other baby had at birth, but she was sure he was the most beautiful and wonderful baby ever born.

"So did he tell you his name?" Jelani said with a hint of fond sarcasm.

Astan smiled. "As I told you he would, *denami.*"

She waited for a moment and then poked him, frustrated. "And?"

"His name is Elliun."

"Elliun, huh?" Unconvinced, Jelani slipped an arm around Astan, moving closer to see the tiny face inside the dusky green blanket. To her surprise, the baby opened his eyes wide and even reached for her. "Hey, baby," she said, lifting her finger within reach of his questing hand.

"He has your eyes," Astan said and leaned sideways to kiss her cheek. "Are you all right? Nothing has been damaged?"

She turned her head to kiss his lips with a soft, gentle touch. "I haven't really looked, but I don't think anything's permanently ruined." The baby squirmed and drew her attention again. "He is wonderful," she agreed.

"I love you." Astan brushed against her arm and her fingers sought his, locking together in a shared moment of connected bliss. "What we have to remember, Jelani, is that we did this," he said. "You and I. Not Daven, not the Circle, not anyone but us." He could not seem to stop smiling. "You should hold him."

"Didn't look like you were going to let him go." Finally allowing herself to relax, she grinned as he settled the wide eyed baby into her arms. "Too bad we can't set a charm to keep the door closed."

"Daven probably could." A dark shadow passed across Astan's face.

"There must be someone else. Perhaps Max," she said, distracted already by the new life in her arms. "We should ask him."

"I will," Astan said. He took her shoulders and maneuvered

her toward her large, round chair, helping her into it gently.

She scooted back into the blue cushion, the baby now clamoring for attention, and she decided that Elliun needed something to eat. She had talked to the staff at Dr. Pitt's office about nursing, and she had read the pamphlets.

Guess this is put up or shut up time.

She loosened the buttons on the front of her gown.

"All right Elliun, let's give this a try. Just don't be too hard on your mother if this doesn't work. Please?"

Astan left them to settle and retreated to restart the fire, which was in danger of going out after the night's burning. A pinch of dust went into the embers, and elven words invited the fire to resume its former warmth. Soon the room's chill, caused by the outside air coming in and out with all the commotion, faded.

Jelani guided her nipple into the mouth of the hungry youngster and he suckled immediately, his tiny hands clutching her breast. "Ouch! They were right. Babies who don't have anesthetic do have stronger reflexes." She thought back to the whole delivery. "I wish someone had just explained that birth process instead of making it such a mystery. I think most human women I know would vote for the elven method in a heartbeat!"

Astan pulled a chair close, admiring them. "I have never been present before at a child's birth, or I would have been pleased to share the details with you."

"I thought you were going to pass out." She watched his face, the lights in his eyes, and the faint rush of red to his cheeks as he acknowledged his vulnerability in the face of open blood.

"I thought I might. Praise the fates that I remained strong before my father."

"You did," she said with pride in her voice. "All the same—"

"All the same, what?" He frowned.

"It's back, isn't it? Your ability? That's how you read Daven." She shifted in the chair making the baby more comfortable. "Your reading was true, too. I could see it in his eyes."

Astan nodded slowly. "No wonder he's been so interested in 'taking care' of you."

Jelani's feelings of sadness and empathy surged at the look on Astan's face. "You know I would never—"

He held up a finger to cut her off. "No need to ever speak of that again. I know your heart, *denami*."

"Are you all right?" Jelani asked.

"This explains many things. Why Daven was so focused on Linnea's rescue. Why he left my mother and she vanished. Why he's been so—present." Astan's dark eyes studied her, cuddled with their baby and a blanket. "That will come to an end. I don't want to ask him for another thing."

"Agreed." Jelani bit her lip, the suckling slowing as the child seemed to finally get his fill. Adjusting her gown into place, she lifted the tiny new person to her shoulder, patting him very gently on the back. She considered the 'threat' Rashia had made, and fear chilled her to goose bumps.

"Do you really believe they would take him, Astan? Steal him from us?"

Astan's eyes glittered like those of his raptor namesake, a flash of passion and pride therein. "They wouldn't dare."

Hearing the conviction in Astan's voice, she could almost believe it. "I promise, Astan, I'll try really hard. Whatever they want me to do. Anything so that Elliun can be safe here with us."

She concentrated on the feel of her son on her shoulder, his tiny, quick breaths, his little mewling noises, his movements, his fingers, his toes. Everything about him was fascinating and perfect.

"You will be just fine, *denami*. We both will. The Circle must come to understand that we do not intend to allow them to dictate how to live our lives." He rubbed his forehead thoughtfully. "Now that Elliun has come, things may change for the better once again."

"What things?" Jelani shifted the child to a more comfortable position for his sleeping, hardly able to take her eyes from his small cheeks and twitching lips.

"Signs," Astan said. "I don't know if they mean much. Like Rashia herself, how she has become less attentive to her wellbeing. It's the same with many of the others. The trees and other plants in the forests have also faded, lost the glow of vitality you gave them. All this has happened while you've been so ill with your pregnancy. But you already look better. Perhaps everything else will turn around as well."

"I hope so." Jelani thought back, remembering how seldom she had been among the trees of late. She had neglected her responsibilities, that much she knew. After she heard that voice in the forest, she had been reluctant to be alone out there, but she had never meant to abandon her purpose.

"How bad is it?"

"Bad enough that it is the subject of conjecture among the clan."

"And another reason why they think I can't take care of Elliun." Jelani steamed in her chair, brooding.

Astan patted her leg, taking a moment to rub her feet. "Don't worry about such things now, Jelani. You have done quite enough for one day." He smiled again, his pride in her quite evident.

"And the day's only just begun." Content for the moment, Jelani let her finger slowly outline her son's cheek, delighted with his perfection. "What does that name mean? Elliun? I bet it means 'adorable.'"

Astan chuckled. "It means 'a new beginning'. Your son is obviously very wise."

"I see. He takes after his father."

With a laugh, Astan got up and pushed his chair back where it belonged. "Let me make sure the vultures are not hovering outside our door, *denami*. You should rest."

"You'd leave me alone?" Where did that note of panic in her voice come from? She had been a loner all her life. This was no different.

No. It *was* different. She had someone else depending on her now.

"Just for a short while." He came past, leaning down to kiss the top of her head. "If I find Iris, I'll send her to you."

Jelani thought about Iris' earlier actions and thought she might be better off if Iris stayed with Daven. What would Iris have thought if she had been privy to the revelations of that silent exchange? "Be careful."

"Always." He smiled as he opened the door.

"Astan?"

"What is it?" His expression showed calm tolerance.

"I—I love you." There. She said it. Her feelings for him saturated every cell of her body, but she never said it enough. She hoped he knew. She bit her lip, waiting for his usual diversionary retort, but it didn't come.

With a wink, he stepped out.

The room echoed with quiet at first, and then slowly the sounds came to her, the snapping of the fire, the birdsong overhead, the soft breathing of Elliun as he curled against her chest. She lay back with her eyes closed, taking it all in.

With this morning's new dawn had come a new day, in so many ways. She prayed she was up to the task.

CHAPTER 21

WHEN Lane's Vancouver connection sent the DNA results by email, Lane had to read them three times before he could absorb the information contained in it. With all the discussion of alleles and chromosomes and RFLP markers, he was way over his head.

What really caught his attention was Walt Janssen's handwritten notation: *Where the hell did you get this DNA?*

"Not likely to tell you that one, my friend," Lane muttered, realizing both that his coffee cup and his cupcake box were empty. He shoved himself up from his chair in the Cave and lumbered to the kitchen for a refill of both. As he walked by, he caught a glimpse of Crispy's legs stretched out on the floor behind the couch.

"You're not playing dead again, are you, Crisp?"

"Very funny."

A high pitched, raspy scream came from behind the couch, followed by a yelp from Crispy. "Hey, I'm feeding you as fast as I can!"

Lane frowned and wandered over, cup in hand. Kevin had given Crispy a big old computer packing box, which had been transformed into a temporary home for the red tail hawk. After Astan restored the bird, Crispy refused to leave it in the forest, insisting it needed personal care until able to fly free again.

Astan had, with a bit of persuasion, restored the bird to life But then Crispy had absolutely refused to leave it in the forest, insisting he needed to care for it personally until it was fit to care for itself again.

"I still can't believe you brought that damn bird in here. You're lucky as hell Grandpa Jerkface next door hasn't called the landlord with all the noise it makes."

Crispy grinned as he put a hand holding a strip of raw meat near a four inch hole cut in the front of the box. "Astan said it would be all right." A long beak darted out of the box and snatched the proffered food.

"Astan doesn't have to worry about getting kicked out of his apartment for violating a no pets clause."

"He's not a pet. He's a patient. He's, um, in recovery. Been sober now eight days." Crispy nodded vehemently. "You tell Grandpa our friend Red's nearly over the shakes."

"Oh. Sure. He'll buy that." Lane rolled his eyes and went on to the kitchen. He filled his cup with fresh coffee and laced it with factory sweetened and flavored creamer. Then he rummaged through the cupboard over the refrigerator for another box of cakes.

"He will," Crispy said. "He's in recovery, too."

"Oh, yeah? When did we get this earth shattering news?" Lane wondered with more than a smattering of annoyance how his socially impaired roommate got the news before he did.

"Two weeks ago."

Crispy finished what he was doing and came to the kitchen to scrub his hands with antibacterial soap. He washed the fronts and backs of his hands and scoured his nails with a small white brush.

"He just dropped that on you at the mailbox or what? Hello, I'm Grandpa Jerkface, and I'm an alcoholic?"

Crispy eyed him. "Don't be an idiot. Actually, Grandpa Tom, that's his name, saw Iris come by a couple of times and he thought she was cute. One day she was driving the agency van, and he knows some other people who get therapy from them. So he asked me if I was in recovery." He smiled a sad smile. "Guess it wasn't really a whole lie to tell him I had seven years in."

"You haven't drugged in that long, dude. I'd know."

"But I had some wine when Jellie was here. And champagne at New Year's two years ago." Crispy appeared more disappointed in himself than anyone else would be in him, for those minor blots on an otherwise unblemished record.

"Not even close to how wasted you used to get, buddy. Don't sweat it." Lane listened for several seconds to the bird beating his wings against the inside of the box. "How long are you going to keep that thing? You should at least take it up to the Rehab so they can prepare him for release again. Tell them you're a friend of Jelly Bean's."

Crispy gave a small, proud smile. "I know. It's just—I saved him. Me and Astan. I just felt really, I don't know. Like a brother to him. I felt responsible."

"You're gonna feel responsible when he gets out of that box and bites me in the ass, too. I'll make sure of it."

The skinny little man waved him off, and Lane returned to his favorite retreat. His email program notified him of a new arrival with a ping and a shouted "For the Horde!" Lane smiled, as he did every time he heard the sound file he had recorded himself. Sometimes, he was just so damned clever.

Going back to his professor friend's email, he scanned down through the report again. The upshot seemed to be that Daven's DNA was compatible with human DNA, although there were several extra chromosomes beyond the usual human forty-six, and the DNA itself had complexities. Walt went off into a fit of jargon at that point, and he lost Lane in the process. But he seemed to say that human DNA was a trimmed down, more efficient version of the sample he had been given.

Lane blinked, not sure what to think of what the professor had said. But when combined with the information he had received at his meeting with the Circle and a mind wide open, he came to the hypothesis that humans might have evolved from elves over the millennia, as some had started losing their powers and their connection to the land on which they had been born.

Rolling back to see what Crispy was doing, he spied his roommate in the kitchen chopping something. Lane's stomach growled and he hoped something was in preparation for the human residents of the house and not just the hawk. He activated a second keyboard and pulled up a genetics program that he had snagged off some university website. Now, to play a bit.

He uploaded the two genotypes, Daven's that he had gotten voluntarily, and Jelani's, that he had lifted from a bottle of water she had left the last time she had visited. All of that television watching was not a total waste, he assured himself.

Thank you, crime scene investigations.

Once the data was in place, he sent the program off to discover the possible combinations. The program was process heavy, and bogged down the machine something terrible. He tossed a beanbag from a basket next to his chair at the screen, willing it to go faster.

An unexpected knock on the door brought him upright. Had this been a government program he had lifted? He couldn't remember. He glanced over at Crispy, who came to the kitchen doorway.

"Are we anticipating visitors?" Lane asked.

"No."

"Maybe it's your friend Grandpa Jerkface."

"Maybe it's your mom."

The way that last came out, Lane couldn't tell if Crispy was teasing or angry. "C'mon, Crisp, I'm in the middle of something. Answer it, would you?"

Sullen, Crispy stared at him for a moment and then went to the door. Lane heard a quiet discussion, and then the shuffle of feet toward the Cave. Crispy came around the corner carrying a box about two feet across and two feet deep, followed by Kevin Briscoll from the computer store with an even bigger box in his hands.

"Whoa," Kevin said as he caught sight of the Cave. "Now that's one heck of a setup." He inched closer.

"What's all that?" Lane asked, eyeing the boxes.

"Had a bunch of books I thought you might get something out of." Kevin put his box on the table and wandered over to study the equipment in the cave. "Old Linux magazines. Some manuals on Perl. That kind of thing. A bunch of parts, too. Couple of machines that I had to write off, but couldn't really return."

Clearly fascinated, Kevin hunkered down to look at the tangle of cables under the table. "How do you—" Leaning closer, he avoided chunks of some red substance and pinpointed something of interest. "Oh, yeah, I see how that works. Are all of those keyboards synched?"

Lane shook his head. "Not yet." He had not been able to afford the tech to make that happen. Those were the kind of parts that didn't turn up on the secondhand market too often.

"You're not gonna believe this." Kevin started rooting in the box Crispy held. He pulled out a gray rectangular box about ten inches long with a dozen cables snaking out of it.

"A KVM switch? That's awesome!" Lane's breath caught. That was exactly what he had been wishing for since he sat up the Cave, a device to allow him to run all his machines from one keyboard. He had to hold it in his hands. The switch was a thing of beauty. Lane admired it as if it had been the Mona Lisa. Or a full-scale model of the space ship *Serenity*. "What do you want for it, man?"

"I got it returned, and I can't resell it. I don't need it." Kevin gave it to him.

Crispy sat down his box and poked through it idly. He pulled out a plush penguin about a foot high. "What's this?"

Lane's eyes lit up. "Tuxbot! Does it dance? Is the little fishy there?"

Kevin laughed. "Yeah. Got that before I went overseas. Our LUG had a raffle, and that's what I won. Software's in there somewhere."

"Linux user group?" Crispy was still digging. In a moment, he jumped back, dropped the item he'd had in his hand, and he scuttled back to the kitchen.

"What? What's wrong?" Kevin looked in the box. "Spider?"

Lane came over to check it out. "Oh." He gave a sagely nod. "Not a spider. A webcam."

"But it's not hooked up." Kevin's brow furrowed.

Lane waved a chunky hand. "Doesn't matter. He figures the government's spying on us anyway." He pawed through the rest of the stuff, trying not to drool. "Now, look, I can't just take this. I'll help with your overflow repairs or something."

"Sure, sure," Kevin said. "I'm not too worried. Anyone who's got a setup like this, they'll be needing more parts sooner or later." He grinned.

"Ain't that the truth." Lane ducked back into the Cave to check on the progress of his analysis.

"What are you running?" Kevin asked.

"Personal project. But this program's kicking my system's ass." Lane gestured to the two dark screens. "I've even shut down half the system to divert resources."

"Huh." Kevin studied the computers with the 'men-around-an-open-car-hood' look. Then a sly expression eased across his face. "You know, all I'm running downstairs is my website and a couple of public service programs today, and my server's got a little power. Want to bring it down?"

Lane braved an immediate flash of paranoia. Considering the subject matter of that program, did he really want that information on anyone else's computer? He eyed the screen, struggling to process. Damn. "How much power?"

"Come on down first and take a look," Kevin said. "Your friend can come too."

"Hear that, Crisp? Your big chance to get out in the world today."

A strangled little sound of distress came from the kitchen.

Lane tried to remember anything that he might have seen downstairs that would entice his roommate to venture out. "Oh, come on. Bet he's got a peppermint."

Kevin winked at Lane. "Mr. Mendell, I think you owe me the courtesy after I loaned you my box to use as an end table."

"For a what?" Lane's head snapped toward the kitchen.

"Table, he said. He needed something sturdy for a small lamp."

With a sheepish smile on his face, Crispy peeked around the corner from the kitchen just as the hawk let out a screech.

Kevin twitched, nearly dropping the cords in his hand. "What was that? A T-rex?"

"Ha!" Lane laughed. "That's your end table."

Crispy hissed and hurried over to the box. "You're bothering him. He needs some rest."

"He?" Kevin still didn't look too sure.

"Show him your soul-mate, Crisp." Still chuckling, Lane

checked the program again. Too damn slow. Muttering, he grabbed a thumb-drive and copied the program and the email data onto it.

Kevin followed Crispy into the living room.

"Don't scare him," Crispy said in a quiet voice. "Now he doesn't like to be touched. And I can only open the box for a minute."

"Come on, man, what is it? A gremlin or something?"

As the box opened, Kevin gave a surprised yelp and dove into the kitchen with his arms around his head. More shrieking erupted amid the flapping of heavy wings. A shadow passed, and Lane ducked just in time to avoid being sideswiped by the bird's talons.

"Crispy!" Lane yelled. "What are you doing?"

Chaos ensued, as the bird bounced off the window and then hit the door, knocking over plants and everything else in its path.

"I'll get him. I'll get him!" Crispy hurried after the bird, eventually catching it with a piece of chicken as bait. Holding its wings close, he quickly put it back in the box and secured the top.

They all heaved a sigh of relief.

"That's a hawk," Kevin said, getting to his feet. He looked up every so often as if expecting another aerial attack.

"He was dead. Now he's mine."

Kevin's eyebrow shot up in consternation. "Oh, really."

"Not really," Lane said, grabbing his coat. "Well, he was dead. But Crisp is returning him to his friends and neighbors any time now. Right, Crisp?"

"When he's ready." Crispy sulked in the corner of the living room nearest the box.

"Right." Kevin appeared to be quite puzzled, but he took the hint from Lane's preparations.

"Come on, let's head down."

* * *

LANE and Crisp followed Kevin to his shop.

Against a brief blast of cold wind, Kevin unlocked his door and then they hurried inside to the warmth.

"This is great of you to offer, man," Lane said. "I can handle most things, but this is something out of the ordinary."

"No problem at all." Kevin led them to the back and held out a hand. "There she is."

Lane's first view of the monster set up across three heavy desks felt like someone had just sucked all of the air out of his respiratory system. A dozen or more computers were stacked, harnessed, and trained all on one purpose: serving their master. He had never seen one of these in person, although he had read about them everywhere. "A Beowulf cluster?"

Kevin's broad grin confirmed his suspicion.

"Wolves?" Crispy asked, hanging back by the door.

"Beowulf cluster. All these computers are hooked together, Crisp, functioning like one gigantic computer. Holy mother of all dwarves. Can I?" Lane gestured to the machinery.

"Sure." Kevin's pride in his creation was apparent. He held out a small dish to Crispy. "You wanted a mint?"

Crispy darted forward to take one of the candies, whispered thanks, and then withdrew again.

It was Lane's turn to hunker down, marveling at the gathering of individual computing power, all combined to increase their individual capabilities. He had read an article years ago about computer superpower Google, and how the company ran its servers off huge collections of old hard drives, so numerous, that when one died off, it did not matter. The others just picked up their load and continued.

"This. Is. Awesome." Lane sighed happily. "You running Open MPI?"

"Exactly. Some Ubuntu mods, but one basic server node, twenty-four clients, all doing whatever I tell them to do." As Kevin touched the mouse several screens flickered to life, including one running screens of data in multi-colors.

"What's that?" Lane asked.

"I'm sharing some of my computer down time with SETI. Letting them analyze some of their data on my server, since their servers can only handle so much of the information they collect."

"SETI? Little green men? Really? Sweet!" Lane beamed.

The door behind them opened and slammed closed. The bell on the outer door rang, and then the sound of footsteps echoed in the stairwell beyond the wall next to them.

Kevin seemed disappointed that Crispy had left. "Something I said?"

Lane chuckled with long practiced tolerance. "Long story." He pulled the thumb drive from his pocket. "When you're ready."

Kevin slid into the chair to insert the drive, bringing the resources of the machine to bear on Lane's problem. "Want me to wait outside? You seemed a little jittery about the subject matter upstairs."

He had been so generous, Lane hated to be rude. "No, that's fine. I just—the problem's kind of personal. And I guess, well, you wouldn't believe it, probably, even if I did tell you." Lane blew air out of pursed lips. "Man, we have gotten into some crazy shit."

"I love crazy shit. Are you kidding? Neighbors who have a zombie hawk in their living room, who actually understand what I'm doing here?" He pointed to his cluster. "We are brothers. Hey, us deeps have to stick together, cause the tank only cares about the medic."

"So true, my brother, so true."

Kevin studied the directory as the thumb drive registered on his machine. "'Elf stuff'? What's that? Your toon files?"

Lane frowned. He could not remember anything like that being on the drive. "I don't know. Open it up."

His fingers tapping on the keyboard, Kevin eyed the screen with great interest for a moment before he turned to Lane. "What's the Circle, and who's the Lelan?"

Surprised, Lane stared at the blank screen. "Where does it say that?"

"Right there." Kevin stabbed at the screen with his finger.

That raised Lane's eyebrow. He stared at the screen, but it was blank. He saw nothing. Nada.

Kevin hesitated a moment, seeing Lane's confusion, and then began to read. "December 20. Got my pound of flesh. Well, pinch of DNA. Met with the old witches of the Circle. Here, just let me print it out. I'll copy it onto my machine and we can both look at it." He tapped commands into his keyboard to transfer the file and then sent it to the printer.

A few minutes later, Kevin handed Lane a stack of printed paper. "Some kind of interview, it looks like. Questions and answers."

Truly puzzled, Lane read over the printed words. "I was going to go up and interview them. The witches. But I don't remember doing it." His gut twisted, just a little. Something had happened to him. Something *they* had done. Had to be. "Wait. Wait. Let me think. December 20."

He pulled his small Palm device from his pocket and dialed it back to the twentieth of the month before. Sure enough, on that date, a notation: *Meet with the Ooga Booga gals, 1 p.m.*

"What's the matter?" Kevin asked. He took some of the papers back and read over what was on the sheets. His face got a little more disbelieving with each page. "Elves? Really? Like faeries, elves, wizards?"

"It's a long story, man. With a Watergate-sized hole in it."

Lane pulled a chair over to the table that held the computer complex and read through each of the pages. He really had gone to the forest. He had gathered the DNA, that he knew, but somehow he had forgotten all about this discussion. It had not appeared, to him anyway, on his computer or in his files. Only when Kevin had transferred it to his own machine had Lane been able to see it.

The file's final notation was that Daven was going to walk him back to Jelani's tree house. The obvious conclusion was that Daven had done something to him, his file or his computer, to alter his perception. The prime reaction was to remind himself to punch Daven in the face next time he saw the devious, deceitful elf.

Kevin waited, mostly patiently, while Lane pulled his thoughts together. Then Lane looked him in the eye, and took a deep breath. "So I have this friend...."

CHAPTER 22

GRIGOR met on several occasions with the disaffected youngers Fontine had brought to him.

Of the group, he found he spent more and more time with the rebellious Vez, who had recruited several malcontents of his own to swell the numbers of their group to eight. Grigor and Vez seemed to resonate on many subjects, especially their mutual dislikes. And also their likes, particularly where the lovely Fontine figured in.

But this is where Grigor was one ahead. He could graciously pass on Fontine as a reward, once she had served his own needs. His eye was set on higher game, anyway.

Grigor and Vez arranged a private meeting at a red-tinged dawn several seven-days after their initial introduction. Vez had asked for the meeting, which Grigor found intriguing. The blue-eyed elf seemed ambitious enough to be included for Bartolomey's consideration. Almost too ambitious.

Was there such a thing?

Grigor would not consider himself in that category. He knew what he wanted, and he would do anything required to reach that goal. It was just a practical matter. He could respect a similar quality in Vez.

He also knew Vez had good reason to hate the Circle because of the way they had refused his foster mother entry into their esteemed number and, by extension, Vez as well. Under those circumstances, Grigor was sure he could twist those vengeful feelings to his own advantage.

His energy strong again, Grigor intended to use today's outing to scout the far boundaries of the clan's territory, testing their defenses. Vez had provided some preliminary intelligence gathered from the other elves, so they had a clear place of beginning.

Grigor waited beneath the branches of a large fir, hidden by the shadows overhead from most eyes. He wanted to force Vez to walk across the open field in front of him, be the one exposed. He watched and waited until he became a bit annoyed that Vez had not appeared and wondered whether he had been found out by the Circle. Or whether Vez was just, as the humans said, 'jerking his chain'.

But he didn't expect the voice that spoke behind his shoulder, causing him to whirl and face the speaker, his heart racing.

Vez smirked, standing relaxed with his hands in his pockets, red hair tied back with a thin band of tanned animal skin. "Miss me?"

Grigor fought to keep his expression hard, not wanting Vez to see how he had been startled. "You're late," was all he said, the words sieved through gritted teeth. "Come on."

They set out to survey the entire territory around the north end of the lake the humans called Flathead, and then westward to the gray granite foothills of the Cascades.

Grigor had not forgiven Vez for his little prank. Sulking, he held back on his earlier intention to scope out Vez's heart. Vez took advantage of the silence to bring up the subject of Bartolomey.

"What makes you think a full-blooded member of the royal family is still available to lead the clan?" Vez asked as they topped a ridge.

Grigor weighed the usefulness of Vez to his scheme. While they believed in many of the same ideas about the clan, Vez was obviously not the sort of sheep Grigor preferred to have at his back. He did not like being challenged. He wanted to be the one cracking the whip.

At the same time, the business ahead called for at least some participants with the stomach and ambition who might also be prepared for violence and deceit. Vez seemed to have the kind of edge honed by frustration that would bring forth those qualities.

Was it time for Grigor to reveal what he knew? Hesitating, he stood near the eastern edge of the rock. The straight drop to the valley below didn't bother him. He had been close to death often enough over these past few months. The prospect of death had nearly lost its ability to cause him fear.

The valley was a blur of brown and gray, the snow having melted somewhat in what the humans called the January thaw. Even in the mountains, the winds would blow a bit warmer for a few days before the onslaught of more cold air from the north. He would be purely visible from the various levels below, perhaps in range of elven arrows. How long did he dare to stand there?

Vez pulled himself up into the lower branches of a nearby pine tree and stood tall, looking out over the same valley. "You don't know anything at all." Dark merriment tinged his voice. "You've just conjured up this thought to dazzle the youngers, impress them with some secret news, something special that exists only in your head."

"I do too!" Grigor shouted, stung by Vez's words and resultant smirk. He had allowed himself to be manipulated. *Shame on me.*

"Then what is it?"

Grigor stepped back from the edge, hands in his jacket pockets. "Something I cannot share with you until I am sure you can be trusted."

Vez stared him down with ice-cold azure. "You know my heart, Grigor Biren. I will not rest until the false queen is destroyed and those who support her are reduced to the least among us."

Nodding, Grigor looked up and smiled. "Then surely you will be among those who join our leader."

A pair of eagles swooped low, passing overhead and then diving into the valley below. Grigor watched them until they vanished into a hole in the rock itself, about halfway down the mountain. When he looked up again, he was startled to find Vez right behind him with a hand almost on his shoulder. He had not heard a sound.

"If you are not my friend, Grigor, then you might be my

enemy," Vez whispered, a depth of dark intention conveyed in his tone and the terse way he delivered his words.

Fighting not to show any alarm, Grigor forced a smile. He turned slowly to face his companion, moving aside slightly to a safer location away from the cliff. "I am your friend, Vez. I have ways to prove that to you in the seven-days to come. You'll see."

"I hear you talk. A lot. What I need to see are your deeds, Grigor. Your words prove nothing to me."

Grigor nodded. Vez was not an easy sell like the others. He would have to work harder to bring him into the fold as a follower. "When the false queen produces her child—"

"The child lives. The midwife brought him forth a seven-day since."

Furious that he had not been notified, Grigor whirled and walked back to the edge. "He is born? He survived?"

"He is reportedly the darling of the Circle. All those witches coddle and make much of him." Vez walked over to stand next to Grigor. "I understand the herbs have already been mixed to force the issue on the queen the next time. She will produce an heir. A female heir."

"No. No, she will not have the chance."

"What? Will you kill her?" Vez smiled, but there was no mirth in it.

Grigor stared out over the valley. "She took what I cherished. I shall do the same to her."

"I see." Vez mimicked Grigor's stance, hands in his pockets, feet facing forward on an outcropping of rock. "And for this you will be rewarded by the true leader of the clan?"

Grigor shot the other a sideways glance. A smile etched itself on his face. "He will be grateful. I'm sure his gratitude will be shown in a multitude of ways." Grigor thought of the sensuous *neris* Firefly. "I, too, can be grateful. For those who support me."

"You have only one thing I want," Vez snapped.

"You'd be surprised how thankful I can be," Grigor said. "Once we have that ill begotten child in our hands, the end will begin for that queen and her false reign. And we will have everything we desire. Both of us."

A sideways glance showed a mysterious smile on Vez's face. "You can count on me, Grigor. Together we will destroy the queen and her child."

Pleased, Grigor stepped back from the edge again. "Very well. Come, let's follow the western perimeter and see how our brethren have let the defenses fail."

He took off at a run toward the south, and a few seconds later, heard regular soft footfalls behind him. The moment had passed. His test had been met. Vez was the one with whom he would share the details of his plan.

* * *

RETURNING alone to his woodland abode as dusk fell, Grigor sensed something different in the air.

Something had passed this way, something looking for him.

He stopped at the exposed root of a large fir fifty feet from his home, observing the lay of the land.

Nothing seemed out of place.

But something wasn't right.

Grigor walked slowly out into the open, half expecting the air to fill with rocks or arrows. His hand slipped into his pocket and his fingers closed around the talisman given to him by Firefly.

"I'm not afraid of you!" he shouted.

And suddenly she was there.

Just a tiny speck of light when he first caught a glimpse of her from the corner of his eye, by the time he turned to watch her emerge from the glow of light around her, she was as beautiful as he had seen her the first time, this time in deep green from head to toe, her silvery hair tucked into a thick braid.

"Nor should you be afraid of me, Grigor." Her voice caressed him like the softest of furs. "I see you have put my talisman to good use."

"I have. Let me show you." He smiled, transformed by the warmth in her indigo eyes. He put out his hand to her but she didn't take it. Stymied, he used it instead to gesture her toward the entrance to his home.

She stepped up beside him and then followed him to the

upper tree level. There they could look down and watch the animals forage undisturbed for winter rations.

Grigor turned to her. "What can I give you? Are you in need of food or drink?"

Her regard had cooled since they came inside. She paced the length of his domain and back, and then turned to face him. Her eyes flashed and Grigor could swear lightning bolts flew from them right into his chest.

Jolted, he stumbled backward, trying to catch his breath again. "What have I done to offend? I don't understand. I'm doing what you've asked!"

"Are you?" The silvery hair pulled back made Firefly look severe, like an old grandmother ready to scold him. "You seem to have done quite a bit for yourself. You have nice clothes, a place to live, food, and drink. You're no longer the starving, filthy elf I met. But what have you done for us, hmm?"

"I have met with the youngers, as you asked. Many have rallied to the cause. I have shown them that what the Circle told them was not true, that an elf does not lose his powers when he is cast out!" Grigor did not understand what had changed. She had just been practically purring. What happened? "You know of my plan to abduct the child, Jelani's child, and destroy him. Surely this will bring the clan into further disorder!"

Still she didn't speak. What else did she expect him to say?

"I serve Bartolomey!" Grigor vowed. Desperate, he considered falling to his knees, but could not bring himself to do it. Not now. Not when he had fought his way back to this point. He could not be so hopeless. He fondled the talisman once more, begging it for inner strength.

She eyed him a few more seconds without speaking, the silence deafening. Finally the wind picked up outside and she relented. "Tell me your plan."

"You will not tell the others in the clan?" Grigor asked.

Lightning again shot from Firefly's eyes.

Grigor screamed in pain and fell back. The talisman remained in his fingers, but instead of making him strong it rendered him weak and lethargic.

She walked over and hunkered down beside him where he lay on the floor.

"Bartolomey knows I am to be trusted, worm. It is not within your purview to question me." She got up, and for a moment looked as though she wanted to kick him with her heavy boots. Instead she turned away. "Get up."

Grigor pushed himself upright, feeling his strength drain away. "What did you do? What's happening to me?"

Firefly crossed her arms and watched him. "The talisman is a powerful gift, Grigor. You may receive great rewards, but the mages do not reward inaction. Until you can show the mages that you are worthy of such a prize, they will decide each day whether it will bring you strength or take it from you. Do you know how they will make that choice?"

Miserable, Grigor looked down at the talisman on his open palm. "But I'm going to do this, I swear on his life I will."

She continued as if he had not spoken. "They make that choice based on your success. Up until now, you have increased the discord in the clan, sending these youngers back in with their minds full of confusion about the truth. The queen herself, has ruffled some feathers, and this too, brings the clan closer to chaos. But the mages do not believe it is enough."

Firefly lunged forward and grabbed his wrist, closing her hand over his, her fingers squeezing his hand closed with the talisman inside. She spoke in a tight, hateful voice. "In order to bring Bartolomey back across the divide, this clan must be shredded, in ribbons, brother standing against brother. Do you understand?"

As she spoke the talisman burned hot, and rays of light seemed to come from within it, slicing through the spaces between their clasped fingers.

Grigor groaned with the heat of it.

"Do you understand?" she demanded again.

"Yes!" he shrieked. "Yes, I understand! I'll do it. I'll do it."

Firefly released him and stepped back. "Tell me your plan."

He wanted to look at his hand, see if his skin was black and peeling as he believed it would be from that pain, but his failing dignity would not let him. He kept his eyes focused on her face.

"I have a way to get back inside the clan territories," he said, his voice barely above a whisper as he tried to sublimate the pain. "I can blame it on the humans. Enough of the Lelan still distrust them. Fontine has opened the door to the possibility of my supposed rehabilitation. The youngers will help me, Yadin, Hidal, Vez, the others. They're committed. We'll rush the queen's house and do whatever we have to do to leave with that child in our hands."

"And then?"

Grigor had not thought that far ahead. "And then...." He looked at her, silently begging her not to hurt him further. "Command me, lady. Where shall we bring the child?"

A cold smile snaked onto her lips, an icy pleasure that chilled him. "Bring him to Bartolomey in the forest. Bartolomey will know what to do."

He nodded fervently. "I will. I will bring him there."

She studied him a few moments, allowing the chill from her eyes to sink deep into his bones. "When will you do this?"

"When? I had thought we had some time to—"

A bright flash of light blinded him but he felt no contact from it. When he could see again, he noted her disapproval.

"Time grows very short. You must act in the very near future. Or Bartolomey and the mages will not only take away the power they have given you, but they will see to it that you live forever in agony."

"Lady, please." He was tempted to throw the talisman as far away as he could. But he remembered how he had lived before that, and he could not go back. He just couldn't.

"Yes, Grigor," she said, suddenly soft and approachable once again. She reached out for his hand and opened it, showing indeed the blackened flesh of his palm. Laying her hand over his, she murmured a phrase he didn't understand and the pain faded away. She showed him his hand, now healed and healthy from her magic.

"The mages do not wish to cause you pain. They can reward. They can give you your heart's desire."

Still holding his hand, she pulled him close to her and he was immersed in her spicy scent. It filled his head, leaving him dizzy and wanting her with all his soul.

"When you accomplish your task, you will receive all that you deserve," she whispered, her breath hot in his ear.

He tried to answer, but nothing would come past his dry tongue and lips. He nodded to show he understood.

"Remember, Grigor." She released his hand and walked away, right through the wall of his home. When it seemed she would have tumbled that great height to the ground, she vanished, in a burst of light, in midair.

Breathing hard, not sure if he had been in the presence of angel or demon, Grigor cradled his hand to his chest. One thing was clear. If he wanted to live, he had to execute his plan to take Jelani's child. Soon.

CHAPTER 23

ASTAN marched along the trail back to his comfortable home, where his woman and his son awaited, but he was not at all settled or happy.

Something resonated in a minor key, a nagging bit of oboe or bassoon that indicated the presence of discontent. No, more than discontent. Almost a warning. But he could not hear the melody in the mystery just beyond his reach.

His abilities had grown as he and Jelani spent more time alone together, keeping away Daven and the others. Astan began to wonder if Daven had purposely dampened Astan's gift to keep him from revelations such as the one he'd had the day Elliun was born. And maybe Djana before that, once she realized his ability. Where did the scheming stop?

Over the five seven-days since Elliun's birth, he and Jelani had managed a stilted truce with the Circle. The old women constantly tried to invade their home under the excuse of being able to treat the little one like the royal child he was destined to be, but Jelani was sure they only wanted to get their hands on Elliun so they could take him from her.

After the vision he'd had, even interrupted as it was, Astan did not know what to tell her. What he did know was that none of them should be trusted. What was it Lane always said?

You're not being paranoid, if they're really out to get you.

How long could the group that had ruled the clan and held its remnants together stand against the true-born queen of the clan? What possible positive outcome could there be?

To create some sort of order to the chaos, Daven had brought the proposal that he and Iris could serve as a clearinghouse for the gifts. Members of the Circle could bring items to the two of them, and Iris would take those she found acceptable to the queen. She had remained a guest in their home, even though she often spent nights with Daven. Jelani didn't seem to mind and Astan was just as happy to have as little contact with his father, or any potential pawn of his father, as possible.

True to his promise to Jelani, he had not asked Daven for anything else after the request for his father to place a lock on the door that could be activated from inside. Daven had even refused that request, a simple task for him.

"What if there was another emergency, Astan? What if Elliun became ill, and Jelani was home alone with no way to get help? Would you really want to lose him because of her childish fears?"

"Of course not. But I don't think her fears are—"

"Astan, calm down," Daven said. He put his arm around Astan's shoulders and handled him.

Damn his magic, Astan thought.

Unable to mount an argument with Daven in that state, Astan swallowed his anger and confusion and went for a long walk.

The truth was, Astan did not think Jelani's fears were at all childish.

Since Elliun was born, she relaxed, she smiled, she became once again the woman he had fallen in love with, affectionate, amusing and more patient with a newborn than he had ever expected. They spent hours in their bed, cuddled close with the baby sleeping between them. Even when the winter wind howled outside the tree, the blizzard conditions driving every animal and elf in the forests into cover, in their small space they were safe, and they had each other.

She worried, though, about the future, and he had to agree.

"Why don't they tell us things?" she had asked him one night. "Like the whole birth thing. Why didn't the Circle tell me what would happen? Every time I asked Rashia she rushed me along without an answer, telling me I'd know when the time came. Lane knows more about elf procedure than I do! He got the chance to talk shop with the Circle, remember? But me? Kept in the dark."

Her righteous indignation provoked his, as well. He smoothed her hair back from her forehead, wanting to bring her comfort. "*Denami,* I'm so sorry. I should have—"

"No, there's no reason why you should have taught me any of that. Daven, maybe, the great talker of all talkers. Or Djana. Or Rashia. Or any of them. Are they not telling me because they think I instinctively already know these things? Like they did when I was supposed to release Linnea from the tree? Or is it worse than that? Are they keeping the truth from me on purpose?"

His thumb stroked her cheek and he felt wetness there. Her sorrow struck him like a blow. "Why would they want you to be ignorant, Jelani? I cannot see how this would serve them in the least."

"You wouldn't think so. Unless it's true that they just want me to play nice until they can have their true princess. Then Rashia or one of the others can slip me one of their horrible potions and get rid of me."

Her tears had started for real then, and reassuring her that he would never let that happen, he held her close until she cried herself to sleep. He could not imagine the Circle he had known, had grown up with, could be so evil.

But the elven world had changed since Jelani Marsh had come to the woods.

He marched on, his task to bring food for the family that evening. He had not seen much in the way of wildlife, though it had been plentiful when Jelani had first started her work in the forest.

Many of the other young elf men and women had said the same, when he met them briefly here or there, and they were not happy about the state of things. They urged him to bring Jelani back into the world, among the trees, to help stimulate growth again. They complained about the Circle and the strict lines of conduct they tried to impose on the youngers. Word even circulated in whispers that those who had been exiled had not perished, but indeed flourished in their lonely woodland places.

Astan knew who they meant: Grigor Biren.

Ever since he had seen Fontine sneaking away to the outcast, Astan had meant to take the initiative to track him down as well. But one crisis after another had risen to steal his attention and time since then, and he had not done it. Soon, he would have to make it a priority. When he felt secure enough to leave Jelani on her own again.

No one seemed content, except perhaps Jelani's friend from the city, Iris Pallaton. She seemed to be head over heels in love with his father, as Astan had suspected the day they had saved the old queen. Doubtless they would soon be family. But no one would expect great things from Iris. She was only human after all.

Astan was even reluctant to access his ability, afraid he might see a black future ahead. If he could choose his own path, he would convey Jelani and Elliun away from here, keep them somewhere far from the clan, safe from their interference, even if he couldn't take them far into the human world. Jelani's occasional timid suggestion to return to the city did not sit any better with him. Elves needed to be connected to the natural world, not polluted air and boxes of concrete. He wanted to see his boy grow up strong and free, in the open air. No, they all needed to be in the wilds.

Astan knew Djana often spoke kindly, but there was a will of iron under her pleasant demeanor. If she believed the queen's child, boy or girl, was at risk, Astan knew she was absolutely capable of taking the child away.

"For his own good," Djana would say. "Jelani never listened to us. Too unstable. Should concentrate on the tasks she can do."

His fury growing as he played out the imagined conversation in his head, he leaned down to pick up a thick fallen branch. At the foot of a huge pine tree ahead he stopped and turned the branch in his hand as if it was a long sword. As hard as he could, he sliced at the trunk, cracking the branch against the thick wood over and over again, trying to release the anger before he got back around any others of the clan. His breath labored, his curses in muttered grunts, he continued until the branch had simply splintered into small bits.

Blood dripped from his fingers where the rough bark had

torn them. Had this been a sufficient catharsis? He hoped so.

He marched on, wrapping his hand in a handkerchief from his pocket, one of the few human items he continued to keep. He found them useful for a number of things. So little of human culture was. Like Lane and his incessant nagging about computers. Of what use were such objects in the elven world? They sucked electricity and resources from the world and provided but random bits of information which, if truly needed, should certainly be obtainable from the natural world, though perhaps not as fast or in the same form. Surely all the knowledge one needed could be gotten from the earth.

Jelani had mentioned that Lane and Crispy were coming up later that afternoon to see the baby, bringing some toys and larger items like a stroller. No doubt that would cause further rumblings among the elders. A stroller in the woods? He could hear the complaints now. But it would make Jelani happy. So be it.

He moved on, more confident now. He was the Guardian. He should be making these decisions about his lover, the Elf Queen. He intended to start now.

* * *

BEFORE Astan reached his door, he found Daven lurking in wait near the tree house.

His self-administered pep talk had set his mind against the Circle and Daven. He was in no mood to be trivialized by his father once again.

To his credit, Daven did not start in as Astan had expected. He didn't pounce, didn't touch him, just kept leaning against a thick tree trunk. "How are you, Astan? You, personally."

"You're worried about me now?"

Daven's lips twitched and then became firm, as if he had to hold something back. "I'm your father. I'm always worried about you. I was a young *nian* once, partnered with a beautiful *neris,* one whose spirit chafed at the traditions. I understand the issues, you know."

Astan poked at the inside of his cheek with his tongue, trying to come up with an answer that had the appearance of deference.

It hurt him that he could not be open with Daven. He appreciated being able to talk with him, since he had returned from Sleep, to bounce ideas off him, to receive advice. Someone he could usually talk to, unlike Djana. Someone who understood the elven implications of things, unlike Jelani. If only his father wasn't allied with the Circle, and therefore always suspect for an ulterior motive.

"I'm glad you understand, Daven. Then you know why I would rather succeed without your help."

Daven chuckled. "As I wanted to be considered grown without my father's constant prodding as well. And that of Djana."

Who was easily as bad as three elf men, Astan knew. They both knew.

"I'm all right. Fighting with myself every day to remain here and do what's right, even though everything in me screams to get away."

Daven stared at him for some time. "You must uphold the needs of the clan above your own," he said in a quiet voice.

Astan stared at the ground thinking of his father's choices. He seemed to be able to live with what he had done. Astan didn't know if he would be able to do the same. Or if he even should.

"Jelani's fine, Father. She's a good mother. She loves Elliun and we are both determined to see him flourish."

So you can call off your dogs, he added silently.

"The Circle is concerned about you both. About all three of you. We only want everything to be the best it can be for the clan, and for you. If you need help—"

"We don't need help." Astan couldn't avoid the edge to his voice that time.

"Astan, I only—"

"No, no, no!" Astan walked past his father, and then half turned back to him. "You wanted a queen. You have a queen. When she is well and happy, and not stressed and panicked about your old witches, everything will be well and happy, too. It's all slipping now, but it's not her fault. It's yours. All of yours!"

Astan's breath came so fast it pained him, and his heart

thudded into his ribs as he let go. "You pushed her into being a queen without telling her what she was getting into. You pushed her into pregnancy before she was ready, when she was just getting a handle on her power. You've pushed and prodded and backed her into a corner, so she can hardly function at all. And then you have the gall to complain that she's not living up to her potential, and so she should be deprived of her son?"

Daven seemed frozen in place, his eyes wide and surprised.

"You will not interfere any longer," Astan continued, his words propelled on a wave of passion that came from the depths of his heart. "If we need assistance, we will ask. But don't hold your breaths, any of you."

He turned and stalked down the path toward the tree house, empty-handed, imagining fire coming from his fingers, toes, any outlet, shooting into the ground and releasing the burden of stress he had carried for both of them. He had meant it. He was done.

Tempted to glance over his shoulder, concerned Daven might follow him, might even attack him from behind, he refused to allow himself to do so. In his mind, he heard the cold howl of a gray wolf, another loner in the night.

He didn't care if he had burned that bridge. The Circle might well take action after all, due to his own rebellion, not Jelani's. That could certainly backfire on him.

He had asked for help, and his father had turned down the only thing he had truly wanted. A simple lock for the door. Was that so much to ask?

So if he, Jelani, and Elliun had to go it alone, they would. If they had no support in the elf clan, her human friends would do what they could. Lane and Crispy might believe Jelani's true family was a bunch of fruits and nuts, but Astan believed the humans loved Jelani very much and would never let anything happen to her.

They would be out to visit later that afternoon. He would talk to them. If he felt safe, and if his ability continued to flow free, maybe he would flick through to a clearer perspective, to help him decide what to do about his family.

CHAPTER 24

"SO how exactly does Jelly Bean think we're going to haul all this stuff up to the Swiss Family Marsh's happy tree house when we can only drive this far?" Lane complained. He thought about the half-mile trek to the clan's environs and muttered.

Crispy climbed out and took down the stroller. "There's not so much snow, Lane. We could do it in a couple trips." He loaded several of the boxes atop the wheeled device.

"She should just move back into town." Still fussing, Lane slung his big computer case around his neck, tucking an arm through it so it hung stable across his body.

"But she belongs here." Crispy sat his own package on top of the carefully balanced stack. "Just like Red."

"Glad you're finally getting rid of that thing." Lane bustled about, stomping his feet to knock snow from them, and peered into the back of the pickup to see what was left.

"No you're not." Crispy's face broke into a slight smile. "You're just taking lessons from Grandpa Jerkface."

"Shut up." Lane covered any showing of emotion with his awkward unloading of several plastic grocery bags full of baby stuff some of Iris's coworkers had sent along. To tell the truth, he had been a little jealous of Crispy's outpouring of care and concern for the bird. But it had sure been good to see Crispy involved in something other than his paranoia. Let him smile. He deserved some happiness to make up for all he had missed those years in the past.

Just when Lane had given up on getting Jelani's presents to her, he caught movement from the corner of his eye. Little elflets, is that what they called them? Youngers? Maybe the equivalent of ages five to ten in human years, half a dozen of them came running out of the woods with Astan on their heels.

Crispy smiled and waved. "See? She has things taken care of," he said to Lane. "It's good to be the queen."

"Yeah, I bet," Lane said.

Muttering to himself, Lane handed box after box into eager little hands, whose giggling owners skittered away toward the tree house. One of the tallest took Crispy's rolling tower and headed off with it, after Crispy had rescued the box with the hawk from the top.

"Glad you're here," Astan said. He stopped first to check with Crispy.

The bird must have sensed a change in the air around him, because he let loose with a loud screech and beat his wings so hard that Lane thought he would come right through the cardboard.

"He sounds ready to fly," Astan observed.

"Can I let him go?" Crispy asked.

"I don't see why not. You have served him well as caretaker." Astan stood back and crossed his arms.

Crispy laid his head on the box for a moment and the bird went silent. "Be well, my brother. Fly free, where no one can hurt you." Wiped a tear from his eye, he stood and pried open the box flaps.

The hawk shot up into the air like a rocket afire. He pirouetted and flipped over, his wings flapping hard to lift him high and away.

All three watched until the bird was a speck on the wind.

"You done good, Crisp." Lane grinned with pride.

"I couldn't have done it without Astan," Crispy said softly. "He's the king. He has the healing hands."

Astan snorted. "Can't say I've been able to fix much lately."

They started walking up the trail, Lane dragging a bit behind as always, because of his ever broken pledge to himself to get back in shape.

One of these days. One of these days.

One of the children, a boy with snow-white hair, slowed to keep pace with Crispy.

Lane studied Astan's downcast eyes and the slump to his shoulder. "So everything's not happy in Elf Country, hmm?"

Astan hesitated, looking poised for a denial. Finally, he shook his head. "No. Everything's not all right. I'm frankly not sure what's going to happen." He shoved his hands in his pockets. "Lane, can I trust you? For Jelani's life?"

"What?" That perked up Lane's ears. "What about her life? Hell yes, you can trust me."

"The Circle doesn't trust Jelani because all the changes that she began to make here when she first came have begun to fade. They're pressuring her, blaming her."

"After all they did to her?" Outraged, Lane compiled a mental list of all the horrendous affronts the wicked old women had concocted, and started to spill them, but Astan held up a hand.

"No need to convince me. I'm well aware. I've had this same conversation with Daven. And more." He sighed and then shared with Lane the sorts of conversations he'd had with Daven and some of the youngers. "Daven still urges me to do my duty," he said as he finished. "But I wonder now where my duty truly lies."

"You better say it's with keeping our Jelly safe." Lane debated reminding Astan how he had failed Jelani before, when Bartolomey's men had taken her and tortured her. But something in the elf's face told the tale even stronger. Astan had not forgotten a moment of it.

"I believe the clan needs her. They need someone to rally around and follow. They should have waited until she was ready." He sighed again. "Everything's falling apart."

Lane did not like the sound of that one little bit. "And when everything falls apart, doesn't that mean the bad guys come out of the woodwork?"

Even as he said the words Lane felt a little chill on his spine, and he kept a closer eye on the tree line around them. "You still have bad guys, right? Just because old Black Bart got kicked to the other world doesn't mean there isn't someone else with a rotten agenda, right?" He thought back to what he had learned in Kevin's back room. "Like your father."

Astan twitched and stopped walking. "Why do you say this?"

"He has all kinds of different agendas. Seems like he's got new ones all the time. He'll tell you one thing and do something else." Lane studied Astan's face, seeing he was puzzled but not in disagreement. "He messed with my mind, the day I came here to meet with the Circle."

"Are you certain?" Again, Astan seemed to be more interested in discovering something bad about Daven Talvi than defending him.

Lane nodded and told Astan everything that he had been able to piece together about the day. "You'd better watch out for the guy. Really."

Astan eyed Lane a moment. "We have our own reasons to be cautious. Based on the actions of both Daven and the other Circle members, we feel the need to take some action. If the danger becomes too great here, Lane, I need to know we have somewhere to hide. Can we can count on you?"

The intensity of Astan's stare was almost painful. Lane turned away first, the desperate emotion in Astan's posture, let alone his face and voice and eyes, felt almost dangerous and overwhelming. Since childhood, Lane had pulled away from that kind of powerful emotion. It usually led to bad things and people getting hurt.

He forced his gaze back up wanting Astan to know how much he meant what he said. "Of course, man. We'd do anything for her. We'd do anything for you too, because of her." He held out his gloved hand.

Astan shook it in the human way. "You are unique among men, Lane Donatelli."

Snorting, Lane broke into a laugh. Anything to avoid his real feelings. Humor remained a good foil. "Oh, my friend, you can say that two times." He let go of Astan's hand and clapped him on the back. "Come on. Come show me your little squirming worm."

* * *

THE scene back at the tree house was chaotic.

The elflets had stayed around, fascinated with the bright

plastic toys, stacking them all around the small nursery. Lane was pleased to see Jelani much more like herself, handing out sarcastic tongue lashings like the old days.

He buddied up to her and slipped an arm around her shoulders for a quick hug. "You look good. You gave up on the Circle cocktails, did you?"

Her smile faded a little. "Yeah. Too much drinking was bad for my health, you know."

He nodded. "You want to know what else I know?"

"Sure." She pulled her chair closer, handing the baby to Astan to rock for awhile.

Lane took out his laptop and set it on the table, remembering belatedly that he had not brought an extra battery pack. "I don't know how long I can make this run," he said with a hint of apology. "But this stuff is pretty damn close to sci-fi here." He pulled up the results of the test he had run through Kevin's super machine. "I think I've discovered that humans are descended from elves."

"What?" Shocked, Astan came to stand behind him, as Lane paged through the DNA analysis. Some of it was pretty obscure, even to Lane, but the basics came across.

"This is how you two could have Elliun together, and Vincent and Linnea could have Jelly Bean before that. Because you're really made of the same stuff. We all are."

Silence fell on the room as they tried to process that information, followed by the flickering of the machine's screen. It went dark, blanking all the data.

"Damn. I thought I had more juice than that." He fiddled with the battery port. "You really need to get electricity up here, Jel. Damn." He scratched his head, looking around for the case. "Oh, well. Do you have any soda?"

"Soda? No. There's juice over there in the box." Astan was having trouble containing the active baby against his shoulder so Jelani held out her arms for the boy. She glanced over to the baby's room. "If you want to put that away, I think the kids took your case in there for safekeeping."

"That's fine. I didn't have batteries in there anyway, I'm

pretty sure." He studied the new mother, thinking she looked happy, if harried. "You want me to hold him?"

"I'd put him down for a nap, if we didn't have a party going on in there." She sighed and bounced the boy on her arm gently to calm him. He settled fairly quickly, the fussing fading to an occasional little mew. "But they're having so much fun playing with all the toys. I can wait a few more minutes."

Astan retreated to the bedroom doorway to discuss with Crispy the care and feeding of damaged wildlife.

Lane helped himself to some kind of red juice and a pastry that had been saved in there, too. He didn't think she would miss it.

His thoughts were spinning. So Astan was worried about trouble in paradise. And he had talked to Lane outside of Jelani's hearing, which meant he did not want to worry her with the problems. *Good man.* Even though the written transcript of their interview showed the old elf women had been sweet to Lane while he had that wormwood talisman, Lane didn't trust them as far as they could throw a cupcake. And Daven he did not trust at all.

If Astan was worried things were bad, they were probably several shades worse than bad. Critical, even. Something to think about.

He turned back to the table and saw one of the little ones futzing with his computer.

"Hey, that's not a baby toy!" Lane called. He went to pull the kid away from the keyboard, but something in the acquisitive way the child's fingers caressed the machine made him hesitate. "Sorry, kid," Lane said. "The battery's dead."

"Dead?" the white-haired boy asked, cocking his head. "Energy never goes away. You just have to locate a new source."

Lane chuckled. "Now a kid is gonna Yoda me into computer rebirth?"

Astan came over to stand near them. "Max is no kid. He is of my age. He just hasn't grown like the rest of the youngers. And he likes machinery."

"Max, huh. Okay." Lane hung back. One possessive hand

twitched toward the laptop every few minutes, as the other manipulated the keys and picked it up to study it.

"Max, this is Lane," Jelani interjected, grinning. "He doesn't play well with others."

The man-child twisted slightly to study Lane with eyes almost an amber color. "You are The Lane. The Circle spoke of you."

"I'll bet they did," Lane said, trying to be sarcastic, fighting a little gush of egotistic fulfillment as he was addressed in the same way as the saintly Vincent Marsh.

"*The* Lane?" Crispy asked. "I'll never be able to live with him now. His head won't fit through the door frame."

Jelani laughed and got up from her chair. "All right, this little boy's tired and needs his room! Thank you everyone, for carrying in the load. Go on home now."

Lane plastered himself back against the wall at the rush of elflets, but they were gone as fast as they had come. "Good thing they came to help or we'd still be out there lugging stuff."

"We could have brought Kevin's van," Crispy said.

"No. We couldn't. Kevin needed it today."

"Who's Kevin?" Jelani asked from the other room.

"Lane's new friend."

"Lane has a friend? Incredible!"

"Ha, ha, very funny." Lane rolled his eyes.

Crispy donned that self-pleased look he wore whenever he was able to zing Lane. "Kevin has a computer store downstairs. He's a WoW guy, too. He built a wolf computer and he's using it to spy on aliens."

"What?" Jelani came out of the bedroom, closing the door part way. "Aliens? Really?" She looked curiously at Lane.

"Seriously out of context, honey. Kevin's good people. Actually, he helped me with this information we were looking at before my computer so gracefully died."

Lane watched with trepidation as Max removed the battery from the laptop to examine it. He looked at it from all sides, and then bent down to the ground, a part not covered with one of the throw rugs Iris had brought up from town. He filled his hand with dirt and stood up again.

"Okay, now just a minute," Lane protested.

Astan shook his head. "Wait. He knows what he's doing."

"Dirt? He's fixing the battery with dirt? Are you kidding me? I'll never get it out of the connections!"

Astan held up a hand, gesturing for patience.

Lane groaned and had to look away as Max rubbed dirt onto the battery, all the while humming some little singsong tune that eventually included words Lane could not understand.

Even Jelani gasped as she saw Max with the dirt. "Astan, you know that computer is like a child to Lane."

Astan shrugged. Lane winced.

Max studied the battery for a moment and then blew away the dirt. He laid a hand on the laptop and in slow motion reinserted the battery. He observed the machine for a few moments and pushed the 'on' button. The fan kicked into life, but after a few moments it started a quiet beeping and then the screen went to black.

"What's that?" Astan asked.

"Low battery warning." Lane shook his head. "I told you this was crazy."

Max made a *tch-tch-tch* noise in his throat and took the laptop again, setting it down on the bare ground. He sat in front of it, legs crossed Indian style.

"Look, man, it's dead. I know it's dead. I'll bring a printout next time, all right? Not a problem. Just don't." Lane protested, As Jelani had said, he felt as if one of his dear children was being misused. "Okay. Okay, listen. Just don't get it full of dirt, huh? I'll have to buy another can of air."

"Now," Max said.

"Now what?" Lane asked.

They watched in amazement as the laptop battery indicator skewed diagonally up in a matter of seconds, showing a complete charge.

With a look of sheer delight, Max sat on the floor and tapped the keys. He brought up several new windows before finally settling on a game of solitaire.

"Holy crap on a cracker," Lane said. "How'd he do that?" He

turned toward Max. "How'd you do that?"

"It's part of the clan now," Max replied, not taking his eyes off the screen, fingers flying across the keyboard.

"It's—excuse me?" Lane stammered. "Did you say *it's* part of the clan? Really?"

Jelani shrugged and crossed her arms. "That's what they did to Elliun. When they made him part of the clan. Me, too."

"But he's a person! Or elf. Or—you know what I mean. This is a laptop. It doesn't get happy. It doesn't get sad. It just runs programs." He stared in disbelief, as Max continued to test out various applications.

"Cool," Crispy whispered, watching from the far side of the table.

"How long will it stay like that?" Lane asked.

"Till it runs down," Max explained. "But it will become strong again when it is one with the soil." Max stood and handed the laptop to Lane. "And I have met The Lane. My life will never be the same." Then the man-child actually bowed.

"Um, really, pal, that's not necessary." Lane felt the heat of embarrassment rush to his face.

"The Lane," Crispy whispered in a mocking voice.

"Knock it off," Lane warned.

Max watched the interchange between the two, his expression solemn. "Life will not be the same for any of us ever again." He twitched and cocked his head, before he turned to look at Astan. "The Circle meets."

Astan's face fell. "I knew it. I should never have told Daven what I truly felt." He turned to Jelani. "Will you be all right here with Lane and Crispy? I want to go find out what they are up to. Just in case."

"I'll be fine," she said, but her fingers trembled where they clasped her arm.

Lane could see she wasn't all right in any way.

Astan took her in his arms and held her tight for a long moment. "I'll be back as soon as I can."

Lane shut the computer and tucked it back in its case. "We'll keep an eye on everything, Astan. Your boy will be safe. I promise."

Astan nodded and left the house, Max on his heels.

"So, want to play some gin rummy?" Lane asked brightly.

CHAPTER 25

SURE he was about to lose his shot at the power he craved so dearly, Grigor summoned his cohorts.

They met just outside the eastern quadrant of the clan territory in the shadow of a tall fir, known to the elves as Tsal, the survivor, because it had lived through a powerful lightning strike fifteen seasons before. The tree had nearly split in half and its trunk had twisted as it healed, its branches now extending at strange, almost violent angles.

Grigor arrived first, anxious to implement his vengeful plan, but he waited the better part of a human hour for the others to meet him. When they arrived, they were full of news of the agitation of the Circle, which was meeting at the same time to discuss what to do with Jelani's child.

"They believe the queen has lost her mind," Fontine said. "And that she's bewitched Astan as well."

"Perhaps if you simply returned to show them how well you've survived, Grigor," Yadin said. "And give them an alternative to this queen."

Grigor shook his head, pacing on the bare area of forest floor in the center of the small circle the others had formed around him, each of them watching him, waiting for him to provide answers. Terzon stood, his arms crossed tight, almost as if he were trying to keep himself warm. Hidal and Yadin, clearly torn between Grigor, whom they had known since they were all young elves, and Vez, who figured now in their daily lives. Fontine, of course, hung on his every word.

Could he just go home? No. Even if the clan did forgive and open their arms to him, that was not how the process had to work. Making himself into the hero, that came second. First, he had to destroy the one who had taken everything from him.

"That will never work," Grigor said. "Astan Hawk would kill me on sight."

"Not if he thinks you're already dead." Vez's dark smile sent quivers through Grigor.

Grigor forced himself to continue to pace for several more steps, though his body nearly froze at the possibilities that suddenly confronted him. Surely Vez didn't mean to kill him here in front of these others, Grigor thought in a flash of panic. No. Of course not. He meant that because Grigor had been left in the woods on his own, he should not have been expected to survive. That was it.

Now he had to concentrate on the next steps. This was Grigor's plan, no one else's. He had thought of it all on his own, after the clan had discarded him, left him alone here in the pitiless rocks, cold winds and harsh rain. He deserved the right to carry it out.

"If the elders are involved in their politicking and complaining, then now is the time to strike," Grigor said, looking Vez straight in the eye. "We should move in and take the child now."

"All the same, if guards are posted, while they may let us in, they will not let you pass," Vez insisted.

"We need a distraction. Something to send anyone who's not already involved in this discussion about the false queen out of our way," Grigor said.

Terzon's face lit up, an idea practically bursting from his lips. "A ground-quake. That would frighten them. Show them we are a force to be reckoned with!"

Grigor knew that capability existed within his childhood friend. But so did the rest of the clan. "They would know you had caused it, Terzon. Inherent in this plan is the ability for you and the others to continue to blend into the clan, to appear innocent, until the queen is deposed once and for all. The same goes for the rest of you. Your elven powers are obvious to those who know you well."

Silence settled around them like a heavy smoke. Grigor had

not thought through all of the details, not while trying to coordinate so many of them, and now facing the open hostility in the eyes of Vez, he struggled to be clever.

"Then we should use human powers," Vez said.

"Humans have no powers!" Hidal cried.

"Exactly. What can we do that will call to the heart of every elf in the forest, that we can blame on humans?"

"Fire," Fontine whispered.

"Yes," Grigor said. "Yes, Fontine, that's just what we need."

Grigor knew that Fontine could start a fire anywhere, just by wishing it into existence. But careless humans had destroyed hundreds of acres of elven territory over the years. The possibility was one the clan feared more than almost anything.

Yadin nodded. "Beckley said a camp of human males has been on the eastern face of the mountain for the last week, hunting for animals."

"This was known to the clan?" Grigor asked.

"Yes," Vez said. "I heard them talking. Here's your chance to be a hero, my friend. And we can hold the humans accountable for all of it. Of course, this would be more believable if you showed the clan you'd put up a fight to protect them." He eyed Grigor. "I think a blacked eye and a bloody nose ought to do it."

"You won't hurt Grigor!" Fontine put her hands on her hips and stamped her foot. "Even you couldn't be that cruel after all Grigor has endured!"

Vez's cold look told Grigor exactly how cruel he could be, and from that moment, Grigor knew Vez was determined somehow to knock him off his position of superiority. That motivated him to even more desperation.

"How far are the humans?" Grigor asked.

Yadin pointed to the east. "Not far."

"Everyone knows humans travel over large areas," Grigor said. "We don't have to go all the way to them. Fontine, go start your fire. Something controlled. Something that won't take many trees, but will be big enough to draw attention. Yadin, you go back to the clan conclave. Warn them the humans have caused this disaster. The rest of us will go ahead."

Fontine slipped into his arms and kissed him with real passion. She pulled out of the embrace and then ran with Yadin to the east side of the glade, where they disappeared into the trees.

Grigor looked at the others, distrust of Vez coloring what should be his perfect day with gray shadows. "We should go," he said. He started for the edge of the glade.

"No need to hurt you, friend," Vez said with a hearty laugh. "Just lay still and do nothing. It shouldn't be too hard for you." He stepped forward and scooped Grigor up onto his shoulder. "Let's go."

Vez started off at a run for the clan meeting area, every step jolting Grigor's ribs till they bruised. Grigor struggled, but Vez was unnaturally strong, his arm like iron across the back of Grigor's legs. He had no choice but to go along.

Shouting ahead stopped the small group, and each of them was questioned by two of the youngers who had been left on guard duty.

"Who's this?" one asked, pulling Grigor's head up by the hair to see his face. When he recognized him, he let go as if he had been bitten. "This one is dead. He was sent away with Bartolomey!"

Grigor concentrated on hanging limp over Vez's shoulder with his eyes closed, loathing the vulnerability it caused.

"Not yet," Vez said. "Those humans, friends to the queen, they found him in the woods and beat him. We happened across him and thought even the Circle could not turn him away when he had been harmed by the outsiders."

The lie came so smoothly from Vez's lips, Grigor wondered what other lies the elf might have told.

The guard hemmed a moment. "I should call Daven Talvi or one of the others to permit this. This *nian* has been assumed dead. His appearance now is—"

"Fire!" came the call from beyond the hill.

Grigor tried to twist around, to see who was coming, but he couldn't move. Vez held him tight.

"Fire?" The guard sounded less sure what to do.

"That's Yadin," said Vez. "He was assigned to patrol earlier today."

Grigor shifted his shoulders just enough so he could see a breathless Yadin coming toward them at a run.

"Fire!" he gasped before he collapsed at the feet of the guard.

The guard whistled vigorously and several more guards appeared from the trees around them. A few words in the elven language set the others running in the direction from which Yadin had come.

"What about him?" Vez asked, indicating Grigor.

The guard hesitated a moment, and then waved them through. "Take them to the Circle!"

"Sure will," Vez said with a little laugh. "Sure will."

The guard helped Yadin to his feet and then the two of them ran through the trees.

After the guard and Yadin were out of sight, Vez dropped Grigor to the ground.

Grigor fell with a grunt and avoided the hand Vez extended to help him to his feet. Pain ricocheting through his midsection, he walked around for a moment, trying to get comfortable enough to continue.

"How far?" Grigor barked.

"Half a mile in that direction," Yadin said.

"She will likely not be alone," Hidal added.

"Those meeting with the Circle will likely go to help put out the fire. Even the saintly Astan will risk his own safety for the clan. It's his way." Grigor rubbed his ribs, trying to redirect his own pain into the anger he was about to rain down on Jelani and her mate.

"We could divert blame for this act as well as the fire, you know," Vez said, leaning on a nearby tree. "Wouldn't it be prudent to have blame fall on the Circle itself?"

A murmur of assent went around the group. The wind blew past and through them, leaving a chill.

Grigor shivered and tightened his jacket, slipping his hand into his pocket to seek out the talisman. Rubbing it through his fingers did not bring the usual comfort. He chalked it up to his level of adrenaline.

Fontine joined them, running up through a knot of trees at an oblique angle to the route they had come. "It's done," she said. "I started just a small fire, but the wind whipped it up more than I'd expected." Her eyes filled with remorseful tears. "They'll contain it, won't they? I don't want the forest to suffer for what we're doing."

"Everything will be fine, Fontine." Vez assured her, before Grigor could speak.

Grigor bristled. Enough of this elf who was supposed to be his subordinate. Grigor was back in charge as of now. His words came out like bullets from a human gun, sharp and painful. "All right. Fontine, you wait for the others, then help put out the blaze. Yadin, you seek out Astan or the human female with the golden hair. Tell them something horrible has happened to the queen, and that it was at the bidding of the Circle. Take your time. We three will need a short delay to arrive at the queen's home and carry out our end."

Vez nodded. "Clever. You may yet be worthy of a mage's cloak." He smirked and turned away leaving the others puzzled behind him.

Even Fontine looked at him with new eyes. "What does he mean? Grigor, is this what you have become? A mage?"

"No. I am not a mage." Grigor ran after Vez, wondering how his dream had been discovered. "Go do as you are bid!" he yelled to the others.

Hidal followed along after Vez, too. The others waited, knowing their journey would be shorter and they needed more discretion.

Grigor panted hard as he ran to catch up with Vez. He needed a charge from the talisman, but Firefly had dimmed its power so much he could barely run at all.

"We don't harm the queen!" Grigor gasped as he finally drew even with Vez. "She must suffer from the loss, as she's made us all suffer."

"I know the plan, my friend," Vez said. His running seemed effortless.

Grigor hated him.

Just a few minutes now. A few minutes more and his revenge would be complete.

CHAPTER 26

JELANI wondered what was wrong.

After Astan left, Crispy settled down with a book pulled from one of the many boxes the youngers had carried, but Lane paced with a trapped tiger look in his eyes.

Lane had a computer at hand but wasn't using it. That was what finally tipped her off.

"So what's going on, Lane? It's not my birthday," Jelani was tired and would have lain down, except something in Lane's bearing wouldn't let her.

"It's what?" Lane turned confused eyes on her.

"Not my birthday." She gestured to the door. "Surprise party? Elli's too young. Astan's been ready to explode the last few days. So something's going on. Tell me." Nervous herself now, she walked over to the door of the baby's room and peeked in, seeing his little swaddled lump in the cradle the elders had sent. Relieved, she came back to Lane. "You told me I could ask you anything about this, starting with that video so many months ago. Didn't you?"

Lane shifted his bulk from one leg to the other, looking everywhere but at her. "Jelly Bean, maybe you best ask Astan about—"

Fury bubbled up in her quickly followed by fear. The evasion and lies made it worse. "I'm asking you. Tell me now."

"Jel, have you thought about moving into town? Get away from those old witches before something bad happens?" Lane's fat fingers twisted against each other as he fought for words. "You know, just to be safe."

"Something bad's going to happen? Is that what Astan thinks?" Alarmed, she went to the door of the baby's room again, looking at the small space where he lay.

"Now, I didn't say it was. I just said if."

"You said before," Crispy corrected.

Lane eyed him with a look like a baseball bat upside the head. "You know what? Never mind. Let's play cards. C'mon, Crisp, you'll play gin, right?"

Jelani hated being pandered to. Or handled. Or lied to most of all. Blood raced in her ears. "The hell with cards. Tell me or get out."

"Can't, Jelly Bean. I promised Astan—"

"To hell with Astan, too. Everyone in the world is conspiring behind my back and I can't stand it!" She snatched up her elven blanket from the papasan and wrapped it around her shoulders. "Get out. Now. I can't stand to have anyone here who isn't fully behind me. Not any more."

When they didn't move, she felt a rush of adrenaline shoot through her and overwhelm her so fast that she started shaking. Something bad was coming. Everyone was against her. Even Astan had bailed to go meet with the Circle. She was on her own.

"Get out!" Jelani ordered. "I swear I'll shoot you if I have to."

Lane snorted in disbelief. "Bull."

"You don't believe me? I have a gun. I do!"

Almost lightheaded with anxiety, Jelani went to a drawer in the kitchen area and opened it. She pulled out a small pistol and waved it at Lane to prove she really had it. She was not a liar. She meant what she said. She could be trusted. She had done her job as queen, she as had been chosen to do even if the others had tried to defeat her.

"I'm not screwing around here," Jelani said. "Get out. I don't want anyone near me who can't be honest."

Crispy, eyes wide, was halfway to the door. Once he saw the gun, he had turned pale as a ghost. "Come on, Lane."

Lane froze. He almost gasped for air, his eyes glued to the gun in Jelani's hand. "No, this is not all right. You can't blame this one on postpartum depression. It's crazy! Just crazy! Put that thing down. Mothers shouldn't have guns. Mothers shouldn't—"

He pulled at his hair, his face looking years younger. "No guns! Just wait until Astan gets back."

She could not stand it any longer. Why wouldn't he listen to her and get out? She pointed the gun at the ceiling and pulled the trigger. The shot echoed around the small room and made her ears ring. An acrid odor filled the space. All she could think was that she had to prove to Lane, to everyone, that she meant what she said.

"Get out!" she ordered.

"Jel!" Lane ducked aside with a yelp. "All right! All right, honey. I'll go! I swear. Please, just please put down the gun. Crisp, go on out. I have to get my bag. It's in the back room."

"Just go," she said. Feeling nauseous, like she could trust no one any more, the sound of the shot echoing in her ears, Jelani pulled the blanket around her shoulders and walked into her bedroom, wishing like hell Astan was there.

"Bye, Jelani!" Crispy called from the door.

Yeah, good riddance, she thought. *I can't even count on my friends. No one except Astan. And maybe not him, since he keeps going behind my back. Just me. I should take Elli and go away. If I wasn't so tired, I'd go right now.*

"I'm outtie, Jelly Bean," Lane said. He hesitated by the door, his computer bag on his shoulder and his laptop under his arm. His face looked strained and hurt. "Please come see us soon. Please?"

She knew she had caused that look on his face. Guilt slipped between her ribs and made her feel sick. But she would not back down now. "Just leave me alone, Lane. I'm tired, okay. Just tired."

"I know, honey. Everything's going to be all right."

He left and the door closed behind him. She walked over to the door of the baby's room again, the small lump that was Elliun sleeping in the cradle the only thing that could possibly bring a smile to her face. Astan would be home soon, and they could talk about the Circle and what needed to be done.

A scratching at the door pulled her attention away from the baby. What now? With an irritated sigh, she walked out to the main room and leaned her ear against the inner side of the tree trunk. "Who is it?"

"Rashia, my Lady. Please. I heard something." A long pause. "I just want to assure myself of your welfare. The welfare of the child."

"Daven went to tell you all to back off!" Jelani growled. "Leave me alone!"

"But, my Lady, please—"

When would they give up? How could she discourage the old biddy? Jelani scanned the room and found the weapon where she had tossed it when she'd pulled that stupid stunt with Lane. Damn it. She shouldn't have run him off. Her hormones were just so volatile.

Her eyes, as if on command, filled with hot tears. "Don't step a foot in here! I have a gun!"

Rashia's voice trembled. "By the Stars, Jelani. You aren't right. Please let me help you."

"Go away! Send Astan back here."

The old *neris* continued to protest, but Jelani leaned against the door until silence replaced the midwife's whining. She waited another several minutes trying to breathe calm into her body. She was fine. Elliun was fine. If all the people who supposedly cared about her would just leave her alone, they would all be fine, too.

She took a deep breath and pulled a chair over to block the door. It wouldn't keep Astan out, but maybe someone trying to break in would at least trip over it. As her adrenaline faded, she was suddenly very tired. She would just rest for a few minutes, in the chair, until Astan returned. It wouldn't be long.

She picked up the gun and laid it on the table next to her, just in case.

With a yawn, she stretched out weary arms and curled up into the papasan chair, closing her eyes.

* * *

SHE woke, she did not know how much later, to a sound behind her. A quick glance showed her dark shadows moving in the half-light between the place where she lay and the door to the outside.

Someone had entered her home. Without getting up, she looked around for the gun, but it was out of reach.

"Astan?" she whispered. She would feel like a fool if it was just him trying to be quiet and not wake her. The shadows moved into her room, then into Iris' room, and she knew Elli's room was next. She could hold still no longer.

"Hey! What are you doing there?" she yelled. "Lights!"

All three shadows startled as the lights came up, and the two biggest ones came toward her. One she did not recognize at first, a large man or elf clad only in dark clothing.

The other was Grigor Biren.

She froze. "No. You're dead. You're with Bartolomey. Gone."

"You wish, my queen," he said, coming closer to her. "Instead I am here to share with you the gift you gave me. The loss of life."

Yes, it was him, tall, strong, and oh so superior. Her heart skipped a beat, and she looked desperately toward the child's room.

"Take my life if you must, but don't hurt my son. Please." Sickened by the expression on his face, Jelani wondered if begging would really change his mind.

"Please." She grabbed the gun from the table and pointed it at him, her hand shaking so much that she probably couldn't have hit him even if she managed to fire.

His pitiless smile flayed her slowly, ignoring the gun. "I'll take what means more to you than life, my lady. Your child. And you'll never forget it. Never."

"Enough talk," said the other one, in the light more familiar as an elf she had only seen occasionally in clan gatherings, a big *nian* who seldom spoke to anyone except a few of the youngers. "Let's end this now."

"No!" She pulled the trigger but the shot went wild, the sound echoing.

She backed away a few steps looking for something else to stop them with, but tripped over the blanket in which she had been wrapped. The big elf jumped landing next to her, and twisted the gun from her hand, lifting it and then ramming the hard butt of it against her forehead.

Pain exploded in her head before she slipped into darkness.

CHAPTER 27

ASTAN paced outside the meeting room of the Circle, sheer determined concentration letting him hear what was being discussed.

Most of the Circle was present. Only two seemed to be missing: Uralia the herb-mistress and Rashia. While Djana expressed concern over Daven's report of his conversation with Astan, nothing seemed to be decided. The Circle chose a 'watch and wait' attitude, which Astan could live with, at least for now.

Before Astan had time to assimilate that news, Yadin came running through the woods.

"Fire!" Yadin cried. "Fire in the eastern woods!"

As Astan just stood there stunned, several of the Circle pushed him aside and burst through the gossamer door that enclosed their gathering.

"Where's the fire?" demanded Daven. "I saw a group of humans at a camp out that way. We should have watched them more closely." He let out a chest full of air in the cry of an angry raptor. Moments later, the glade filled with elf men and women.

"Some of the youngers are already there, trying to put out the fire," Yadin huffed. "But we weren't enough. Help is needed."

Daven called again and others appeared from the trees. Word spread quickly. Daven had quite a fighting force of volunteers, including some members of the Circle who headed east to deal with the crisis.

As Astan started to follow them, he noticed Yadin hung back as if trying to catch his eye. Yadin's shoulders were hunched over and dark circles lay under his eyes.

"What is it, Yadin?" Astan asked. "You wish to speak with me?"

"I worry about the clan, my brother" Yadin turned and took several steps in the opposite the direction from which the others had gone.

Astan fidgeted, torn between dealing with whatever was afoot with Yadin and helping to put out the fire before it consumed the lands of the Bitterroot. "And how so?"

Yadin bent at the waist, gasping to catch his breath. "The queen may be in danger."

"From the fire? Of course. Let us go extinguish it for the sake of all of us." Astan started to follow the others, but Yadin grabbed his arm.

"No." Out of breath, Yadin wheezed as he walked. "From the Circle."

A flood of dread washed over Astan. He turned and stared moment at the Circle chamber, its door fluttering open in the wind. "No, I heard them. I listened to their counsel. Daven persuaded them not to take the child. I heard it with my own ears. They said—"

A strange expression crossed Yadin's face, and then he shook his head. "They lied to you, brother. Even your own father cannot be trusted. Something's happening, right now." He followed Astan's glance, and his voice hardened. "You let yourself be distracted."

"No," Astan insisted. He released Yadin's arm and headed in the direction of the tree house. Had he left Jelani just as she needed him, again? "You go help with the fire. I'll go home."

Astan ran toward the tree house, his thinking only for his feet and how much speed he could generate. When he came within sight of the home, his heart sank. The door stood open.

Where the hell was Lane?

He dashed across the threshold and skidded to a stop.

Jelani laid on the floor, wrapped in her blanket, blood dripping from her forehead. Azrael sat next to her, his tail twitching in distress. Their possessions were scattered across the room, including the new toys Lane and Crispy had brought. The distinct odor of burnt gunpowder hung in the air.

He had been distracted, just like Yadin said.

Damn the Circle.

Damn them. All of them. Especially Daven.

His throat choked with anger and pain, he returned to kneel beside the unconscious woman on the floor.

"Jelani?" he croaked, as he wiped blood from her face.

Her cheek was warm. She was alive. But the blood was nearly dry, which meant this had happened some time ago. Relief mingled worry. Cold fury bubbled inside him.

"*Denami*, please wake up," he whispered.

As he considered what he would do to the Circle for its treachery, Jelani's eyes fluttered open and then widened as she focused on him.

"Astan? Oh." Jelani groaned, as Astan slipped an arm around her shoulders and helped her to sit up. Then she stiffened. "Elliun!"

Startled, Astan looked toward the baby's room and noticed the cradle was knocked askew. "Jelani, what happened?"

"Help me up," she murmured.

Astan slid an arm behind her back and eased her to her feet. She stumbled, half-dragging him to the baby's room.

There was no mistake. The cradle was empty. Elliun was gone.

Astan buried his face in Jelani's shoulder, feeling sick. "They took him. They took him. I thought I'd lost you both."

"Grigor," Jelani said.

Astan's eyes narrowed. She must have been hurt worse than he thought. "What?"

"Grigor. And two others. They came after I fell asleep." She looked around, anxiety written on her face. "They were right here." She pointed.

"Where was Lane?" Astan helped Jelani into a chair. "Lie still. I'll get ice for your head." He walked across to the box and came back with a chunk wrapped in cloth, which he handed to her. With a second cloth, he wiped the remaining blood from her face. The wound was smaller than he had expected from the amount of blood.

He should call Lane.

No.

He shouldn't call any of them. None of them could be trusted.

But Grigor? It made no sense. Grigor was gone, or at least weak and powerless in the forest. Daven had said so. How could he have done this? He returned to his question. "Where is Lane? He promised me he'd stay with you."

"I made him leave. Him and Crispy both. They were lying to me about where you were, what was happening. I knew. I knew you were coming right back." She rolled her head sideways with a little noise of pain. "I should have—"

"It smells like gunpowder in here," Astan said. "Grigor had a gun?" His jaw tightened with gritty anger. Astan remembered quite well how that particular *nian* could handle a human firearm.

"No. It was mine. I brought it from the city. I fired it. Up there." Pushing the blanket off her, she pointed at a dark shadow above them in the top of the room. "Lane wouldn't leave. I don't know what I was thinking. I wouldn't have hurt him. Really."

"In my vision, I had seen Rashia running into the old forest with Elliun. Yadin said—"

"You had a vision about Rashia?" Jelani's eyes grew wide. "She was here. I wouldn't let her in."

"Come to think of it, I didn't notice Rashia at the meeting of the Circle." Astan felt heartsick. "But Grigor was here? Are you sure?"

"Do you think I'd forget the elf who shot you?" Jelani asked. "Ever?"

The reality of their loss began to sink in.

Jelani wiped away angry tears, the gesture pulling at the wound on her forehead. Astan reached for her, but she shoved back his arm. "He said he wanted to take my life's meaning from me, the same way I had done to him. He knew just what he was doing. Our son's gone, Astan."

Lost. That word summed up Astan's whirling thoughts. He had been ready to blame the Circle, but he knew how evil Grigor could be. If one with such a black heart had possession of his child, Elliun was as good as lost. All the petty arguments with the

Circle, their resentments, even his will to live melted into a fiery wash.

If Grigor wanted to destroy Jelani, he had certainly chosen the most likely method. Astan saw the beginnings of deep sorrow creep into her expression. They could not just sit here. They needed to act.

He grabbed both of her hands. "Think, Jelani. Think. What did you see? What did you hear?"

Astan opened his mind, the emotion running between them easily as high as the moments after Elliun's birth when they had shared Astan's ability. Maybe it wasn't too late.

He concentrated on the scene inside the tree house, as it had been when he left. Max had just finished with Lane's computer and left with Astan. Lane and Crispy milled around the room, as Jelani put the baby to bed. When he had that picture solidly in his head, he opened his mind.

Flick.

Lane's terror when Jelani pulled the gun.

Flick.

Jelani, exhausted, asleep in her chair.

Flick.

Dark figures approached the door, activating the elven mechanism to open it. Three of them. He did not have to see Grigor's face to know which one he was. The second was an elf named Vez, an orphan who had joined the clan some months before and with whom he had hunted. The third was Hidal, an elf he had once considered a friend.

"Traitors!" Astan hissed.

"Yes," Jelani concurred.

Flick.

Darkness. Swaddling. Close quarters. Unable to move.

"Elliun," Jelani said.

Astan agreed. That sense definitely came from a place which felt like their son. "He's alive, *denami.* He's alive."

He pulled her into his arms, holding her in silence a long time before he spoke. "We'll find him. I promise we will. If it takes the last drop of my blood. I swear it."

"How will we? How?"

The ache in her voice nearly tore him apart. He would not fail her. It was not an option. "If we can sense him, we can track him. Wherever Grigor has taken him. He is a heartless bastard. He'll draw out whatever evil plan he has for as long as he can. But we need to hurry."

She gave a slow nod.

Through their touch bond, he felt her resolve come to bear. He knew the woman in his arms could be a pillar of strength. He had seen it. It was how they both needed to be at the moment, strong like stone, like the granite of the mountains around them.

The one thing Astan knew for certain was that he could not trust anyone. "We need to get away from here in case they return. Fontine knew where Grigor was hiding. Even if she has been deceived by him, I cannot believe she would let him hurt an innocent child. We can find her. We can find them. We *will*. Come on, *denami*. Let's pack."

As quickly as possible, they shoved clothing and food into a couple of knapsacks.

"I know where we can go, Astan. Some place we'll be safe." Jelani pulled a long flat basket out from under the bed. She dug out envelopes, which she then tucked into the pocket of the heavy green jacket she now wore.

The door flew open.

"Astan! Jelani!" Daven called. "Where are you?"

"Tell him nothing, Astan," Jelani hissed. "We can't trust anyone. Isn't that true?"

Astan hesitated. Despite his duplicity, Daven had seemed to understand their point of view, at least for a time. He always spoke to Astan as a mentor and guide, handing out advice like religious pamphlets. But where had he been during this attack? With those treacherous witches.

He nodded in agreement to Jelani and shouldered his pack.

Stepping into the other room, Astan looked around the doorframe first to make sure Daven was alone, blocking the door with his own bulk in case he was not. "We don't want your help. Leave us alone."

"I met Yadin at the place where we put out the fire. He said you'd been attacked." As Daven looked around the room, a look of what appeared to be genuine shock contorted his face. "Where is Jelani? Is she hurt?"

Astan's eyes narrowed. "Don't you mean, where is Elliun? Isn't he the one everyone's worried about?" He crossed the room about halfway, trying to decide which action to take if Daven challenged him. They had asked Daven to help them once, to make a spell to block the door so that something like this would not, could not happen.

Daven had refused. He should have protected them. He was the one who had failed, not Astan. He was the one who should pay.

"Something's happened to Elliun? That's not possible, Astan. The Circle decided not to take action, Astan. We trust you and Jelani, even in light of—" He looked past Astan's shoulder. "Jelani, you're hurt. Who has done this?"

Astan's mind played visuals in a dark loop. All he could think about was what could have happened to Jelani while fearing what was happening to their son. How alone they were in the world.

"Who has done this?" Astan demanded. "You all have! You lecture me about duty? You demand that we sacrifice everything in service of the Bitterroot Clan? But what duty do they owe us? A little confidence? A little protection? A little support? I'd say those were lacking here."

He approached Daven, who did not move.

"What are you doing, Astan? Where do you think you're going?" Daven looked at Jelani and saw her tear stained face then looked to the empty crib. "Where is Elliun?"

"Gone, damn you," Jelani said, her voice breaking. "Damn you to hell."

A paleness crept up Daven's face. "He is truly gone? Who has taken him? Not the Circle. Not the Circle, Astan. I swear to you."

"Then what was Rashia doing here?" Jelani said her voice so cold it burned.

"Rashia?" Daven's jaw worked. Was he chewing out a lie?

"Shut up," Astan said, voice gruff with sublimated guilt for not handling the traitor Grigor himself. He should have known. "All your talk about how we should allow the traitor Grigor Biren access to the clan again. This is what that talk has brought! Get out of my house."

"Grigor? Not possible. The runes never. No." Confusion dragged his feet to a standstill and painted his face with questions. "Please, let me help you," Daven begged, holding out his hand, first to Astan, then to Jelani.

"We don't want your help now. It's too late!" Astan's pain surfaced with an urge to vent his fury and sorrow through violence.

"Let me call the clan's trackers. Djana can—"

"No!" He could not let Daven stop them here. Even a few minutes' delay could mean the difference between life and death for their son. There was no time for this.

Astan grabbed a chair from the table and swung it at Daven, hitting him in the forehead. Daven dropped first to his knees and then to the ground.

Astan stared a moment in shocked silence. When Daven didn't move, Astan turned to his mate. He had not intended to kill his father, as much as he blamed him for what had happened. "Do you think—"

"It's not time to think, beloved." Jelani stared down at Daven without expression. "There, he moved. He'll be fine. I hope he lives forever with the guilt of what's happened on his conscience."

She went to the door and took a quick look outside. Azrael shot out the door when she opened it. She sighed.

"Az will go home to Iris, I'm sure," Jelani said. "But if we're to have any hope of catching up with them, love, we need to go now. It's time to decide, Astan. Do you choose the clan, or do you choose your family?"

Astan looked at the barely conscious elf on the floor, knowing what Daven's answer had been. Astan did not intend to make the same mistake. He reached for Jelani's hand, feeling it warm in his. They would get through this darkness and come out on the other side, where the light and their new beginning would be waiting for them. The hope shone from her eyes as well. It was time.

"Let's go, *denami*. Quickly. Our son waits for his mother and father to rescue him."

And they were gone.

CHAPTER 28

GRIGOR Biren heard only the rustle of clothing, as he and his followers sprinted atop the snow, leaving no footprints as they retreated to the place he had constructed for them in the trees.

Beside him ran his lover, Fontine.

Directly behind them was the me-too follower Hidal with Astan's former friend Yadin at his elbow.

To the right ran several others with the brooding presence of the hulking Vez bringing up the rear.

They had to run, to hide. They had exposed their treachery to the elf clan in their attack on the elf queen. They were outlaws, all of them, in a way even Grigor had not been before.

Grigor had only followed the commands of the elf king Bartolomey, and his handmaiden, Firefly. Grigor's plan had been ingenious, or so he had thought.

Sneak into the clan's gathering.

Take the newborn prince.

Destroy Jelani's life, as she had destroyed his.

It had seemed so simple.

Behind him, Vez spoke a few words, and Grigor sensed that the others stopped running.

Grigor turned to see what was wrong.

The icy wind ruffled his blond hair, lately grown long and thick thanks to the powerful talisman given to him by the mysterious mage Firefly. He didn't feel chilled, though, his elf powers restored through that talisman. At least not until he studied his companions. His eyes searched the faces watching him, now in a half circle. Only Fontine looked troubled. The others' faces were frozen, cold as the granite under their feet.

"What?" Grigor asked.

"What?" Vez repeated in a voice lined with velvet derision. "It is we who should demand an explanation from you. You promised we would have the queen's son. We followed you, believing you had the sanction of the forest mage. That's what you said."

Grigor bit his lip to keep it from trembling, so hard it hurt. That had indeed been his plan. But it had gone horribly wrong. When they had arrived at the queen's tree house, they had found her alone.

"He wasn't there!" he exclaimed. "She must have known we were coming!"

The faces reflected only stony condemnation.

"How would that have happened?" Vez's brilliant turquoise eyes looked as hard as cut glass. He turned to survey those standing with him. "None of us would have betrayed the rest. Would we?"

"And you killed the queen," Fontine said in a half voice, her frightened blue eyes flicking from Vez to Grigor. "The clan will not let this stand."

Vez scoffed. "She is human. Who knows if that killed her? Perhaps she will only wake up with a huge headache and go on to make the clan miserable."

Hidal jammed his hands in the pockets of his rough brown jacket. "But what about the baby?"

"We all revealed ourselves as conspirators to accomplish this task," another grumbled. "We cannot go home, and we still have proved nothing."

Grigor could only think of the beautiful face of Firefly when she had come to him so angry, pushing him to act, act, act or else lose his power. That murderous light had frightened him, pushing him to move before he was ready. This was her fault, not his. He hadn't wanted to try this yet.

"Firefly—" He stopped short, biting off what he really waned to say.

He could not appear weak, not if he wanted to maintain control of this little group. Vez would take it from him in a heartbeat, had been threatening to do so for some time.

"We'll try again," Grigor added, the words sounding lame even before he finished speaking them. "The false queen must be taken down."

"Of course she will," Vez said. "Come, my friends, let's celebrate the next plan!" he cried, a smile splitting that previously unsympathetic face, his expression suddenly jovial. He wrapped an arm around a puzzled Hidal's shoulder and started for Grigor's bower.

Unsure, the others followed him, Fontine and Grigor trailing the group.

Grigor struggled to find something to say.

Fontine hung her head. "Perhaps Daven Talvi read my mind," Fontine whispered. "It could have been me. Without even meaning to. I should tell Vez."

"No," Grigor snapped. "You did everything I asked you to and more. This is not at your door, love."

"What are we going to do?" She looked up at him, no loss of adoration in her dear face.

"I'll think of something."

"You always do." She smiled and leaned over to kiss his cheek. "We will yet restore the clan to its rightful place in the world."

Grateful, he took her hand and squeezed it. "That we will, Fontine. That we will."

Vez stopped suddenly, looking back over his shoulder. "Did you hear that?"

"Hear what?" Hidal eyed the direction from which they had come.

"They must have followed us," Vez Said.

Grigor's heart skipped a beat, or several. He had to take the lead here, or he would be lost for sure. "All right. The rest of you go on. I'll go back and draw them off."

Vez seemed surprised, but nodded. "Fontine, take the others and wait at Grigor's place. I'll stand here with him. He shouldn't have to do this alone."

Queasiness shot in Grigor's stomach. He would have preferred any of the others to Vez, but the others were already nodding with appreciation. When Fontine hesitated, Grigor urged her to go. "We'll come along in a few minutes. Be safe."

Hidal took Fontine's arm and led her away with the others following him. When they were out of sight Grigor looked at the path they had taken and then to Vez, "What was it you heard, exactly?"

"Sounded like Astan's little whistle, you know? The one he thinks sounds like a hawk?" Vez's disdain for the queen's partner echoed in the cold air.

"I didn't hear anything."

"Maybe you don't want to hear anything. Maybe you don't want to face the consequences of what you've done." Vez turned and walked toward the forest.

True enough. Grigor did not want to deal with the clan, or Astan Hawk, not now. Even if he didn't have the baby, they wouldn't care. But he couldn't retreat, not with Vez here.

"Vez, come on," he said. But all he could see was Vez's broad back. Vez gave no sign that he had heard.

"Vez, we're walking out in the open here. If we're about to be attacked, shouldn't we take cover?"

Still nothing.

Grigor stopped. He glanced back over his shoulder. He saw no one in any direction. "Vez."

Vez turned to him. "You're right. We'd better blend into the trees." He took off running.

Finally, something that made sense.

"Coming," Grigor said.

He picked up his pace, trailing after Vez on a path among the pines. Once he was among the sparse shade of the thin trees he realized he had lost Vez. A furrow digging itself between his brows, he went to the right a little way and then stopped to listen. Where could he have gone?

Suddenly Vez appeared right behind Grigor's shoulder, his hand reaching for Grigor's neck. Grigor jerked away but Vez had him by the front of his jacket, his hand digging inside.

"Leave me alone!" Grigor said, swinging at Vez.

"I can't. The mages need someone strong to help them

destroy the clan. You're useless." Vez's hand closed and jerked back, the talisman appearing in it. "And now you're powerless."

Grigor eyed the stolen talisman with dismay. "That's mine! Firefly gave it to me." He lunged forward, grabbing at it, but Vez pulled away.

"You don't deserve it." The broad-shouldered elf turned and ran into the forest.

"Give it back!" Grigor ran after him, his stomach clenched with fright. He knew what would happen to him without it. He would lose his elf powers again. His bower would fade into dust. He would starve. He would be cold.

He would die.

"Damn you, Vez!" Grigor chased him, tripping over the logs in the snow, no longer able to lightly step along its crust. His shins ached. He kept running, sensing some movement ahead of him in the trees. If he could only get that talisman back. "Firefly, please. Master Bartolomey, please. I can strike a blow for you. I can!"

Suddenly Vez appeared, standing still and dark against the snow ahead. Grigor's momentum carried him almost to Vez's feet when he heard a loud snap, and then his right ankle exploded in pain. "What the—"

He looked down to find huge steel jaws clamped on his ankle above his boot, blood soaking his pants leg. The pain was excruciating. He tried to pull his foot away but the trap held tight. A sound issued from his throat, something between a whine and a whimper, as he realized he was caught.

"Fitting, don't you think? Now that you're only human, to be the victim of a human trap?" Vez's smile froze Grigor's blood.

"Vez." Grigor looked back over his shoulder wishing for any of the others to appear, hardly able to think because of the pain. "Please, help me. You can keep the talisman. I'll give you Fontine. I'll give you anything. Please."

Vez slipped the talisman into his pocket. "I don't even know if I can, but I'll try." He bent down and reached for the steel clamped on Grigor's leg, but instead of loosening it, he twisted it, slicing the skin open.

Grigor screamed in agony, but could do nothing.

Vez soaked both of his hands in the flowing blood, and then rubbed it on his own clothing.

"I'll take good care of Fontine, Grigor. Don't spend your last hours worrying about her." Vez looked into the forest around them. "Don't make noise, now. You might attract a wolf. Or something worse." He stood, his expression one of scorn.

"Vez, no!"

"Goodbye, Grigor." Vez turned and walked away, leaving no footprints in the snow.

"Vez." Grigor, panting in panic, his leg ravaged, tried once again to pull it loose but the trap was chained to a tree. He was going nowhere, his perfect plan to become a mage fading into mountain mist. He fell into the snow, his life ebbing away.

* * *

VEZ hurried back toward the place where they had left the others, tearing his shirtsleeves and wiping the remainder of the blood off of his hands and onto his clothes.

That weakling Grigor would not last long. What he had to do now was to send the conspirators to a place of safety until the clan could be handled in the proper way.

And he knew just the right one to do it.

Working himself up as he broke into a run, he rehearsed his story in his head.

By the time he reached Fontine and the others, they were confused at the vanishing of Grigor's elven bower, and shocked at Vez's disheveled appearance.

"What's happened?" Fontine said taking Vez's arm. "You're hurt!"

"Where's Grigor?" Yadin asked.

"No time to explain," Vez said, hardly slowing down. "They're coming! Hawk and the others—the queen really is dead! They destroyed Grigor. They almost got me. They're coming for all of us! Come on!"

He half-dragged Fontine as he sprinted past the place where Grigor's home had been. "I know where you'll be safe."

The others, a little slower to understand, finally caught his desperation and started to run after him.

Vez did everything he could not to smile. This would be easier than he thought.

He sent his thoughts ahead to his contacts, knowing that they were somewhere near the bend in the river.

I'll be waiting.

Vez slowed down to make sure all his chicks followed. Their faces showed varying degrees of disbelief and shock. They would be reassured soon enough. He smiled just a little to encourage them. "Come, my friends, we'll soon be safe," he promised.

Minutes later they came to an open space by the river, where a single *neris* waited for them, a female elf with beautiful violet eyes, brown skin, and silver hair. She welcomed them with soft words and a reassuring pat on the arm for each of them.

"I'll take you to a place where you will be appreciated and protected," she said. "Rest yourselves now for a few minutes. Have some water. Sit a moment. Everything will be fine."

The young male elves walked away, grouping themselves near the water. They talked quietly among themselves.

Fontine, however, looked lost.

Vez crossed the space between them and held out a hand to her. "Fontine, Grigor was brave in meeting his end. You have to be proud of what he tried to do. But we have to move on, make new plans now." He squeezed her chilled fingers. "Will you be all right?"

"I don't understand," she muttered.

"The mages of the forest, Fontine, they're real. Grigor was right. They have chosen us to be their warriors." He reached his other hand to cup her chin, his fingers registering the softness of her skin. She was his now.

"Oh, Vez," she said as she melted into his arms, tears running down her cheeks.

Yes, she was his now. Vez felt the pride of possession burn through his chest all the way to his heart.

The silver-haired elf watched Vez from the shadow of a tree, a smile playing across her lips, her arms crossed. "You've done well, Vez," she said.

"Thank you, mother." He smiled back at her.

Fontine pulled away and turned to the other woman. "You're Vez's mother? Are you the one Grigor calls Firefly?"

"That could be," she replied. "But my real name is Veraena."

THE END

Acknowledgements

* *My wonderful group of friends and readers, who praise me when I'm doing good work and tell me that I'm full of it when I need it, especially Michele, Debbie, Sue, Kellie and Gina.*
* *Linda Caler, who has gone above and beyond to share the story of our Bitterroot elves with her huge troops of friends and family in Montana and beyond.*
* *My writing critique group, who each bring their own gifts to share as we pass on our stories, one to the other—Tom, Jeff, Dave, Gene, Carm, Paul, Linda, Ginny, Christy and particularly Jean, who reads every word, wields her red pen like Zorro's sword, and makes me want to write as well as she does. Thanks, too, to Ed for the wonderful review of The Elf Queen—hope you like this one as well!*
* *Eric, without whom plot holes would become plot pitfalls, who always knows "how to" do any kind of wacky thing, and who taught me everything I know about epic drops and Beowulf Clusters.*
* *Terri Branson, who shared a vision with me and continues to push the creative process along as this story comes into your hands.*

About the Author

Lyndi Alexander dreamed for many years of being a spaceship captain, but settled instead for inspired excursions into fictional places with fascinating companions from her imagination that she likes to share with others. She has been a published writer for over thirty years, including seven years as a reporter and editor at a newspaper in Homestead, Florida. Her list of publications is eclectic, from science fiction to romance to horror, from tech reporting to television reviews. Lyndi is married to an absent-minded computer geek. Together, they have a dozen computers, seven children and a full house in northwestern Pennsylvania.